Kunal Basu was born in Calcutta and has travelled widely. He
teaches at Oxford University and is the author of two previous
acclaimed novels: *The Miniaturist* and *The Opium Clerk*. He is
married with one daughter.

By Kunal Basu

Racists
The Miniaturist
The Opium Clerk

Racists

Kunal Basu

PHOENIX

A PHOENIX PAPERBACK

First published in Great Britain in 2006
by Weidenfeld & Nicolson
This paperback edition published in 2007
by Phoenix,
an imprint of Orion Books Ltd,
Orion House, 5 Upper St Martin's Lane,
London WC2H 9EA

3 5 7 9 10 8 6 4

A CIP catalogue record for this book
is available from the British Library

ISBN-13 978-0-7538-2150-3

Typeset at The Spartan Press Ltd,
Lymington, Hants

Printed and bound in Great Britain by
Clays Ltd, St Ives plc

The Orion Publishing Group's policy is to use papers that
are natural, renewable and recyclable products and
made from wood grown in sustainable forests. The logging
and manufacturing processes are expected to conform to
the environmental regulations of the country of origin.

www.orionbooks.co.uk

for Ajlai

I

If they are human,
they descended from Adam.

ST AUGUSTINE

1855

A boat on a sea. A tiny speck out on a lazy drift, basking under a sun that tantalises. She appears content, anchors drawn and awnings spread, as she skims the waves, folds and unfolds the sails passing a string of islands close to the coast – suitors encircling the dark queen. Bence, Gorée, Santiago, Arlinda, Anamabo. She cruises *La Petite Route*, that classic passage from Europe to Africa, holds a steady course till Cape Verde, waiting to scurry down the pirate coast and strike east into rivers with inland ports to land and load cargo. It's a well-travelled route. Traders have known it for centuries. Cotton, wool, iron, gunpowder have come down these waters, and much has flowed back: ivory, gold, beeswax, hardwood. Slaves.

A trader she isn't, more a flute-ship by her looks, or a refitted man-of-war. A few dozen hogsheads of rum, a score barrels of wine, kegs of water biscuits, a reasonable supply of gammon, hoops, calavance and black-eyed peas, a firkin of butter and sides of beef in her hold won't tempt an eager chief waiting ashore or his half-caste agent. The crew numbers a mere twenty, and that includes the captain, the mates, the surgeon, the cooper and the carpenter. Not enough hands or guns to foil a raid, should pirates chance their luck.

Nor is it a *négrier*, one of those stinking floats packed deck upon deck with black gold, carrying the necessary evil to America even after the trade has been banned, flying the flags of their smuggling captors – a Portuguese *Bom Jesus*, a French *Minerva*, or a British *Charming Sally*.

Up close, the Cupid figurehead gives her away – the *Rainbow*, a perfect beauty, guns and binnacle shining. Her captain is more famous even than her looks – Captain Perry, a gentleman dilettante with not too gentlemanly a past, a veteran of both traders and

3

slavers. He is the lion of these waters, rumoured to have carried everything, from the corpses of a dead garrison to the English Queen, as indefatigable spinning his yarns as he is resourceful, on sea and on shore. A busy raconteur. Show him a man, it is said, and Perry will have him in fits!

A lull in the passage brings the captain out of his coop. He struts up the foredeck to amuse the most eminent of his guests, Professor Samuel Bates of the Royal College of Physicians, the master craniologist. With typical aplomb, he announces their passage through the islands, telling a juicy tale or two about each to the professor. Gorée's scandal, with its slave prison passing off real apes as slaves! Santiago's brothel, finer than the finest of Liverpool. His guest barely listens, frowning at a passing island as if it were a deviant student in his laboratory, eyes fixed on the banks of dark shadows cast like blemishes on its slopes.

Spurned by Bates's silence, the captain starts to go below deck to find his other eminent guest, the Frenchman, a member of the Société Ethnologique de Paris, a traveller no less travelled than himself. He stops, knowing that Monsieur Jean-Louis Belavoix will already be asleep, snoring, fully dressed on his bunk as if about to deliver a long and important speech to the Société. Used to a roaring audience, the captain grumbles at his luck – the *Rainbow* turned a ghost ship by the deathly silence. Only Nicholas Quartley, Bates's English assistant, will be keen, stopping his inspection of their precious cargo – boxes of scientific instruments riding the hold – to flash his obedient smile and listen to the captain. He could have Quartley to himself for a few minutes, before the young man returns to his scraping and scrubbing, delicately opening a box's lid to check whether an instrument has suffered from last night's swell.

Even on the long shipboard evenings, with the door of the spirit-locker open, the captain has not been able to capture his audience, the three far too immersed in their own thoughts to rise to his hints and teasers, offering a resolute defence to his yarns. The same thought swirled in each of them – the one that has set them off on their journey, to an exceptional venture unlike the usual run of traders and slavers.

In the faint evening light, the captain observes his other guest, the nurse travelling with the three scientists. Norah, forever in motion, marching the deck from end to end, clutching her two bundles to

4

her chest. A short but appealing figure, with a slim waist, brown eyes beneath fine brows. Her neat features flawed only by a sad mouth. He watches her closely to see if she is immersed too, eyes on the wooden deck marking out her own thoughts. He wonders if she'll stop, put her bundles down, if she will change trajectory and come up to him, to listen with her eyes only. He feels sorry for the girl, her mute lips unable to utter a single word.

A week is all it takes for the *Rainbow* to reach her destination. Halfway down *La Petite Route* she has changed course to cruise the islands, waiting at an inlet for favourable winds to draw near the tiniest of them all: Arlinda. It is a plain and unlikely stop. The grinding anchor stirs the scientists finally to life, brings them out on the foredeck to watch the captain lower the outrigger. The assistant is the first to go down with the boxes, followed by Bates and Belavoix, and then the nurse joins them on the boat. All eyes are on her two bundles, strapped firmly to her side, now twitching in the fresh sea air as they make their way over to the island. She rocks them gently to soothe the moaning and whimpers, parting the wraps for a glimpse of what's inside. They see the babies.

A black boy and a white girl.

ARLINDA: 1860

Rising from the sea, the island resembles a catamaran with green sails floating between two layers of white – a line of breakers and a band of clouds. Closer still, the horizon stretches out into the surf, the beach and the forest. Nothing in the shape of a harbour can be made out. Neither smoke nor any sign of human life is visible, not even a fisherman or two. Just an empty coast lying motionless by the sea. As the light summer breeze brings the ship within sight of landing, the island appears to her visitors exactly as it did when they glimpsed her for the very first time on Captain Perry's *Rainbow*. Each recalls his first voyage down *La Petite Route*, and the several that have followed since, Arlinda turned familiar by their visits over the past five years.

The fears have faded now. Of an ambush along the way. Fear of the island – of disease, wild beasts and unexpected visitors. The shadow of the Dark Continent no longer stretches across the luminous sea to worry the scientists. Arlinda is safe, just as Perry reassured them even before they set foot on her for the first time. A few hundred nautical miles south-west of Gibraltar, she keeps the company of notorious neighbours. But even with the slave islands breathing down her neck, she is free of the troubles that come with the black gold. Her size is her flaw, and her saviour. Circumnavigated in less than a day, she is small compared to the other islands that dot the African coast, lacking the flat stretches needed to build barracks and fort, church and brothel of a proper slave colony. With an easy approach and a pleasant climate, she tempts many a venturer, but her beauty is worthless. The rocky landscape arrests the eye, but turns its back to seeding and cropping, refusing the settler a regular staple. None has thought to bring animals here to start a farm, or their favourite creatures to raise as game. An island without food, without sport – nothing to capture a passing captain's interest. Even her coast is too open, without an estuary or lagoon, leaving no place to hide from pirates. Arriving on the *Rainbow*, the scientists found a barren Arlinda, just as promised, free from the smell of humans or animals.

Dropping anchor, they gaze upon the wild red flower, the African tulip, the island's only prize – the 'flame of the forest', as Captain Perry taught them to call it. It brings a smile to each face, knowing that the days of crawling bugs and nights of nausea are now over.

When the sun rises, it leaves one half of the island in shadow as it lights up the other. Early beams run into dark slopes of what's more than a hill but less than a mountain: a hill with a modest crown keeping an eye out for the whole island. A solitary ridge, steep and treacherous, the only birthmark left by the sea's eruption. For the most part, the foliage hides the loose rock that makes up Arlinda's crust. The forest is dense and prickly round the lower parts of the hill, rising comically to halfway up in circles, like an army of lofted fists. The trees are evergreen and many bloom all year round, including the arlinda after which the island is named. It yields a fruit with a kernel as hard and dark as loose rock and just as inedible. It rots on the forest floor. Portuguese merchants once collected a few sacks and made a poison to kill ship rats. But it didn't kill them – turned them blind instead, made them run helter-skelter and fall into the sea.

A sulphurous stream borders the foot of the hill on one side, separating it from the patch of land that runs into the beach. Where it comes from, no one knows. It collects rocks, covering them in moss, and keeps them warm. It's a witches' cauldron, hissing with lizards and frogs and snakes that stay coiled up around the stones, rarely moving for years. There might once have been a colony of birds on the island, but most have disappeared except for the gulls that turn endless circles around the beach. Otherwise there's no sign of life, not even the small animals one would expect to find burrowing under the shrubs, likely repulsed by the poisonous fruit.

The two camps are set a mile apart. One is lit by the morning sun, while the other is still in the shadow of the hill, one on the rising flanks halfway to the top, the other close to the beach. The stream flows between them. A goat path, narrow and winding, leads up to the visitors' camp on the hillside with its clear view of the other below it. Built for the three men – Professor Samuel Bates, Monsieur Jean-Louis Belavoix and the assistant – it's just what a shipwrecked sailor would need as he waited for the natives to repair the hull of his stricken vessel: a log cottage with three rooms in a row under one roof, joined by an open veranda. An adjoining shanty serves as the sanitary lodge. The smell of oil-soaked wood fills the rooms, a cloying odour that masks the fecund soil beaten into a hard, slaty floor throughout the camp. The rooms are dark but airy – a curious geometry of turrets cut into the wooden walls facing the veranda. Each is fitted with a trunk, a mattress and a tin-pan lamp lit by palm oil. A clay jar for water stands by the door of the cottage. A hammock, the only mark of leisure, lies rolled up like a ball of rope in a corner of the veranda.

Bates is always the first to rise, eager to make the best use of the first morning in Arlinda. The journey seems to affect him least. With a rap on his assistant's door, he marches off to the sanitary lodge, barking out commands over his shoulder. The boxes of new instruments are to be taken out of the ship's canvas bags, the log is to be marked carefully where the last entry was made six months ago. He orders Quartley to be ready in the blink of an eye. Then, stamping back to the veranda, a foot struggling inside his breeches, he examines his face in the mirror – features heavy with impatience.

It is a face to scare any assistant. A cranium of exceptional size, sporting dark eyes and a square jaw. At fifty, a full head of hair and sideburns. Scars over the brows from thinking things out. A wrestler's neck, constantly alert for a glint of opposition. A face that has fitted all the names given him over the years by fearful assistants.

Nicholas Quartley senses his master's impatience. He is an unlikely assistant for a scientist like Bates, a simple village boy with a clever pair of hands, a specialist in cadavers, a frequenter of morgues. He has won Bates's favour, impressed the craniologist by keeping his eye on the object – whichever object has caught his master's fancy over half a dozen years at his London laboratory.

'Don't forget to string the goniometer's needle.'

'No, sir.'

'And balance the orbiostat before—'

'Before we take measurements, sir.'

8

'It'd be a mistake to assume the samples' familiarity with procedures. We may have to repeat everything we did last time.'

Quartley nods. 'And what if they turn violent again?'

Bates narrows his eyes. 'They weren't *violent.*'

'Well, sir . . .'

'They were . . . suspicious.'

In his mind, Quartley tastes the trickling blood on his fingers. 'We must be ready if they become suspicious again, sir.'

Polishing his pince-nez and raising them to squint at the sun, Bates resumes his examination. 'And what instructions are you to bring down to the nurse?'

The young man searches for words. Does Bates mean the things she must do while they are here on their visit? Or is he quizzing him on the rules? He rehearses these quickly. The rules are to remain unchanged for the full twelve years of the experiment, and the nurse is obliged to follow them, observe them scrupulously with their two samples. The rules that she has learned on her voyage down to Arlinda on the *Rainbow.* Does Bates wish him to remind her of them?

'I've to tell her not to swinge the children, not even if . . .' He starts to recite the list, before a frowning Bates cuts him short.

'I don't mean the Ten Commandments.' With a quick look at Belavoix's closed door, he gets ready to leave. 'Never mind about the instructions, Quartley. You've clearly forgotten. Just mind your way with the boxes.'

With his assistant stranded on the veranda, a box in each hand and the log precariously under an arm, he repeats his command: 'Don't dither, Quartley!'

As they set off down the goat path, Bates striding resolutely ahead and Quartley struggling a dozen steps behind, they hear the Frenchman call after them.

'Wait!'

Bates strides on. Afraid to stop, Quartley turns for a quick glance. He sees a monk in a cassock, arms waving frantically from loose sleeves, limping down the cottage steps.

'Have you forgotten me? You're leaving your friend behind, Mr Bates. Mr Bates . . . !'

With Bates still set on his course, Belavoix starts to hobble down, pleading with the two to slow their pace. 'Ah! This path . . . it is dangerous. One mistake and that'll be the end! It's fit for the *chevreau* . . . the baby goat, not men. Tell me, why must we live up there –' he points back at the scientists' cottage – 'when we're so interested in what happens down there?'

The Frenchman carries a heavy sack over his shoulders. It is full of notebooks, some filled, most still empty. Only his face betrays his youth – a prominent nose, a head of boyish curls. A fashionable Parisian moustache kept waxed to a point at each end. A giant and suffering frame holding up a disproportionately sweet face. His chin quivers as he comes up behind Quartley, grumbling at Bates's silence.

'How English! Punishing himself for no reason.' He raises his voice once more. 'Why can't the two camps be closer together? Was it your idea to put them so far apart, or the mad captain's? You're trying to keep me from Norah, aren't you? – like Romeo from Juliet!'

Suppressing a laugh, Quartley offers to carry Belavoix's sack, inviting a suitable protest before he accepts with obvious relief.

'The English assistant is kind . . . *much* kinder than his master,' Belavoix mutters under his breath, glancing slyly at Bates. 'And smarter too, I've been told!'

The stream slows Bates down, having him cross a bridge of stones they themselves laid on their first visit. Stuck firmly on the loose bed, the steps appear undisturbed by the currents or the assorted life around them. The stream has bowed to the visitors' intention, covering the rock steps with a thin layer of moss. It is more a trick than an invitation – a slip sure to land the intruder in its bubbling cauldron.

The three of them are together now, each treading with caution over the bridge. Belavoix seems relieved, barely a step behind Bates. He pants almost into his ear.

'It's too early to rush down . . . No? Too early for work?'

'Rubbish.' Bates points up at the sun, now illuminating all of Arlinda.

'Ah! But you slept well on the ship. You drank French claret with the captain and snored in your cabin. I heard you, Mr Bates!'

Bates gives him a puzzled look.

'Your mind is fresh . . . as alive as the fishes –' Belavoix points down at the stream – 'ready to gobble up our samples!' He makes a gesture of helplessness as Bates strides ahead once again, now barely yards away from their destination.

'I didn't sleep a wink on board. Not for a whole week! A horrible rash covered every inch of me . . . a case of minor scarlatina. Quite dangerous!'

'Nonsense!'

The cottage at the other camp is larger than the visitors', but not by much. A substantial kitchen at its heart, there are three smaller rooms as well, two on one side and one on the other. The steps lead straight into the kitchen, which is bare but for a table of solid oak in the middle and a few cane chairs. An iron stove with grates for burning twigs holds a far corner, a bench or two around it. A partition screen hides a modest larder. The door at the back of the kitchen leads not to a garden patch but to another small chamber, which looks like a locked cupboard. It houses the instruments. Although the walls are built of the same oily wood as the visitors' cottage, they smell different, of stove smoke and food.

The camp is fenced on all four sides and surrounded by an overgrown hedge whose prickly leaves are easy to burn. Piles of logs stand next to a vegetable garden, a vain effort betraying the cultivator's plans, some recent, some failed ventures.

This is Norah's camp and cottage, where she has lived with the two children since they arrived five years ago in Arlinda. For them, unlike the visiting scientists, the island is home – a home they have never left for a single day, not even for a leisurely sail on the luminous sea. She and the children are the only human inhabitants here, their camp well hidden by the tall arlinda trees from passing slavers and traders.

This is her room by the kitchen, where she spent the first night ashore with the twitching bundles. She pulled her blanket over them that night to stop the roaring sea from reaching their tiny ears, suckled the babies every time they woke. She spent her first sleepless night on the island, worrying not over her tasks but about the dark sea and the dark night, and the days ahead when the scientists who accompanied her would leave. She knew that the cottage would be hers, the camp, the island.

The kitchen has been her fort from the beginning. After a few false starts, she has learned to guard it against dwindling stock and decay.

She has mastered the trick of passing messages, leaving the list of things she needs each month in a small hut by the beach and raising a flag over it. Then she'd wait for one of Captain Perry's ships to replenish her larder with supplies, bring her food and fresh water. She'd ask for tinctures and drops, clothes, provisions for her cottage – everything to keep her going on the barren island. She'd leave a letter for Bates as well with her list, her monthly report on the children. In the five years, the camp has turned her into an invisible trader, a letter writer and a nurse.

From her kitchen window she sees Bates arrive at the fence. He leaps over the waist-high rampart, followed by Nicholas Quartley and a struggling Belavoix. Although the sun has risen high, the camp seems brighter than the island's other parts, somehow more open. The eye is free to roam through the slender tree trunks towards the horizon. The sea near by makes it alive, the unbroken surf and the squealing gulls. The wheezing breeze. The hedge attracts an army of black flies. Like the garden's cultivator, they have plans that baffle the observer, rising up in tall columns or swooping down on the pile of logs wet with morning dew. The arlinda trees have thrown a canopy of branches over the cottage, a touching gesture that'll soothe when the sun is even higher. But the undergrowth is kept free of the poisonous fruit.

At the cottage steps they find the boy crouched on the ground excreting worms, each about six inches long, a dozen of them coming out in a looping coil. Seeing Bates, he leaps up, runs and catches hold of his hand, shrieking and blabbering through his full lips like a glib-tongued monkey. He greets Quartley and Belavoix in turn, pointing and gesturing with his hands. Ignoring the boy, Bates walks up the steps to the kitchen and enters. He ignores Norah at the table, heading for the cupboard that houses the instruments. The boy clutches Belavoix's cassock, buries his little face in the billowing folds. With Quartley out of sight, the Frenchman takes the boy's hand, kneels down to blabber back to him. The two set off on a trail around the prickly shrub, the boy leading, pointing at the swirl of black flies. He makes as if to leap up and catch them, taking a tumble after a few tries. Then, perched on Belavoix's shoulder, he returns to the cottage, all stirred up to see the camp from this new height, wriggling like a rare beast in an exotic forest.

The sound of boots as Bates and Quartley enter the cottage brings the girl out of her room. Barefoot, wearing a scanty dress, hair roughly tied back. To the visitors, both children seem to have grown a few inches since they last saw them half a year ago. Both, at first, appear to be of the same colour: a dull sun-burnt brown. Up close, the girl looks a touch fairer, her upper arms and chest white. There are scratches all over their limbs. Blackened nails and chafed palms speak of digging dirt and rock. A layer of fine dust on hair sends out small puffs each time the children run or tumble on the floor.

They seem familiar with their visitors, but not familiar enough to take their eyes off them. The encounter seems novel, yet tinged with memory. The girl looks more worried than the boy. She has withdrawn to Norah's side and is sitting on a bench by the stove, chin on her chest, but darting glances at Bates as, lighting up his pipe, he curses his damp matches. Fear strikes as she is startled by Belavoix's yawn that sounds a cross between a howl and a sigh. The Frenchman has let go of the boy and sits on a cane chair, one foot up on the table, sipping fresh coconut water served by Norah, his own remedy for yet another 'condition'. The girl's eyes follow Norah, as she dips a rag in a pot filled with boiling water and starts to wipe the table clean. She winces as Norah's hand marks an arc close to Belavoix's foot, as if a touch could set off a terrible explosion. But it's the sight of Nicholas Quartley that stiffens her young muscles – Quartley bringing the craniograph to the table, the instrument gleaming through its chamois cover.

The boy has disappeared again. Belavoix whistles, and Norah goes off to look for him.

Bates eyes the craniograph on the table silently. His earlier impatience has gone. The absent boy doesn't cloud his absorption, his mind taking in the measure of every knob and needle, octant, gauge and mirror – a mother bee giving her honeycombs a thorough once-over.

They hear Norah beating a tin pan with a stick, a rapid pattern repeated over and over. Left alone in the kitchen with the three men, the girl cowers even lower on the bench. Through the open door, they see the boy bounding up, bare-chested as before but wearing a pair of indigo pants down to his knees. He comes in, laughing and babbling, much amused by the gleaming instruments on the table. The gloss and shine send him into a frenzy, as he reaches up on his toes to touch the objects of his admiration.

The scientists observe him silently. Any attempt to protect the instruments from the boy's clumsy hands will excite him further, they know. He mustn't be coaxed or prodded in any way, not just yet. They must wait to see if he remembers the procedure from their earlier visits – if he makes their task simpler, approaching the right instrument and adopting the right posture for measurement. Everyone, apart from the boy, holds their silence, Belavoix peering through his keen eyes, capturing every gesture and babble in his notebook, Bates waiting calmly. The girl sinks her face in Norah's lap.

At a nod from Bates, Quartley draws the craniograph to the table's edge and releases the trap-like door. He kneels, slipping his head into the frame, and beams an invitation to the boy, who goes into a delirium. There's much dancing around the table and giggling. Then, as Quartley withdraws his head from the instrument, the boy rushes to insert his own. Snapping the frame shut, Bates peers closely at the boy's head and breaks his silence, announcing the reading for Quartley to record in the log.

They spend the next hour with the boy, Bates and Quartley measuring his little cranium with half a dozen instruments. The longitudinal diameter. Mastoid arch's width. The length between the parietal bones. The snout's elongation. Belavoix makes his own notes. Their subject appears perfectly at ease. He doesn't need any more reminding or cajoling. The routine has returned to him in a flash while his head was in the trap. He is an imitator no more, leading Bates and Quartley on from instrument to instrument, crouching or twisting his body to assume an odd posture – the little scientist followed by two large assistants.

The log fills in Quartley's hand, tiny black marks inserted in neat boxes. The assistant's eye climbs up and down the columns as he records Bates's readings, pausing briefly at an entry that looks different from the rest. He knows the importance of these numbers. His master will spend hours peering at them, add more lines to his forehead unlocking their mystery. The log is Bates's prize. With it, he'll look inside the boy's head. It'll prove what he knows to be true.

The final bit turns out to be tricky. This is the most difficult of the morning's readings, the torsiometer covering the boy's face in a maze of steel, a coil wrapped around his lips. It is more vicious than the craniograph's trap – a head-crusher. The boy is silent, his gaze dead still through the maze. When he has finished taking the reading, Bates rises from the table, ordering Quartley to release the boy. There'll be a few moments' break before they start on the girl. As the boy is gradually unfastened, his eyes come to life. He lets out a squeal and bites the coil around his lips – bites hard, refusing to let it go.

This is the moment Quartley has been dreading. He remembers the last time – the incident with the torsiometer. It was just the same: the boy up to his mischief, biting the coil, determined to hang on, in spite of Quartley's efforts. He tried tapping the boy's cheeks, tickling him behind the ears. He made faces, hoping to make him laugh. Nothing worked. Then Quartley risked his fingers, using them to pry open the boy's lips. He managed to release the coil, but not before the boy had bitten his finger. Bitten it hard, blood spilling down onto the table.

Quartley remembers the scene vividly. His scream startled everyone. Belavoix's notebook dropped on the floor with a thud, Bates's head snapped up from the log. Norah rushed in with arms outstretched for the boy, and a look of angry accusation at Quartley. He remembers the violence. His blood on the boy's teeth, trickling down his lips.

Is he waiting to taste blood again . . . ? The little monster!

But this time he is safe. Quartley taps and tickles, and then, miraculously, the lips part as the boy is startled by Belavoix's extraordinary yawn.

Measuring the girl turns out to be more difficult. She gives a sudden start, shaking herself like a dog, knowing it is soon to be her turn, and heads for her room. Norah runs after her, but she shies away, struck suddenly by a horror of being touched. They run around each other in the kitchen – a merry game, ending with the girl's capture. She starts to wail, face turned away from the instruments. Nothing stops her. Not Quartley, who tries to distract her by tapping a mallet on the table, beating a low drumming sound; or Norah, inserting her own head in the goniometer's trap to encourage her. Notebook open on his lap, Belavoix merely chuckles.

Bates starts to pace the kitchen, sweating from the midday heat as he glares impatiently at the girl. She only screams louder and shakes her head as Norah drags her over to the table. Quartley has caught hold of her shoulders, and tries to squeeze her tiny frame into the instrument. She starts foaming at the mouth and choking for breath. Then Bates stops them.

'Let her go.'

Thwarted on the verge of success, Quartley gives him a puzzled look. 'But . . .'

'I said let her go. *Now.*'

'Won't we need to measure her too . . . ?'

'Not the way she is.' Bates makes a motion with his hands to release the girl. 'At this rate, she'll cut herself, or worse, tip the instrument over. Can't risk that, can we?'

With a shrug, Quartley obeys his master; the girl rushes out of the kitchen back to her room. After pausing for a few moments, Norah returns to her stove, while Belavoix, groaning under his weight as he rises from the table, announces his intention of taking a stroll. A disappointed Quartley starts to put away the instruments. They'll have to measure the girl another time. The log will have to wait. The instruments must be locked safe in their boxes for future readings, guarded against the moist breeze and blowing dust.

'It's always the same with the girl, sir.'

'You mean her fear?'

Quartley nods. 'She seems quite silly . . .'

'Difficult, not silly,' Bates cuts in. 'She'll learn in time.'

'And the boy, sir? Will *he* become difficult too?'

Bates frowns. 'What makes you think that? The happy boy will grow up to be a happy man. Inferior but content.' He brushes aside Quartley's worries. 'It'll be all right later. You'll see.'

In the afternoon Bates brings along a flask of laudanum from the scientists' camp, and gives it to Norah to make the girl swallow it. Seeing the men reassembled in the kitchen, the child's eyes fill quickly with fear. She drinks with her face turned away from the table of instruments, the scene of the morning's ordeal. Within half an hour, her drowsy eyes droop as her face lulls to sleep. Lifting her off her feet and bringing her over to the table, Norah places her face inside the trap. Bates reads out the measurements, just as before.

'Eighty-seven degrees. No, make that eighty-eight.' A smile crosses his face. 'She shows the promise of her race!'

Away from their camp, the children head towards the forest after the scientists have left for the day. Skipping over the stream's rock steps, they arrive soon at the foothills. But the goat path is not their favourite. There are other paths, hidden by the shrubs and the dark shadows of Arlinda. Narrower, steeper – fit only for baby goats.

She leads him, her tiny feet hugging the jagged turns with the assurance of a seasoned explorer. She follows her own trail, clearing the sharp branches before her with a stick for the boy to pass behind unhindered. More than an explorer, she appears to be the path's caretaker – removing a clutch of loose rocks that have slid down the slopes to block their climb. Where the patch is hard, she leaps over the surrounding shrub to land on yet another narrow clearing, urging the boy to follow with a quick sign.

The two seem to carry their own map of the island in their tiny heads. This is not the Arlinda the visitors know, all hill and sea, camps and stream, but a universe hidden inside the forest. They know which flanks of the hill have secret passes that lead to flat meadows, lush like grasslands – a string of private gardens guarded by tree walls; gardens that echo, that are free of the poisonous fruit.

The forest shows their true colours. The shrubs stand dark against the girl's pale limbs, a shy white hiding under a veil of cinnamon. Greens draw out the orchid-pink under her arms, a hint of gold in the matted hair when the sun is high and strong. The black boy is no darker in the forest. The light and shade cut him in half – a blur of blunt copper and glistening raven feather. The two form the halves of Arlinda's special breed – a speckled serpent hugging the forest, a two-headed Medusa darting among the trees.

Digging for roots in their private garden, they strike early treasure: a cone-shaped bulb, like an egg. Both have their heads down over the spot, digging – the girl with her bare hands, the boy with a piece of jagged rock. The bulb sticks out of the middle of a shallow crater, waiting to be plucked. The boy rips it out by its roots and passes it on to the girl, who draws it close as if to plant a kiss. It passes from one to the other rapidly, till the boy bites into its berry-brown skin. The sharp taste makes him gasp, juice squirting all over his bare arms.

Dropping their prize, the children move to another digging spot, one they suspect holds another egg. From close up they appear as normal a pair of young children as one would find anywhere, except that they exchange no words. In place of speech, they have their own grunts and babble – a language of gestures made with their necks,

17

arms and agile faces. And their laughter, starting as suddenly as it stops, varying in pitch, rising and falling like a duet, as if phrases spoken in a secret language.

The nurse's defect has caused them to be this way. A dumb Norah, unable to teach them words, and their visitors, the scientists, unwilling. But they are normal in their intentions, digging for roots and bulbs, tasting and hiding their treasure, stealing from one another with howls and moans announcing such misconduct.

That the two are unalike is obvious. The boy shows extreme energy that can turn to sloth without warning. He needs to be drawn out of his sullenness with patience. With the girl, it's being outside that makes all the difference. Here she blows light as a breeze – not the cowering sort but a different being altogether. Each is skilled in their own way, perhaps reflecting their mind, and yet their minds seem at one with their limbs – digging, scraping, lunging at their treasure.

A splendid tuber is their prize next time. A grand specimen far superior to the first, a purple core studded with milk-white thorns, like a queen on her throne. Neither shows any haste plucking her from her roots. They lie about on the dirt soil around their freshly dug crater, admiring silently, like earthworms too full to reach for their feast. Itchy fingers shy away. Veterans of the forest, they know perhaps her secret: a sting more painful than the poisonous fruit.

A raindrop wakes them. They fill up the crater in a flurry, burying their treasure, and leave their private garden. Alert to danger, they break into a trot crossing the grass meadows, not once looking back. The hill tracks will turn treacherous with rain, they know; the rocks will come unstuck in the muddy soil. The path will turn into a steep slide, with nothing to hold their feet. It will snap the goats' tender limbs. Now each takes turns leading the way, the boy grabbing the shrubs by the path to keep steady, the girl following with her heels dug as deep as possible into the wet soil. The torrents drown their shrieks, and they must grimace at each other to warn of a rapid turn or a tricky patch. The stream isn't far away; its banks announce the end of the slopes and the comfort of flat earth. The rock steps are not as slippery as the hill tracks. It is a lesser danger. If one falls, they can stand still in the shallow pool and wait for the other to pull them ashore.

They slow for a moment at the stream. Rain reminds them of the sea. Then they go bounding again, with dazzling speed through the mushy shrubs, heads down towards the ground. Running past their camp, they reach the surf in a flash, between lightning and thunder.

'It's the cottage they're living in. The experiment will fail because of Norah's cottage.'

Bates glanced up from his book at Belavoix. It was early evening. The two were resting on the veranda at the end of the day's work, Bates on his chair sipping a drink and Belavoix lying in the hammock.

'You want it right next door, don't you? You want your Juliet right by your side?'

The Frenchman appeared more agitated than usual. An argument had started to brew after two quiet days on the island. They had eaten their evening meal down at the children's camp. Belavoix had sat quietly, hardly nibbling, reading his notebook and glancing absent-mindedly out of the window. But the slow climb back up to their own cottage had put him in a foul mood. Whatever he was thinking, it seemed ready now to spill out on the veranda.

'It's not just *where* it is, but *how* it is.'

'Would you care to explain yourself?'

Belavoix toppled out of his hammock. 'It's not how I dreamt it would be. It is . . . too clean and pure. Too perfect. Almost . . . beautiful!'

'Beautiful?'

'Yes, beautiful. Like an English cottage. Where's the rose garden . . . *je me demande!* Maybe it's on its way, coming by Captain Perry's supply ship. Why the fence, I think, why the nets covering the windows . . . why?'

Bates stared back coldly. He recalled more than a dozen skirmishes between himself and Monsieur Jean-Louis Belavoix. His mental notebook opened on the page marked with the Frenchman's name. A baby-faced genius, a mischief-maker. Arch-heretic of racial science. A whimsical amateur, deluding himself and half of Europe with his half-baked ideas. A master of surprise.

'Would you prefer it if the children's cottage was . . .'

'No, I wouldn't. Whatever it is, it shouldn't be "normal".'

'What's wrong with the window netting? Do you want the flies to kill the samples?'

'Ah! But *that's* what it's all about, Mr Bates. Have you forgotten why we are doing this experiment?'

In his turn, the Frenchman's keen eyes took the measure of Professor Samuel Bates, of his immense stature. The father of craniology, a mind as precise as his instruments. Ruthless by reputation, eager to stamp his authority on his opponents. A collector of skulls, his collection covering each and every race known to science. *He has examined dead men but never seen them die*, Belavoix thought to himself, as he prepared to surprise Bates.

'We agreed that our experiment would be held in a wild forest, no? Not in a garden, but in a *real* jungle. A jungle full of dangers. We agreed that our samples would live like . . . Adam and Eve!'

'We aren't short of dangers here, I think.'

'What dangers, Mr Bates?' Belavoix spoke in a mocking voice. 'The danger of a half-poisonous fruit? The danger of a thunderstorm?'

Eyes back on the book, Bates seemed unwilling to prolong Belavoix's agitation. It was the Frenchman's way not to finish what he had started. His notebooks, Bates was certain, were filled with records – some the result of observations, most conjured from his imagination.

'There's the danger of starvation,' Bates began. 'If the supplies are late reaching Arlinda, for instance. The risk of accident. The children are very young, after all, and not always within the nurse's sight. Then think of the flies and—'

Belavoix interrupted in a whisper, as if he hadn't heard Bates. 'Our experiment is about danger, disease, death. To see which one of the children wins against all three.'

'It's a challenge' – Bates's voice betrayed his annoyance – 'which they must have a chance of winning, not one that condemns them to die.' With a sip of his drink, he shot a glance at Belavoix. 'Would you like us to invite some pirates to Arlinda? Have them hunt the children down as game? Or shall we throw them into the high seas, see whether they swim or sink?'

Belavoix stood immobile before Bates for a few moments, face red, his mind racing faster than his tongue. 'In their English cottage here, they will grow up civilised, as civilised as children back in Europe. Fed by Norah. Bathed. No lice or germs, no enemies to fight . . . the very conditions we didn't want for the experiment.'

'We agreed' – Bates uttered each word carefully – 'to conduct our experiment for twelve years. To keep the children alive. Observe and measure them from infancy to puberty.'

'Twelve years!' Belavoix let out a snort. 'That long? Do you really expect the children to live that long?' Shaking his head of curls, he slumped back into his hammock, glancing over at Quartley, who was dozing on an empty instrument box. 'Are we ready for seven more years of this?'

'Polygenist!' Samuel Bates muttered under his breath. The continental plague threatening all of racial science. The scientist of doom. His rival.

'Twelve years! Will *we* live that long? I hope you've built a graveyard too in Arlinda, Mr Bates!'

NATURAL HISTORY

Nicholas Quartley sat gazing at the islands from his favourite lookout. The sea had turned them into hazy anthills barely rising over the shimmering surf. He tried to gauge their distance, drawing imaginary lines in the air with the tip of his finger. He watched the floating anthills shift course, stretch or shrink each time he let them out of his sight.

It was a game he often played, leaving the scientists' camp to climb up the tricky path to the top of the hill, when the others were resting after lunch. It was his afternoon's diversion – a break from the log and the instruments, from worrying over the experiment's future. The sea calmed him, the nauseous sea that had kept him awake on the journey down. With a finger raised, he tried measuring the most significant distance. From Arlinda to the Madhouse – the laboratory in London, the little brick house he shared with Bates, and Bates's collection. It was greater, he knew, than the simple sum of nautical miles that Captain Perry would proudly announce as they drew near England. A distance measurable only by the length of the argument between his master and the Frenchman. The immensely long and weighty argument behind their experiment.

As a country boy, it had taken Nicholas Quartley more than a few slips and sighs, and a fair dose of scolding to catch a glimpse of that argument. It was luck that had found him a job as an assistant with Professor Bates at the craniology laboratory of the Royal College of Physicians – a job he couldn't have dreamt of as he grew up in Wallsby, his tiny village in Lincolnshire. His father, a quiet and suffering man, had died of consumption when Quartley was still very young. Luckily, he had been spared these qualities, inheriting instead his mother's. She was a courageous woman, a herbalist, always on the move visiting her ailing neighbours, taking her son along with her. She had passed on to him a country quack's intuition, the skill to puzzle out things for herself, and a scavenger's memory that allowed her to squirrel away the secrets of her trade. He had grown up a fine-looking lad with an upright build, pleasing features and a winning smile. His mother had wanted more for him, and urged him to leave their village to seek his fortune elsewhere. He had gone to London when he was twenty, ready to become anything – a coster at the Brill market or a captain's lackey – but a pair of skilled hands had landed him a job helping a taxidermist, where he had learned to dissect and clean a cadaver. It was a short journey from taxidermist to morgue, exchanging one set of tools for another – bullet forceps for a chainsaw to cut open a corpse.

His lucky break had come then. Sir Reginald Holmes, President of the Royal College, had spotted the young man during his rounds of the city's morgues, and recruited him to help his now famous student, Samuel Bates, at the recently started craniology laboratory.

From the beginning Bates had treated him without sympathy. He had shown no kindness, putting Quartley on a par with his despised students, the pick of the universities. He wasn't spared the growling and glaring, the gritting of teeth when the callipers were misread, or one specimen mistaken for another. 'The great man has the patience to learn but not to teach,' his admirers said of Bates. Students left crushed after their course of study with the master craniologist, no wiser for their time spent at the Madhouse. Quartley had survived by virtue of the skills he had learned from his mother. In time, he had impressed his master, become Bates's shadow – his assistant. He had achieved the impossible, managing to keep his job for years, where others before him wouldn't last months.

Wherever he accompanied Bates – to the academies, the great museums, or to the Royal Society – his instinct never left Nicholas Quartley, his smell of things, that often ran faster than reason. He'd surprise his master by the bluntness that showed beneath his obedience, and a clear wit choosing between the half-good and the half-bad. But for the most part, he kept his own views to himself, making the best of his lucky assistantship.

The tragedy of a dead father didn't trouble Quartley much. Bates was the father of all beings dead and alive at the brick laboratory, which sat on a quiet street not far from King's Cross. Bates's rivals had dubbed it the Madhouse. They had refused to join forces with him, stung by his eccentric views and by his temper. It was perplexing to others how Bates, a Cambridge man, had withdrawn from a glittering life in the academies to spend night and day working alone in his laboratory, how he had abandoned the whole corpse in order to study just a small part of it: the cranium. To understand humans one must examine skulls and nothing else! believed Bates, ready as ever to challenge those who thought otherwise. The other scientists had left a mad Bates to occupy the Madhouse by himself, to set up his laboratory in one part of the building, leaving the rest empty. True to his reputation, he had chosen to sleep there as well, uncomfortably, a far cry from the pleasures of his wife's mansion, which he rarely visited. Rumours about his wife added to the mystery of Bates – a sick and rich wife who stayed away from her husband, but kept her eye on his laboratory.

But there was more to the Madhouse's madness than Bates. There was the collection: the skulls. Bates had over three hundred of them, from each race and tribe the world over. A large room of the laboratory, built like a crypt, was reserved for them. Cabinet after cabinet with locks on their doors. A lock and a number marking each inhabitant.

The skulls were almost as famous as their collector. Bates had spent a decade collecting them, exploited every possible source. He had befriended fishermen in order to acquire the drowned that caught in their nets. He had visited lunatic asylums and gaols, paid for the unwanted dead, dealt secretly even with bodysnatchers. His admirers, a small band of wealthy patrons, rewarded explorers and ships' captains handsomely in exchange for the skulls of foreign devils. Nothing like the collection was said to be found anywhere. Some even doubted its very existence. Enquiries about the skulls came from budding craniologists from as far as the Americas. They were the inspiration and basis for Bates's brilliant thesis *Cranial Variations in Man* – the bible of the new science of craniology. They were his evidence and argument, the weapons he wielded to crush his rivals.

The skulls had brought Bates to Arlinda, Nicholas Quartley knew.

A smile crossed Quartley's face as he remembered his first encounter with Bates's collection. He had dreaded entering the crypt. From his desk in the laboratory, he had heard sounds coming from behind the closed door. Moans and whispers, laughter. He hadn't been afraid of cadavers, but feared the skulls. From time to time, Bates brought out a specimen for measurement. They looked harmlessly dead on the laboratory bench. But locked in their cabinets, Quartley was sure they were alive – alive and made evil by their sheer numbers.

'Bring me number 88,' Bates had barked one day, soon after Quartley had started working at the Madhouse.

He stood frozen before his master.

'What is it now? Don't you know where to find it?' He wrote the number down on a slip and held it up. 'Go!'

Quartley felt tempted to ask Jenny, Bates's witch-like caretaker, for help. She was the only other inhabitant of the Madhouse, and knew more about it than anyone he had met. Jenny had been hired to serve a whole army of scientists who were expected to work alongside Bates, but had ended up serving him alone – cleaning the rooms, lighting up the gas lamps, running errands and supplying tea and titbits. The skulls didn't scare Jenny. But her cubbyhole was empty. The dark laboratory, stone-cold, set his heart throbbing. He started to walk towards the crypt, holding the bundle of keys. Number 88! – the most frightening specimen of all, the prize of Bates's collection. Quartley knew all about it from his master's lecture to the students. Buffalo Tail: a fiery Seminole warrior shot in America by an adventurer, the skull brought back to England as a trophy and sold to Bates. A notorious bandit when alive, felled by a single shot from an 88 calibre revolver to the head.

With each step, Quartley could hear Bates's voice: '. . . Gentlemen, observe this member of the American family. The lofty forehead retreating between the parietal bones. The remarkable height of the cranium. The quadrangular form is typical of its race. From the shape of the coronal suture, I am certain the owner was a devil when alive – a thief and a liar. Now observe the fatal shot . . .'

The gas lamp in Quartley's hand lit the room. Tall cupboards split into rows lined the walls, floor to ceiling. He could smell the ugly desiccator vapours that kept the air dry. Boots creaking, he carried the ladder over from the door to one of the cabinets and started to climb. It took a few tries of his shaking hand to pick out the right key from the bundle and unlock number 88.

In the dim light, the skull seemed different: much larger, glowing in the dark. Bringing his face closer, Quartley saw the lofty forehead and the crushed lapidal nodes through which the whistling bullet must have passed. The empty eye sockets stared back. From the top of the ladder, he was aware of the doors of the other cabinets opening. He gazed in alarm at number 91, the Red Devil, saw the Mongol grimacing at him; number 63, the dwarf, with its flattened skull and tiny anterior shaped like an ape. He turned his face from wall to wall in panic, as the cabinets burst open in rapid succession, exposing all three hundred inmates: the ghastly Hottentot, the Eskimo from Baffin Bay, the bronze Malay, the enormous Lap-lander, the bulbous Egyptian, the drowned sailor from the Hebrides, the New Guinea cannibal, the Mississippi Mermaid – that black wench from the American South – and many more. Shaking, he turned, about to climb down, and stared into the face of number 50 – the Villain – a lynched baby-killer; not his skull but a rotting face with a bludgeoned head.

Quartley stumbled on the ladder and fell. Number 88 slipped out of his hands and landed with a thud. Flat on the floor with his face down, he heard the sound die, and another grow with each step coming down the corridor towards the collection room. It stopped at the very edge of his head. Looking up, Quartley saw his master's gigantic frame looming over him.

The fear had gone with time. Working with Bates, he had learned all about the skulls, got used to living with them. It hadn't taken Quartley long to grasp his master's method. He had fallen into the routine of cleaning the old specimens whenever Bates wished to demonstrate them to his students, or to conduct measurements on new ones when they arrived at the laboratory. He had learned to operate the instruments, each designed to measure a skull in a particular way, comparing the results between different specimens. Saxon to Celt. The Caucasian family to the Native American. Comparing a European skull to that of a Negro.

He had surprised Bates by his willingness to learn, but it had taken him much longer to grasp the reason behind his master's method. 'How many more skulls must we measure, sir?' Quartley had asked one day. 'Must we go on till the new ones are no different from what we've already got here?'

Startled, Bates had offered him a rare smile. 'It's not difference we are after, Quartley – not for its own sake. We're here to understand

26

what makes one race superior to another. What makes it stronger, wiser, the winner.'

'Do we know what it is, sir?'

'We'd have no need of you, would we, if we did?' As he left the Madhouse, Bates had thrown his words over his shoulder.

Quartley's luck was in – the luck of the rising number of assistants busily working their hands, feet and weary eyes for the benefit of their masters in the most brilliant century for science. Never since Newton's *Principia* had there been such fervour, such hope. A time to rejoice, as scientists finally turned their minds from the mystery of things to the mystery of man. From arranging the millions of stars neatly into a universe, to arranging the motley races strewn higgledy-piggledly across the earth. From discovering nature's laws to building a theory of the human species.

For centuries, sailors had returned from unknown lands with strange tales of beast-like men and man-like beasts, spreading rumours about creatures that were the very opposite of themselves: black skin, curly hair, flat noses, thick lips. Travelling merchants had brought home accounts of plunder and rape – not committed by them, but by foreign devils. A whole ship burnt by sea gypsies. Hill Indians threatening to swoop down on Spanish gold miners. The New World rife with nightmares – masters, mistresses, overseers, entire families murdered by their dark servants. A black slave raping his fair lady in Jamaica.

Starting with the early Jesuits, missionaries had been filling diaries with laments about the heathen. Brooding tales of cannibals, tribes fighting tribes with cudgels, picks and arrows then singing and dancing together at night. Butchering innocents to placate their gods, sacrificing their own children. Was it lack of faith that made them devilish? Or were they devilish by design? Now at last, Civilised Europe was waking up to the mystery of human variation, ready to solve it once and for all.

It had been a century of collectors. Ships' captains, idle colonial hands and traders had gone into a frenzy. To these gentlemen the scientists owed their greatest debt – gratefully receiving the treasure they brought home. After a century of mammals, birds and fossils, the specimens too had changed. Grave-digging explorers sent home spectacle after spectacle: a whole Inca skeleton; a curious stillborn from Benin preserved in salt – half-boy, half-baboon. Shields and totems, finely woven loincloths. Racks of skulls wrested from headhunters.

Three museums opened in Paris alone in less than a decade. Two in London. Antwerp boasted that its Athenaeum would overtake even the British Museum. Cologne, Edinburgh, Leipzig, Copenhagen weren't far behind. The Queen of Holland offered a generous benefaction to scientists to document the peculiarities of her subjects abroad. The King of Sweden was said to have a keen eye for shrunken heads brought back from New Guinea headhunters, to display to his privileged guests. Even guildsmen and sugar barons felt tempted to abandon their morbid lust for building more cemeteries in order to erect new temples to science.

The scientists' assistants were the foot-soldiers in the grand campaign, lorded over by their masters and their academies. Working silently behind the scenes, they nevertheless rode the crest of the new wave. The study of human variation, christened 'racial science', attracted men from the old sciences – biology and zoology, geology and palaeontology, botany and linguistics – and even some from the recent ones, like craniology. There were annual meetings of scientists from all over the continent at Florence's Academici, at the Société in Paris, and the British Association for the Advancement of Science to debate thorny matters such as human origin, racial types, or the consequence of racial mixture.

Not since Galileo's inquisition over his scandalous treatise on the movement of the earth had science seen so many rivalries. Each scientist claimed to have trapped the ageless mystery of human variation along with its solution in a jewelled box, giving a simple explanation for differences between black skin and white, the savage and the civilised. The meetings saw many such jewelled boxes displayed. Dr Rudolph Müller, the Göttingen anatomist, claimed that the races were different in blood. The Austrian, Tiedemann, vehemently opposed to his Saxon cousin, flaunted a complex formula involving the limbs of the European and the Negro. The Frenchman, Jacques Leconte, was certain that all races had been the same colour in the beginning, with the African simply burnt black by the sun. Octavio Sanchez, the learned Portuguese missionary, suggested that the solution was in the tongues, in the languages spoken by the different races. Captain William Coleman, an occasional visitor from

America, offered a curious view. Early men, he argued, were black, a few having turned white over the years as civilisation advanced.

In Samuel Bates, racial science had more than a pedlar of novel explanations. He was brave enough to throw his jewelled box into the fire of proof. All races belonged to the same species, claimed Bates: each was a member of the Race Adamique. But like siblings they weren't all the same, were not all equal. It was the mind that mattered, made one race superior to another. The brain was the mind's organ, and the cranium the brain's home. Measuring the home would reveal the true worth of its owner. His instruments, some of which he himself had invented, stunned his audiences no less than his skulls. It was a common sight: Bates arriving at a meeting with his assistant behind him sinking under the weight of his boxes. 'That the Negro is more a monkey than a man can't be denied. But why is it so . . . ?' He'd open with a puzzle then offer answer and proof in public, producing instruments and specimens like a magician. He'd compare the skull of a European – 'the race that has produced Newton and Shakespeare' – to one of a Negro: 'the inferior sibling, unable to count the numbers of their fingers'. It was more than colour of skin, he'd thunder on. The savage and the civilised were separated by nature where it mattered most: in the brain. Like Aristotle's *scala naturae*, Bates's Chain of Races charted the entire human species, based on the cranial features of each race. At the top of the chain stood the European, the very best, while the bottom was reserved for the Negro: 'A man he is, like us, but a *lesser* man!' he'd announce to general applause.

Then there were those who disagreed with Bates and believed the very opposite. The polygenists – the likes of a Jean-Louis Belavoix – came to the meetings and displayed their own jewelled boxes. They claimed the races to be unrelated altogether – not siblings but strangers: the European was to the Negro as the eagle was to the raven.

She sits, an elbow on her crossed arm. The cottage is empty with the children playing in the forest and the scientists resting back in their camp. The kitchen table is bare, the instruments locked away in the cupboard. The rough-hewn table top has seen tears and blood, but for now the ordeal is over. There won't be any more measurements soon, she knows, just the other tests for the children.

She sits at the table, staring down at the floor. Not a single muscle in her body moves. Not even a twitch. A droning bee fails to distract her from whatever her mind is turning over. The drizzling rain doesn't arouse a flicker. Mute and paralysed. As if she has the skill to expel her mind from her frail body, and all the nuisance that goes with it – worries, pain, hope. But there are traces of invisible thought in her still pupils. The ticking of the mind. A pure mind dwelling on pure thought.

What does Norah think?

Perhaps the rising sea has reminded her of the passage to Arlinda, the long hours pacing the deck to keep herself from being sick. She hears the creaking masts, the winds of a full sail. Her mind's eye scans the empty corridor before the cabin she shared with her two bundles. The sailors' din. Bates and Belavoix.

Nicholas Quartley was the only one to speak to her during the passage. He would knock on her cabin door, enter and sit awkwardly on the berth facing her. *He has come to do Bates's work for him*, she thought at first. She remembers his hesitation, how he shifted on his seat, glancing nervously at the sleeping children before beginning to speak. The rules. Five years later, she still remembers how Quartley recited them to her on the *Rainbow*. Rules for the children and for her. The Ten Commandments, as she had heard Bates call them.

The children must be raised free – free to roam, play, fight, rest. They must be protected from danger, but left alone to do as they please and to learn from their own mistakes. They are never to be smacked or spanked – their actions are to go uncorrected, unpunished. They must never be allowed to nibble the carrot of praise. Nothing should force the two to be together or apart. The children must choose for themselves.

The nurse must keep them alive. Nothing more. Bring them food from her larder, which the scientists will replenish as long as the experiment lasts. Captain Perry will bring supplies over each month, and she is to leave her list of requirements in a hut near the beach. 'You can have anything you want . . .' Quartley said, trying hard to sound kind. In exchange she was to leave letters, full reports on the children to be carried back to the scientists. 'Write to us about them' – Quartley pointed at the bundles – 'if they are sick; if anything happens . . .'

Neither child should be favoured over the other, she was warned, not even if one turned out to be an angel and the other a devil. She mustn't teach them games, as one would normal children. Simply keep them alive.

And then the last rule. The assistant dropped his voice, barely audible over the creaking of the ship. 'We don't want you to be their mother,' he said. 'They are not to see you happy or sad. No tears, no hugs, no . . . Do you understand, Norah . . . ?'

She nodded.

She breaks from her paralysis into a frenzy. As if her limbs now know no thought, nothing to give pause as she darts from the kitchen to the small garden patch – to her other island, her world of fruits and flowers, wild hedge and stumps of failed trees. She has remembered the berries, now ripe for picking, imagines the children's shrieks as they fight over the brimming pail.

Skirting the hedge, she frowns at a failure – a plant she has stolen from the forest for her garden. Luxuriant red, with a leaf like a rose petal. She has tried once before to have it grow around the prickly shrubs, but it died. She notices the second death and shrugs. It won't stay in her garden, she now knows – not without the precious sap of the killer fig that surrounds it in the forest. She sighs knowing that the wild too have their rules for living and dying.

Bates was the first to hear Norah and the children in the garden patch. He was, as usual, a dozen strides ahead of Belavoix and Quartley, as they climbed down to the children's camp for their evening meal. This was the best time of the day. After weeks of a ship's diet, Norah's simple fare tasted like a grand feast. She had a knack of turning frugal supplies into mouth-watering treats. Salted meat and barley flour, yam from the garden, and sweet palm wine – a gift from Belavoix, bartered from natives on the passage down through the islands. She waved the wand that changed the rustic camp into a home – a change that didn't trouble the Frenchman while the table was full with food.

Quartley walked behind his master, keeping pace with the animated Belavoix, who was describing one of his visits to the Dark Continent, days of hunger followed by a grand but inedible feast at the home of a tribal chief. 'Salted crocodile and cassava! Food for the dogs!' With one eye on Bates, Quartley followed the story, salivating

31

for Norah's table if not the chief's. He saw Bates come to an abrupt halt at the cottage steps, then go around to the garden rather than up to the kitchen. As they rounded the corner, they heard what had attracted Bates's attention.

The children and their nurse were playing a game with berries in the garden. A whole pail lay upturned, a pile of gleaming red. The girl ran around the patch while the boy grabbed handfuls of berries and rushed to the centre to build a small pyramid of fruit. Then it was the girl's turn to build a pyramid, while the boy set off for a run. Norah clapped, egging the children on without words. After a round of running and dashing, the three pored over the two small pyramids – Norah counting the berries in each through her silent lips and the children with their fingers. The builder of the bigger pyramid was the winner, and was rewarded with the berries from both piles.

As they watched silently, Norah hugged the loser, then set both children off on another round.

The words still frozen on his lips, Belavoix instinctively reached for his notebook. His face turned red in excitement, as if he was witnessing a crucial scene, far more important than the daily measurements.

Suddenly, Bates's angry voice burst on them. 'What do you think you're doing?' He leapt over the hedge, landing almost on top of Norah. 'Don't you know the rules?'

Norah's body stiffened instantly. She sat, eyes down, arms close by her side, like a kneeling prisoner. She looked like a tree snapped by a storm. Grabbing her by the hair, Bates jerked up her head to shout into her face. 'How dare you break the rules! You wretch! Do you think we brought you here to teach them games? I'll teach *you* a few things!'

Quartley froze to the ground, struck by Bates's rasping voice.

The girl dashed forward a few paces to grab Norah's waist, burying her face against her flanks, a moan muffled by the nurse's skirt. Even before the eruption, the boy had spotted the visitors. He had started to run towards Bates, a grin on his face. A yard or so now from the kneeling Norah, he stood still, alert and wary. As if his head was once again locked in Bates's trap.

'You have taught them to count,' Bates said, his anger giving way to a frightening calm. 'You were told not to. You were told never to play games with them.'

The girl's moan grew to a wail. Suddenly, the boy came alive, dashing towards Bates with a cry and hurling himself on his back. Bates raised a hand to brush him off without letting go of Norah's head. The boy fell down, picked himself up and set off again, bent on pulling Bates away from Norah, still yelling at the top of his voice. Quartley caught him just in the nick of time, before Bates could hit him. He struggled to keep the boy away from his master, and darted a glance at Belavoix. What would the Frenchman do? Would he let Bates rage on? Surely he'd intervene, distract him with an argument, or step in to separate him from Norah? Still grappling with the boy, he saw Belavoix engrossed in his notebook, his face flushed.

'You want to spoil our experiment, don't you?' Bates went on viciously. 'You can't! You are *nothing* to us. Nothing.' His face hardened still more as he stooped to whisper into Norah's ear. 'Wouldn't worry us a bit if we had to get rid of you and get another nurse.'

She sits on the steps listening to the sea. The children are asleep in the dark cottage. The visitors have gone back to their camp; the kitchen table is bare again. Now her thoughts are deeper, barely rising to her still eyes. Not even a flicker. What does she think? Is it the evening's ordeal, her mind running back over Bates's words? Her ears still ringing . . . Is it guilt that feeds her mind? Does she reflect on her sins, the rules that she has broken? Does she mull over life on Arlinda, a life without games, living like a stranger with the children?

Or is it her other tragedy that occupies her, the one that is even older than the experiment? The thoughts that are at the very bottom of her heart, deeper than her guilt or the wounds of a scolding . . .

Which is the deeper, she thinks. The sea or the bottom of her heart?

Lying on his camp bed, Nicholas Quartley goes over Bates's outburst. No stranger to his master's temper, he suffers still for the inmates of the other camp. Their few days of calm seem to have been broken. He wonders what Bates will do next. Take Norah back with them . . . replace her with another . . . ? In the meantime, will they begin to pay more attention to the children, stalk them all over the island, spy on their games? The seven remaining years of the experiment loom ahead. He thinks again of the distance between the two worlds: the Madhouse and Arlinda; the skulls and the children. He thinks of the sea, trapped between two continents, dark and fair.

THE EXPERIMENT

That he was of a hostile breed, there was no doubt. Like Bates, a fighting man. A gambler, not simply a roller of dice. A warrior who didn't hope but *knew* he'd win. A sower of discord. A mischief-maker. A philosopher of 'errors'. Logical to a fault, like an English lawyer. An extreme daydreamer. A murderer, committing his crimes in broad daylight. When he challenged his rivals, his letters, such as the one he sent to Bates, reeked of scorn.

Pity those who read the Bible as science! who believe we all have come from the 'original couple'. Of what race was Adam? If the Jews are to be believed, he must have been a Red Indian, for Adam in Hebrew means red! If fossil diggers are right, he must have been black like a Negro, turning white with civilisation. If we listen to the linguists, he was brown, as brown as the Hindu, whose language is the mother of all languages. How absurd! Did all trees come from one tree? All birds from one bird? Every fish in the ocean from the roe of a fertile salmon?

Their first encounter had been in Florence, at the Palazzo Vecchio, during a meeting of Europe's leading race scientists. Bates had just finished demonstrating yet another new instrument to an enchanted audience, members of the distinguished Academici Investigantes. The goniometer measured the facial angle of the cranium between the slope of the nose and the line joining the ears. Bates had applied it to a marble bust of Jupiter, and read the result: 100 degrees. Then it was applied to a European skull: 90 degrees. Then to a Negro's: 70 degrees. And finally to an ape's: 60 degrees. This was Bates's proof. His demonstration of the natural order of races.

Jean-Louis Belavoix had stood up amidst the applause that followed Bates's exhibition, and had begun all at once to speak in a loud
voice. 'How absurd, Mr Bates!' He called down. 'Are we really to
believe that men differ from each other simply because of the funny
angle under their noses? Is that why the German is stubborn, the
Italian greedy, the English cunning, the Finn dull, and the French . . .
charming? Will your facial angle explain why the Greeks were slaves
to the Romans? No! You're carrying it too far!'

Before an astounded audience, he had plunged his knife into
Bates's famous Chain of Races. 'And what about our Semitic
saviour? If the Englishman is going to be at the top and the Negro
at the bottom, where will the brown Jesus stand in your chain?'

Members of the Academici were troubled by the outburst, coming
as it did from a man whose reputation as a race scientist was rapidly
spreading across Europe. Although incensed at the time, Bates had
chosen to ignore the much younger man, refusing to dignify his
outburst with a reply. Then in the days following the scene at
Florence, when he was still smarting over the vulgar attack, he
had received a letter from Belavoix, written in a milder tone but
unrepentant. The paper bore the watermark of the French Société: a
flying lark. 'Of man's origin, we know nothing,' Belavoix began.

It is sad we are so far apart in our views, separated by a simple
belief. The races are mostly alike, you think, in spite of some
differences. But I believe the opposite. That they are really very
different, in spite of a passing resemblance.

For you, creation is as neat and clean as an English house – an
orderly chain. For me it is mad. To study man, you have taken out
your knife, cut him up in small pieces, sliced open his skull. We
French have followed him to his home, not to the morgue.

The *perturbateur*, Belavoix's own treatise on race was arch-heresy
in the eyes of most scientists. A sad solution to the mystery of
human variation, born of a curious pessimism at odds with his
energy and the legendary charm that made him so irresistible to
women. After a bout of medical studies at Val de Grâce hospital in
Paris, he had joined L'étrangère – the French Foreign Legion – as a
recruit, and travelled to dangerous parts of the world. From early
days, he had been drawn to disease, fascinated by the rare ones

that afflicted soldiers and wiped out entire regiments. He'd search under rocks, learn the languages of tribes, observe their rites – filling notebooks as rapidly as he had mastered the art of tantalising speculation.

Arriving once in a remote Nubi town in northern Africa, the Legion had witnessed the aftermath of a grisly massacre. There had been a war between neighbours – a darker southern tribe invading the rich north, storming the adobe forts and overcoming the Nubi by their sheer numbers. Plunder had ended in butchery. What they saw appalled them: a whole city crawling about without limbs, without arms and feet, like worms, half-alive, trailing blood on the sand.

Hardened soldiers broke down and wept. Why . . . ? they asked each other. Scenes of senseless cruelty made the onlookers suffer as much as the victims. Jean-Louis Belavoix, the young doctor, had raised his comrades' spirits one by one, comforted them with his explanation. It was a germ. The germ of racial hatred had caused the massacre. The same germ that was found everywhere, from the Great Republic to the desert kingdoms of Africa. It lived within murderers, victims and saviours – couldn't be destroyed or suppressed for long.

The explanation had stunned the assembled members of the Société when he returned to France, just as it had stunned his comrades in the desert. He had managed to convince his audience with the science of the germ. A science born of deathly journeys, witnessing murder, plunder and rape. A smelly science, with laws that took root under the blinding sun and the arctic frost.

The germ lay in Belavoix's jewelled box, gnawed away at his rivals. The races, he'd announce in his singsong voice, were distinct – they were different species. 'Two hands and two feet, a head and a belly don't make the same animal!' However similar their bodies, the minds were strangers to one another. 'It isn't that the Negro is inferior to us,' he argued, 'but that he is *unrelated* to us. Would you compare a horse with a zebra?' The races were equal only in one thing: the germ they shared. And it woke in them when they met, turned them into two species of fighting animal, driven to covet and conquer the other. That was their *only* similarity. According to Belavoix, *all* races were doomed, doomed to plunder and be plundered, to murder and die. It was a curse, a flaw that must've been in the seeds of all Adams – white, black, yellow, red.

His sweet face smiling, he would deliver judgement on the past and future of all races. 'War is inevitable! If the European doesn't suppress the Negro, the Negro will suppress the European and make him his slave.'

Belavoix's letter had offered Bates a proposal: an experiment. 'There is only one way to prove which of us is wrong. The only hope for science is *l'épreuve*!'

They met in Bates's study in the Madhouse. Unlike the stark laboratory, it was a hoarder's room, every inch taken up with stacks of paper, rolled-up charts and broken instruments. The walls were pasted with skull drawings, some faded, the ink still fresh on others. A brass fumigator with a spherical bowl sat on Bates's desk, a reminder that the craniologist had once been a dissector of corpses.

Bates sat with Quartley facing Belavoix. Sir Reginald Holmes was present as well, sitting on the window sill – the great statesman of science, holder of many titles: President of the Royal Society, Director of the British Museum. He was considered by many to be the most trusted guardian of racial science. A kind uncle among scientists, just as he was a fiend to the financiers, a ruthless scavenger of funds for worthwhile ventures. He was Bates's champion, a self-appointed spokesman for his craniology.

'You have measured many skulls, Monsieur Bates,' Belavoix said with a charming smile. 'Do you know anything more that you didn't know before?'

Bates chose not to rise to Belavoix's opening shot, and began calmly. 'Every new specimen has advanced our knowledge of—'

'And what will you achieve when a million more have been measured?'

Familiar with Bates's temper, Holmes intervened lightly. 'Are you suggesting that physical measurements are irrelevant, Monsieur Belavoix?'

The Frenchman crossed his legs carefully, eyes twinkling. 'The human form is deceptive, Sir Reginald. Very deceptive. If Mr Bates left his laboratory, he'd be astonished, I'm certain. On the shores of Patagonia he'd see men taller than us, taller than the tallest, reaching well over six feet! In the jungle of Congo, he'd find a tribe of albinos. They are quite white, you know – milk-white eyebrows and hair. The sun brings tears to their weak eyes, but they see very well in the moonlight, for which reason they are called "moon-eyed".'

'Are you suggesting that what we do here is futile?' Bates repeated Holmes's question coldly.

'What if you were to examine the skull of a white woman, only to learn she was really a Berber from Africa?'

'Freaks appear in every race.'

'Freaks?'

'Yes. Think of dwarfs, hunchbacks, homosexuals.'

Belavoix rolled his eyes. 'Even if the skulls are different, what does it prove? Nature is full of differences, isn't it?' This time he turned to Holmes, expecting a genial nod.

Bates's crisp voice signalled the start of the duel. 'It proves the superiority of one race over another.'

'Superiority!'

'Yes. *Natural* superiority.'

'I believe one race can win over another, Mr Bates. But not by *natural* superiority.'

'Then how?'

Belavoix smiled. 'By what the English call *chance*.'

'Chance?'

The Frenchman ignored Bates's frown. 'The chance of a mistake on the battlefield. A sudden stroke of luck, a miraculous turn in the weather, or . . .'

'Are you suggesting then that the Creator is hiding behind the clouds and decides who wins and who loses?'

'Every race loses in the end. We all do!'

Even Holmes seemed at a loss for words at that moment – a man known for his exceptional power to blend both sides of an argument. A shadow appeared in the doorway, and Belavoix sprang up to greet Jenny, who entered with the tea tray. 'Ah! Tea time! How wonderful! In France, a lady brings nothing but trouble!'

After a suitable number of sips, Holmes recovered his magisterial tone. 'There are differences, as we know, in our views. But if one were to disprove the other –' he looked at both Bates and Belavoix – 'we must find a better way than endless arguing.'

'But I have already found a way. Haven't you . . .' Belavoix struggled with a slice of bread going laboriously down his throat. 'Haven't you spoken to Sir Reginald of my letter, Mr Bates?'

'About the experiment, do you mean?' Holmes appeared relieved to have it aired at last.

Belavoix nodded.

The senior scientist opened a file that was on the desk, and fished out an envelope. 'Let's see what it is exactly that you are proposing . . .' Then he started to read from Belavoix's letter.

What if we were to bring up two children in an isolated place? Each of a different race. Without any influence from outside, without anyone telling them who they were, or which race they belonged to. We could both examine them at frequent intervals to see if they change in any way as they grow up. If one becomes naturally superior to the other – in morality and intelligence – or if they remain equal. We can keep them hidden from the world for as long as we want. In the end, we'll have proof; the experiment will tell us more about the races than all our silly arguments.

Holmes cleared his throat. 'And this will settle your difference with Mr Bates, you think?'

'Absolutely!' Belavoix replied.

Leaning forward, Bates appeared suddenly intense. 'And you suggest that we measure the specimens as they grow up?'

'*You* measure, Mr Bates.' Belavoix smacked his lips. 'Use as many instruments as you want. We will both observe them.'

'A Negro child, and a European?'

'Yes!'

'Placed under the same climate, furnished with the same diet, and left to roam cut off from all civilised intercourse?'

The Frenchman leapt from his chair in excitement. 'In the wild, lost in the forest! We shall clothe them and feed them, but only just . . . They'll grow up without words, without song, without games.' His chin started to quiver. 'Without punishment. Without God.'

'And what will these children . . . these *feral* children show us?' Holmes asked, still playing the dutiful sceptic.

'These children of nature will show us the truth about the races.'

The study fell silent once again. Quartley fidgeted over his notes. Holmes waited for Bates's reaction. Slices of bread and butter went down Belavoix's throat one after another.

Head turned towards the window, Bates eyed puffs of clouds, addressing them as if they were his students. 'The races are born identical. A black child is the same as a white one. With time the *cutis vera* fills with blood. Changes occur very quickly in their crania. They *become* different – one becomes superior to the other. It isn't just their bones –' he turned to look Belavoix in the eye – 'their minds are stamped by nature. The white is cleverer and kinder – the leader. In a pure laboratory, the changes would be clear, one could—'

A normally patient Holmes broke in. 'And so you predict what?'

'I predict natural superiority. If the children are left from infancy to puberty under such conditions, the white will leave the forest superior to the black. It will prove that the Negro is inferior not because he is kept as a slave but because of the way he is – *naturally*.'

The statesman of science looked triumphant. Turning to Belavoix, he demanded to know what his prediction would be.

'The children,' the Frenchman replied with a sweet smile, 'will grow up equal. Equal in the *pure laboratory* of nature. Not one cleverer or kinder than the other. And then, something will happen.'

'Something? What do you mean?'

'An accident.'

Holmes raised an eyebrow. 'Accident?'

'Yes, an accident will happen. One will murder the other.'

Leaving Bates back at the camp, Quartley and Belavoix went up to the hill top just as the sun was about to dip into the sea. Despite their rivalry, Quartley found the Frenchman jovial company. The two often wandered off after a long day of measurements and observations. In the few hours they spent together, Belavoix dwelt on his favourite diseases, ones he was undeniably suffering from.

In the early years of their visits, he had complained constantly of giddiness and a headache that rose during the day and refused to go away at night. It was common among legionnaires, he had confided in Quartley, an unfortunate consequence of 'untreatable malaria', capable of causing paralytic strokes. He also had a history of digestive troubles, which had been worsened by his travels. Chilblains to trismus, dropsy to Asiatic cholera, he described the strangest of afflictions, and their even stranger cures, the secrets of which he claimed to have learned from primitive tribes.

'Africa has the most magnificent diseases of all!' Groaning under the pain of a troubled knee, Belavoix's face nevertheless betrayed the thrill of an explorer. 'Do you know how many species of flies there are in these bushes?'

Quartley shook his head.

'More than all the species of animals, birds and insects found in Europe. And each is capable of carrying a deadly germ.' He cast a quick look at Quartley's alarmed face, then went on. 'The female blackfly's bite causes blindness. Just one sting from the pig-fly is enough for the skin to break out into lesions, through which the Guinea worm can enter the body, feeding on the flesh inside and growing to more than three feet in length.'

Shuddering, Quartley scanned the hill top for the deadly species. 'How can we protect ourselves, sir . . . ?'

Belavoix smiled the hopeless smile of the seasoned explorer. 'Europeans have tried everything: netting for the windows, soaking the wooden beams of homes in resin, sprinkling ocean salt on the floors . . . But all it takes to die is a sting from a single fly.'

The cool air at the top did nothing to dampen the Frenchman, or calm his lust for deadly diseases. 'Ah! Forget the flies, Quartley,' he sighed; 'the sea is even deadlier!' Pronouncing the name with great difficulty, he explained the meaning of *thalassophalia*. 'The noblest of diseases! found only among the noblest of races: the Greeks.' It started, according to Belavoix, with a simple love of the sea, gazing at the waves, progressing gradually to abandonment of all earthly pleasures. 'The victim forgets everything, everyone. Music, wine. Even love . . .' In the final stages, Belavoix went on, the victim drowned himself.

Quartley turned his face away from the dark horizon, towards the slopes that ran down to the children's camp.

'Could the children be struck by . . .'

'No, no!' Belavoix was quick to assure Quartley of the unlikelihood of such an event. 'Fortunately, the noble disease has never been known to strike the Saxon or the Negro. The children will suffer from common troubles – *les maladies banales*, as we say in France.'

'Like worms?'

'Yes! That's why the boy is always hungry! He wants to eat your finger!'

'And the girl? She appears to be healthy, but . . .'

'Healthy!' Belavoix snorted. 'She's far from healthy. In fact she shows every sign of a dangerous disease.'

'Dangerous?'

'Drowsy all day, sleeping at night with a nervous twitch on her face. If she could speak, she'd complain of a throbbing head, and a cutting pain all over her body.'

'But she appears . . . quite normal, except for her unreasonable fear.'

'Normal!' Belavoix laughed. 'Is that what you call normal – an absence of outward symptoms? Inside she is far from normal, I tell you. Apoplexy of the brain affects both body and mind. Most dangerous!'

From their perch they looked down at the children's camp rapidly darkening under the shadows, erasing all memory of the day's work. The inhabitants of the camp seemed far more mysterious than was revealed by the cranial log. As if by instinct, both thought of the third inhabitant.

'And what do you think the adult is suffering from?'

'You mean the nurse, sir?'

'Call her what you wish, Quartley. To me, she is the Bird of Paradise!'

It hadn't occurred to Quartley that Norah could be suffering from anything more severe than her impairment. 'It is her lack of speech . . .'

'That's a condition, not a disease.' Belavoix shook his head vehemently. 'Every man or woman, whatever the race, must suffer from something or other . . . no?'

Her 'condition' had surprised Quartley when he had first seen her at the Madhouse. *She is more than pretty*, he had thought, as she had turned to face him. Not a coster-girl or a street tramp, almost as delicate as a lady. He had seen a smouldering something in her eyes, giving just half an ear to Jenny as she rattled on. She was an exceptional girl, Jenny had said – knew how to read and write, all her gifts sullied sadly by one single blemish. Jenny had started to laugh, then stopped, seeing Quartley's look. She had had a tragic life, minders who brought her over from her asylum had said.

Bates's choice had surprised Quartley. He had asked his master for an explanation.

'Why must she be dumb, sir?'

Bates had given him a mocking smile. 'You haven't worked that out yet?'

'No, sir.'

'To keep our samples ignorant of their races. How else can we prevent them from knowing who they really are?'

Holmes, who was also present, had nodded in agreement. 'Even without words, the caretaker could, of course, influence the children, but . . .'

'But our rules will forbid that.' Bates had squashed any remaining doubt.

Sitting on the hill top, Nicholas Quartley puzzled over the Frenchman's words. He thought hard about Norah, examining her from head to toe in his mind. All outward symptoms pointed to an energetic body – too energetic perhaps, unrelenting in minding both the camps, keeping an eye on the children and their visitors. Was she prettier now than when he had seen her first? From what was visible to the eye, Quartley failed to detect any sickness in Norah.

'It is difficult to know, sir. Maybe there is a defect in her . . .'

'Yes, I wonder what her defect is.' Belavoix fell silent, then his eyes twinkled as he rose to leave. '*That* is a mystery far greater than the mystery of our experiment!'

'You were wrong to scold the nurse, Mr Bates.'

His boots grinding to a halt, Bates turned to face Belavoix, coming down to the children's camp in the morning.

'It was silly to stop the children. It was, after all, only a game they were playing.'

'Wrong?' Bates bit into Belavoix's word.

'Yes, a mistake.' As he followed Bates and Quartley at his leisurely pace, the Frenchman appeared serene. 'A false obsession with rules. How very English . . .'

'It is no mistake. The rules are there to protect the experiment.'

'And how could the little berry-race spoil it?'

Bates remained silent for a moment. Perhaps his rival had genuinely overlooked the obvious, or was he simply bent on provoking an argument? 'The game that you speak of was artificial. We must do nothing to stimulate the samples.'

'Ah, artificial!' Belavoix had caught up with Bates now and stood facing him on the goat path. '*Je comprends* . . .'

'If the children had come up with it by themselves, we'd have no difficulty.' Bates appeared to soften at Belavoix's attention. 'But it was the nurse's game.'

'But everything here is artificial. The two camps, the kind English *nourrice* . . . everything. What was so special about the game?'

Bates narrowed his eyes. 'Are you suggesting we rear the samples as normal children, as we would back in Europe? Teach them games, rhymes, to count their numbers . . . table manners even?' He took a step forward, looking Belavoix straight in the eye. 'I thought you were arguing the very opposite just the other day. I thought you wanted the samples to live like wild animals in a jungle full of dangers.'

'No, no . . .' Belavoix waved his arms about madly, as if trying to fight off a swarm of flies. Then he composed himself, and started to explain as one would to a novice: 'A jungle, a *real* jungle, is unpredictable. In it the children would discover a new world every day. They'd learn to live in that world . . . fight for food, learn to amuse themselves . . . But here, in this *sheltered* world, *we* must create the dangers and delights for them. In the absence of natural surprises, *we* must surprise them. Teach them games to see who wins and who loses. Only then will we know how different they are from one another.'

'I am sure there are amusements enough to be found here.'

'Yes?' Belavoix laughed. 'Can you show me a few, Mr Bates?'

Bates knew his answer, but appeared to dwell on Belavoix's argument. 'What you say is worthy of some thought. But it has nothing to do with the game they were playing. We couldn't have detected true differences between the samples from it.'

'I disagree.' Belavoix seemed to sense victory over Bates. 'This is another example of your English stubbornness. The children were playing a game designed by nature, giving us a chance to observe the natural bent of both.'

'*Designed by nature!*' Bates almost broke into a laugh. 'Would you care to explain yourself?'

'Yes, I'll explain. I'll explain so simply that you can follow easily.' As he stood before Bates, his large frame swaying, the Frenchman began in an almost poetic voice. 'Imagine Norah as Nature herself: a mute mother forced to raise her children, powerful and helpless at the same time. She can feed and clothe them, but can't teach them good or evil. She lives for others, not for herself. Your rules for her are like God's rules for Nature. You've taken away her tears, forbidden her to love the children. Her game is Nature's game. It is born not of a clever mind but an idle mind. It is the only thing *not* artificial on Arlinda.'

Bates glared in silence at Belavoix for a few moments, then clicked his heels and turned to march ahead, crossing the spring in quick steps and reaching the children's camp. From the far bank, Belavoix called out to him.

'We must pay more attention to Norah, Mr Bates! She's more valuable than your goniometer . . .'

A lizard. Its tail as long as the boy's palm is wide, the body half the length of its tail. In captivity, it looks tame, lying dead-still at the bottom of the pail the children have stolen from the cottage. A dark prison it is, just a thin light-shaft allowed in through the lid – dark and empty, without green moss to wrap around its belly, or loose gravel to strike up a shower of dust with its tail. It is hard to tell if it can change its colour, or if it is of the other kind, always a muddy green, in sun or in shade. Mustard seeds dot its head, each like a blinking eye, make it lizard-like – not a twig, but alive, assuring its captors that it is still there after three long days and nights.

When the lid opens, two faces peer down: one white, one black. Proud and curious. Eyes take in the full measure of a tricky task, achieved not without the full stretch of their young minds. A task that has pitted them against a vastly superior creature, one capable of rapid retreat into impenetrable craters, darting across the sand with weightless feet at lightning speed. For three days, they have simply prised open the lid to watch, to see with their eyes what they thought impossible, without any desire to do more with their prisoner.

They spotted the head first. A beetle, they thought, till they saw the raised tail – two creatures joined at the neck, with one head. It was different from water-lizards they caught in their palms while swimming in the spring. Sharp scales pricked their skin, the wriggling beasts giving up after a few minutes of struggle, feigning a quick painless death, then returned to life as soon as the children left.

They chased the lizard for a whole afternoon, keeping their eyes fixed on the spotted head for fear of losing it in the tall bush and the burnt-brown reed. The boy yelped as he ran, dragging a gnarled branch behind him, striking tree trunks, setting flight to bees and wasps, scattering and scaring everything except their prey. It chose its own battlefield: a narrow patch between the wet sand and the steep boulders at the foot of the hill. In a close encounter, the girl swooped down from a low hanging branch to trap the lizard. But it escaped through the narrowest of gaps under her arm. They chased it up a tree, sprinted after it along the beach, hoping it'd stop at the edge of the waves and surrender. They thought they would be able to simply scoop it up like a dead seahorse.

The girl disappeared after a while, running back towards their camp and returning with a wooden pail, its lid banging against its side. She had stolen it from the kitchen, from the row of pails that stocked their supplies, each smelling of overripe turnip or rancid cabbage. The two examined the pail, exchanging notes with their eyes. Then it was back to the chase, but now they had a plan.

The lizard looks up from its dark well. It remembers the fatal error: the illusion of a nest, a small cave at the root of a dead trunk. The heat of the chase caused it to blunder, to run into the pail, which lay on its side with the lid open in invitation. The girl, hiding behind the pail, turned it upright in a flash and brought the lid down with a thud. A simple illusion had led to its capture at the hands of an inferior. What would they do now? Start a new game, or do as captors do to prisoners, squash it to death?

After three days of observing, the girl reaches into the pail to pick up the lizard. She tries to touch its belly with the tip of her middle finger. It squirms, darting past her outstretched hand, running around in circles. She misses every time she tries, pursing her lips in disappointment. The boy tries next, but he is no more successful than the girl. The chase starts all over again, the prisoner managing to stay free of their touch inside the pail.

What has drawn them to the lizard is hard to tell. The girl seems to take after the gulls, happy to poke sand all day with their beaks. There's a gleam in the boy's eyes whenever he looks at the creature. Does he want to bite off its head? Perhaps the worms are turning in his belly, demanding a feast.

The last attempt to catch the lizard ends in pain. The girl uses both hands, grabbing at last its soft middle, then raises it to her face as if to plant a kiss on its head. It hisses, lashing out its tongue, wriggles to be free. It bites the girl's little finger. She drops the lizard back into the pail with a scream. Her face reddens. A drop of blood stands where the nail-sharp fangs have pierced skin. Quiet at first, the boy starts yelping. He dashes round and round the pail, circle after circle. Then both run towards the stream, splashing into it at the same time and throwing up a wave that floods the stone steps.

Face up, they float, Clouds criss-cross the blue sky, appearing like the lizard, the sunbursts matching its mustard spots. Even though the pain has gone, the girl sniffles; her eyes flicker as she remembers the surprise attack. What will they do with it now? What use is it to them? Unlike the water-lizards, they can't kill it simply by holding it in their palms . . .

As the lid opens, the lizard sees two faces. Expressionless. The lip of a pitcher appears, then tilts down. Water rushes into the pail – warm spring water laced with coiled-up weed and rubble. Gurgles down like the spring itself, water rising in the pail inch by inch. The children are busy now, dashing to the spring and dashing back, taking turns lowering the pitcher, snitched like the pail from the kitchen behind the nurse's back. Each time they remember to shut the lid before going for the next fill-up.

Telescope to one eye and notebook open on his lap, Belavoix observes them from the tree house that Quartley has built for him. He smacks his lips as he scribbles down the points, looks up to see if the job is complete. He sees the children staring down at the pail filled to the brim, a dead lizard floating inside, belly up, its head turned the same colour as its tail.

TABULA RASA

boy and a girl. A *black* boy and a *white* girl.

A frown had appeared on Sir Reginald Holmes's elegant face, a question written plainly in his prominent blue eyes. Gathered with Bates and Quartley in his library, he was taking stock of the most important scientific venture of his illustrious career. Bates had come well prepared to report on preparations prior to their journey to Arlinda with the samples.

'A girl . . . ?' Holmes appeared to be confused by the unexpected choice. 'I thought you wished to study differences between the black race and the white.'

They sat in a room befitting a gentleman, walls wrapped in walnut and sporting stuffed game-heads, a bay window drawing in a fine garden. Smoking his pipe and gazing out of the window, Bates prolonged his mentor's confusion.

'The selection of the samples could be quite tricky. We'd need a pure *tabula rasa*. Nothing short of it.' Holmes paused. 'What if it was defective to begin with, unable to compete against its rival?'

'You mean our white child?'

'Yes . . .' Holmes continued, his confusion giving way to concern. 'What if it wasn't the best example of the white race? If it was a weak child born of a sick mother? A freak even . . .'

Bates nodded, refusing still to explain his unusual decision.

'It must be superior and consistent . . . both. I wouldn't choose an Irish or a west-country Celt, or a Scot for that matter: their range can vary enormously.' Holmes gave Bates a serious look. 'We must have an English boy.'

'What's wrong with an English girl?' Bates turned his gaze from the window. 'What do we know about the human female, Quartley?'

'The female is inferior to the male, sir.'

'*All* females or just those of a particular race?'

'Brain size and facial angle are less for females of all races compared to the males. One finds the same result in the Saxon, the Gaul, the Mongol, the Hottentot . . .'

'Yes.' Bates looked satisfied with his assistant's report. 'The mental faculties are more energetic in males than in females. The white male is far superior to the white female, whose mind is closer to those of children and savages.' He looked at Holmes with a faint smile on his face. 'Even the Egyptians knew that, didn't they, studying their subject races?' Bates appeared to tease his former mentor with his unfinished argument. 'But that doesn't answer your question, does it? It doesn't tell you why we can safely use a white girl in our experiment.'

'No . . .' Holmes's face showed a hint of calm, as he waited for his favourite pupil to surprise him once again with his brilliance.

'Now let's ask ourselves how the inferior white compares to the superior black. What can we say about a white female and a black male?'

'The white female on average has a brain size of seventy-five cubic inches and a facial angle of eighty-one degrees,' Quartley started, as if on cue. 'By contrast, the black male's brain size is about seventy cubic inches, and the average facial angle is only seventy-one degrees.'

'So the inferior white is still superior to the very best that the Negro race can offer?'

'Yes, sir.'

'Her sex is less important than her race, which makes her superior, *far* superior, to her rival. If we trust our craniology, we'll have no reason to fear the result.' Bates appeared to rest his case, before offering his final argument. 'It is the *right* sample for us. The white girl's victory will do more for our racial theory than anything else.'

The skull doctor! Quartley had marvelled at the display – his master's unrivalled skill in winning a sceptic over. The pattern was always the same: weeks of drudgery poring over obscure facts, jotting down page after page of notes, measuring and re-measuring skulls from his collection, then a discovery that stunned everyone and seemed all but obvious, as natural as an apple dropping from the branch of a tree.

Once Holmes, acutely questioning beneath his genial nature, had agreed to have a girl as a sample, the attention shifted to the search for the children. The Frenchman could be asked to procure the boy, Holmes thought. After all, there was no shortage of baby slaves in their African empire. A white girl wasn't a rarity either in London, awash with orphans – unwanted fruits of the opium sot flooding in from the marshy fens. Just a small hint of doubt remained.

'Do you think Monsieur Belavoix will be happy with your argument about using a white girl? Will he find the female acceptable as a sample?'

Bates thought for a moment, then brushed off Holmes's concern. 'I don't think that will worry the storyteller. He'll have more yarns to spin now, won't he?'

His face appears different in the scientists' camp from inside his London laboratory. Turned in profile, holding a drink in one hand, an open book in the other. The lamp flickers on the page, pegged down by a thumb. His gaze rises from the book to the dark night around the veranda then turns back. Eyelids flutter. Lashes stay frozen over a line that has arrested his mind. It is a dreamer's face. Nothing to suggest the mighty will and the sharp temper. Until a sudden twist of the fist turns the book into a swat to kill a gnat drawn to the lamp's flame.

Then back to the unread word.

It is hard to know what he thinks, what turns inside the skull of the skull doctor, as he retracts his eyes from the fireflies' dance to the flickering page to read an account of life in Botany Bay written by a missionary's wife. Does he imagine another place, sitting on a veranda in the company of the author, watching . . . *those miserable, wandering, homeless and lawless savages, fleeing like bears and wolves at the sight of the civilised man, falling at the mere touch of his hand to the earth along with the ancient forests which alone have afforded shelter over centuries of their savage lives* . . . Does he regret the absent savages? Does he secretly agree with his rival, wishing upon themselves an even wilder Arlinda?

Perhaps his mind hasn't travelled so far as the shores of Australia, but is still hovering among his own kind. Not to Botany Bay but to York and Aberdeen, Nottingham, Bristol, among the leading lights of the civilised world. Leading lights! He frowns between rapid sips of his drink. A frown that is reserved for his enemies. The lettered clowns, false pedants, sophists, splitters, the masters of poisonous slander. The frozen toads. Does he see such a one as an Edward Burnett? A mind like a milk jar, trumpeting his theories as superior even to those of the great Samuel Bates? Or does he think of the gold-vested Lord Skeene, walking on his toes and striking out his chin? Skeene, the lover of disputes, little more than a hobbyist and a quack. A dozen more like them? Does the night resurrect them all, those waiting back in Europe to tear him to pieces?

Holmes was initially in favour of rallying them as well to the cause. 'The greatest experiment in racial science needs all its able soldiers,' he said. 'It would be foolish to fight a solitary duel with Belavoix, better to attack him from many sides, strike fear into his heart.' But Bates objected. The Frenchman was more than equal to these twaddlers: they'd hang themselves even before they began. To win, he, Bates, had to fight the duel on behalf of English scientists.

The idle hours he passes on the veranda with his book, giving occasional thought to his rivals. The experiment will resume in the morning. It will be time again for observations, rejecting error and excess, keeping the instruments well oiled. He must measure and re-measure the children every day, using up all his instruments during his visit, just to ensure that the log is as reliable and accurate as it can be. He must wait to discover the awkward facts, the dirty secrets. In that he will be alone, he *must* be alone. Unclasping his pince-nez, Bates stares down at his empty glass. Does he see the face of a kind statesman? He thinks of Holmes back in England, the skilful trimmer, supreme in the art of compromise, the knight in shining armour, the one he must rely upon to silence the army of toads on his behalf. Holmes can be trusted to carry his dirty facts to the academies. He'll know whom to tempt, whom to warn, how to reap due rewards for squashing the Frenchman.

'There's nothing like the rivalry of nature,' he thinks – a *pure* rivalry, unlike that which exists among men. It always yields a clear result, clear for those with keen enough eyes to see.

The light has dimmed in the children's camp. A solitary star shines down on the island. This is Norah's time with the children, time for going over the two looking for a scrape or a cut, feeling the skin for bumps or rashes. Water boiling on her wood stove, she pretends an injury or two, prompting the children to come out with their own.

Sitting on the kitchen floor at her feet, they feign a sudden fall, or yelp as if they have been slashed by something sharp. The girl points at her head, swollen by a falling nut; the boy mimics her with a worried look on his face. Their nurse is led astray by the grunts and groans, until she discovers a real gash and brings out her tidy medicine box. The treatment interests all concerned, drawing silence around the table, unless, of course, it is far nastier than usual – a deep-seated thorn begging the treatment of a sharp needle.

Or lice.

The girl is a frequent victim, never the boy. Her tousled hair is peppered with nits, a head full of active lice and many more dead and hatched eggs. Red eyes speak of sleepless nights scratching her scalp, unable to dislodge the tiny creatures who are after her blood.

Norah is quick to spot the lice faeces dotting her tunic. She drags the girl over to the stove, spends hours crouched over her on the floor. Six-legged creatures scurry past her fingers, hide in the table's cracks, or run for their lives over the floor, only to be chased and stamped to death by the boy. He misses the ones that climb over his arms, black lice blending with black skin.

The *Pediculus capitis* is harmless, she has heard Bates say. Doesn't cause any damage beyond an itching scalp. It is the least of their scourges. She remembers that, as she picks one from the floor with her fingertips and drops it into a pan of boiling water.

From the veranda he can imagine the scene in Norah's kitchen. He follows the events even after the palm lamp has been blown out and the children sent off to bed. Where is the nurse? He raises his eyes over the maze of fireflies, as if to gauge her whereabouts. On her bed, ready for another night in Arlinda? He imagines her on the cottage steps. The breeze fluttering her sleeves. Hair tousled like the girl's. Listening to the sea.

Belavoix and Quartley are yet to return after their walk. It seems late for the two to be out. As he raises his glass to his lips, he finds a dead gnat. It must've escaped his attention when his mind was further away, and managed to drown in his drink. The sound of smashing glass quietens the night sound. It resumes after Bates rises from his chair and starts to pace the veranda, a hesitant drone hiding at first behind the noise of creaking boots.

'*Bonjour*, Norah . . .' He remembers Belavoix greeting the nurse during her morning visit to their camp – lips pressed together, frown on her face, hands busy with broom and pail. He recalls the Frenchman's flattering glances, his attempts to slow her down with his mischief. 'Bird of Paradise!' He hears him whistling under his breath. 'I have my doubts,' Belavoix said, addressing Bates, 'that she really *is* English. Are you sure, Mr Bates? Couldn't she be a fair-headed Corsican just as well? A Slavic queen from Russia . . . no?' He gave Quartley a sly look. 'Maybe she's French! From Brittany. Lovely and naughty at the same time!'

He comes to a grinding halt, makes a half-turn to face the cottage below. Invisible. Even his gaze can't pierce the darkness. Might she be on the beach? All by herself, face to face with the roaring surf . . . ? Might she be *in* the sea? He pours himself another drink as Holmes's words ring in his ear: 'Who will take care of your caretaker? How will she survive twelve years with just savages for company?'

Slowly, he brings his mind back to where it was at the start of the evening: to his rivals. This time to his most important rival – the French mischief-maker. He makes a mental note to scold his assistant next morning for his trolling about with him. What if Belavoix were to fall on the goat path and break his leg? Or be bitten by his favourite fly? What if the island wasn't really free of wild animals, as Captain Perry claimed, and they met with a prowling predator?

His rival must be kept alive: alive and healthy, to be defeated in due course. Otherwise everything would go to waste. *Winning is crucial*, Bates thinks, else he'll have to go back to arguing again, proving his point over and over to the toads, too weak to make up their minds.

It won't be easy with Belavoix, he knows from their previous meetings. Privately, he agrees with Holmes. It's his mind, his confidence, not his arrogant speech, that worries Bates. The Frenchman thinks his predictions infallible. He has managed to convince even his own suffering soul of his fantastic tales.

He knows the hankering. The puzzle of human variation won't rest till a solution has been found. All of racial science is waiting for the verdict. There can't be anything short of a clear answer. It'll have to be his or Belavoix's. His arguments or the Frenchman's tales. Eternal hope or gloom. He pricks up his ears at the sound of boots slowly making their way up to the camp, resumes reading the accounts of Botany Bay.

The missionary's wife tells the terrible tale of the fateful voyage of one Dr Barker and his wife around the Cape, of the brutal ambush and rape of the poor lady by a band of runaway slaves. Bates grimaces, then reads her lament . . . *I had believed the inferiority of the savage not to be an ingrained trait but a result of his condition. Free the slave and you'll find an equal man, I had thought. But the rude awakening has come . . .*

He knows how fragile it is. The mind of the author and the reader. A few horrific tales are enough to demolish the very best arguments in the world. Shutting the volume, he takes a long sip then breathes out into the still air.

The log appeared worn. It had aged faster than the children, the foolscap pages creased and shrivelled at the tip from years of turning. A page or two showed signs of damage. Their repair was clever: a glued strip holding the torn pieces together at the back, the front left untouched. For the most part, they read as if they were recorded all in one go, without a pause between the pages. All in the same ink too, the same twirl of the pen from the flowing hand of Nicholas Quartley. Not a single word appeared anywhere, just numbers in boxes, and a few strokes here and there marking points of significance.

A tireless recorder, Quartley understood more about the log than Bates suspected. Sitting at his assistant's desk in the Madhouse, he had overtaken Bates's frightened students, as he listened to his master's thundering answers to their timid questions. He had learned to construct a full skull from reading its cranial measures, to identify as well the race to which it belonged, its merits and flaws. Even before the students had had a chance to run through the full details of an unseen specimen, he could tell if it was a native of Tonga, or an Inca – the tribe known for its curious practice of cranial mutilation. His instinct and bluntness had helped, whereas the students were far too afraid of Bates. He wasn't shy passing judgement on a new specimen, arguing with his master if he thought it was a fake. 'Do what you're told, Quartley. Stop jabbering!' Bates would demand, pointing his finger at the crypt, ordering his assistant to store the new skull in a box. Every now and then, he'd prove Bates wrong, save him a few blushes by his disobedience.

With rain threatening to spoil a whole morning's work, Belavoix snoring in his room and Bates sulking, Quartley opened the log. The pattern seemed clear enough. The twice-yearly measurements of the children's heads from the start of the experiment held few mysteries for him. The samples had turned out entirely as expected, which in truth was the most resounding significance of all. To Quartley, there seemed no need to go on for the full dozen years. The experiment was all but complete just five years from its start.

'Do we really need any more measurements, sir? The evidence seems to—'

'Not today, Quartley,' Bates replied in a gruff voice, cross at his assistant for reminding him of a wasted day. 'You and your friend can't go romping today as you did last night.'

'I meant do we need to measure the samples *ever* again. The evidence that we have already gathered seems quite clear.'

Bates looked up surprised, distracted from applying a coat of glue to the spine of his book, damaged by last night's swatting. 'What evidence are you talking about?'

'The children, sir.' Quartley wetted his lips, holding the log open before him. 'In five years their crania have changed. The girl's brain is now bigger than the boy's. The front of her skull too is larger than the back, which is the exact opposite for the boy.'

'And so . . . ?' Bates kept on frowning.

'She has now become a member of the race *frontalis*, and the boy one of the race *occipitalis*.' He pronounced the difficult words just as he had heard Bates do. 'The white has *become* a white, sir!'

Bates turned his attention back to the book. 'And is that the evidence we've been looking for?'

'It shows that the white is better than the black.'

Not relishing the interruptions, Bates spoke each word clearly with a cold look at Quartley. 'It shows cranial superiority, not *racial*.'

'But . . .'

'Do you think we have come this far, spent so much time, just to prove that racial features take five years to show fully in a child's cranium? Couldn't we have found that out sitting in London?'

Quartley said nothing.

'A bigger skull, a better skull, doesn't by itself prove what we know to be true. It doesn't show that the owner is cleverer, kinder, wiser, undisputedly the superior. For that we must have more.'

A cloud of doubt descended as Quartley took in his master's words. He had considered the log their most powerful weapon. Time after time Bates used it to silence his critics. Perhaps the Frenchman would bow before it too, he had hoped.

'We must know how the children behave – with us and with each other. Which one becomes more human-like . . .' Bates took a look at his assistant's puzzled face. 'The one with the superior cranium, *and* superior wits and morals will prove itself to be of the superior race. For that we must wait. Wait for the girl to show her true colours.'

Which of the two becomes more human-like . . . Quartley's thoughts left the log and travelled to the children. Could they be sure that it would be the girl? If anything, the children seemed wilder each time they visited the island, neither showing signs of retaining a full memory of their earlier visits. One moment they would be rushing into the arms of their visitors, chattering madly, as if they had sorely missed their presence in Arlinda. They would jump into Bates's arms, the girl climbing onto his shoulders and tickling him behind the ears. Not even a slap could stop her. At other times, they'd watch the men silently from a distance with grave eyes, pricking up their ears at the sound of boots marching towards the camp, fleeing into the forest at a trot. It would take Norah hours to hunt them down and coax them back into the cottage.

'They're both like animals.' Quartley doubted Bates's optimism. 'Will the girl ever become like girls in England?'

Bates appeared to give serious thought to Quartley's question. 'I don't say she'll turn into a civilised human. No. It took early man a few millennia to achieve that, remember. But there will be signs, I'd say.'

'What sort of signs?'

'She'll become curious and confident. Not unduly cruel. Kind enough to share whatever little she has with her brother. The signs will be small and we may have to look hard to find them, but they'll be there.'

'They already seem quite cosy together, sir.'

The faculty of sympathy seemed to have developed between the two children. It wasn't uncommon to find the boy, slipped into a trough between steep banks for instance, howling with fear, and the girl darting to him through the woods in utmost distress. It wasn't uncommon to see them swimming together, or eating out of the same bowl in the kitchen, sleeping curled up like pups on the floor.

Their sympathy was their defence, Quartley thought, against the intruding scientists. Held in the cottage against their will, at times the two of them started a game, shrieking and gurgling, appearing hysterical, as if it was their ploy to exclude others from their company, drawing a veil of laughter around themselves.

'Yes, but with her, there'll be no hanky-panky. Also, you won't find her indulgent with her own body, as he is . . .'

Quartley recalled Captain Perry's words as he stood with him on the *Rainbow*'s deck, watching Norah with the children. *They'll have a jolly life on the island. The little savages! Won't take them long to find a serpent and a fruit, mark my words . . .*

He decided to probe Bates further. 'But the boy's a real dare-devil! He isn't afraid of anything.' In his mind, he played over the scene: the boy climbing a tree to steal from a honeycomb. 'I'd say he's as courageous as the girl.'

'No, no . . .' Bates shook his head. 'You mustn't make that mistake.' Resigned to more rain and a snoring rival, he put his book down and started on a proper explanation, the sort he only offered reluctantly to his students. 'In the Negro, a deficient cranium produces an animal courage – a bent for haste and rashness; an impulsiveness that leads to costly mistakes. The superior cranium of the European, on the other hand, leads to a *reasoned* courage. That's the difference between the boy and the girl.'

Yet both turned cowards at the sight of Norah ready to give them a wash in the camp's courtyard, scattering like chickens before her determined gaze. Quartley laughed, then begged his master's pardon. 'Both can be quite silly at times, sir. Even the girl.'

'But, of course, Quartley. She's no more sensible than some of her visitors, shall we say?'

Reasoned courage!

How could she reason without words? How could she fight her fears? In addition to pointing and squealing, wouldn't she need something else? Wouldn't she need a secret language? That she had a sharp sense was clear. Her gestures were more precise than the boy's. Apart from her fear of instruments, she seemed perfectly at ease with their daily routine. But she'd need more than that, wouldn't she, to prove Bates right? Quartley felt sorry for the girl, tempted to press on with his questions.

'How will she learn to reason here, sir?' He cast his glance about, at the desolate rain pouring down on the desolate island.

For the first time, Bates showed real interest. 'That's what scientists have been asking themselves for decades. How did primitive man learn to think? How did the pre-human *become* human?'

'Do we have an answer, sir?'

'We know some did faster than others. The higher races got there before the lower ones. That's the argument.' Bates nodded, his forehead creased, as if he was reasoning with himself.

Quartley thought of the boy, sitting at the bottom of the chain, his dark eyes unblinking. 'And the boy . . .'

'The boy will become human too. A lesser human, but . . .'

It was a chance one must take, Bates had told him, when he had doubted if the experiment would last the remaining years. 'What if something happens to the samples, or to us . . . ?' Quartley asked.

'It's a chance worth taking for science.'

He listened to the rain drumming down on the flimsy roof, after Bates had retired to his room, lulled at last by Belavoix's melodious snoring. What if it all ended with the rain? The island sunk in the sea. The chance of a lifetime lost.

Mist covered the island when the rain stopped, rising in steep columns like the smoke of a forest fire. In parts, it seemed the bush had been set ablaze – such was the density of the fog. To a passing ship it must have appeared an inviting place, a dark and dreamy land. An island of geysers and springs, shimmering in criss-crossing beams. A rare gem hard to pass by. If he was a horticulturalist, a ship's captain would have expected to find a miracle plant here – a wildflower or a root-bulb – hidden under untrodden moss. Or precious herbs. Profitable timber, for which these parts were known. The red flower glimpsed through the mist might have reminded of past conquests and successful discoveries that had earned the crew a good name. The rain would have been a further draw, bringing the prospect of fresh water amidst a salty sea.

Passing captains, eager to exploit the island's riches, held their temptations at bay, warned of her reputation. Arlinda was a mirage: dreamy but desolate; an empty patch at the edge of a teeming continent. There were rumours about why there were no slaves to be found there. Some blamed it on a possible uprising, or a pirate raid with survivors fleeing in wooden canoes to neighbouring islands. Some brought up an even more frightening prospect: an epidemic, the horror of graves dug up on the beach and baby slaves floating like dark specks on the sea.

The Sugar Islands on the other side of the ocean sparked happier thoughts. Santo Domingo, Haiti, Cuba, Puerto Rico. Bustling havens, they offered more. Trading captains could have their fill of tobacco and sugar, silver dollars and rum in exchange for the very best of Africa: not the frail Luso, the litter of the Portuguese and their Angolan mistresses, or a Beninese whose line was corrupted by Arab blood, but the pure Negro, as pure as the sap of the great camwood tree.

They would have sailed on, leaving Arlinda to the rain and mist.

The tree house hid behind the haze. It wasn't a proper tree house, but a perch big enough for a couple of brave climbers, a dozen or so feet above ground and jutting out from a forking branch. It overlooked the spring and afforded a view of the sea as well, a chance to spot the children in two of their favourite places.

Bates had opposed the idea of building the lookout at first. It was a source of potential danger and no part of the original plan. 'I thought your gout would rule out a climb,' he had said to Belavoix. 'Gout! What gout? These legs are as good as a gazelle's,' the Frenchman had replied, pointing at his feet. 'Never a problem since I took a sip of the Dayak broth made from viper flesh!' It was an argument that Bates would lose. 'But *you* can have what you want, Mr Bates! You can bring as many instruments as you wish. You can bring a new one each time you come. The tree house is *my* instrument.'

It was left to Quartley to build the house, and fulfil Belavoix's wish.

Getting up there, though, had turned out to be trickier than winning the argument. The ascent would begin with Quartley holding the ladder firmly against the tree trunk, and the Frenchman cursing each rung as he climbed, as if it were an arch-rival. Taking a well-deserved rest every few minutes, he'd accuse Quartley of suffering from the English love of 'obstacles'. 'You should've chosen an easier tree, Mr Assistant.' The expedition would exhaust him each time, yet when he reached the top and entered his 'observatory', all else would be forgotten in the rush to spot the 'little savages'. Snatching his portmanteau from Quartley, he'd bring out the telescope, pointing it all around him like a shipwrecked sailor.

The descent would be even trickier.

On one of the early days, the Frenchman had been stranded up the tree, with Quartley back at the camp with Bates, the two busy repairing a faulty instrument. They had forgotten to fetch him from the tree house on their way down to their evening meal, till they were reminded of his absence by a volley of shots. It had brought them to a sudden stop, Bates stiffening instantly as he turned towards the sea, expecting perhaps a surprise visitor. Was this the *natural* danger, arrived at last? A shock had passed through Quartley. Taking quick stock of the situation, Bates had let out a deep sigh, pointing up to the tree house. 'It's the gazelle. He's trapped. Your friend needs you to bring him down to earth. Go on, Quartley . . .'

After two days of constant pouring, the end of the rains brought a significant spotting: a red flag flying over the messenger's hut on the beach. Fluttering in the breeze, it was plain to see without a telescope. Norah ran to fetch the letter, while the men assembled in the kitchen for their morning work. As expected, it was from Captain Perry. The *Rainbow* would arrive, he wrote, in a week or so to take them back. His messenger, a passing ship, had left them a small gift with the letter: a sack of succulent black walnut, infinitely superior to their own arlinda fruit.

As always, the letter changed the way they lived the remaining days on the island. Just as their arrival led to a flurry of activity, the prospect of departure shifted the mood for both Bates and Belavoix. The craniologist spent the remaining days going over his measurements, checking and re-checking the log for missing entries, and salting away the instruments in the cupboard next to Norah's kitchen. He drove Quartley mad. It was time to plan their next visit to Arlinda, with Bates jotting down lists of things to do for the nurse, leaving it to his assistant to read them out to her.

For Belavoix, the letter signified the end. He regarded each departure as final. Not simply to their visit, but possibly also to the experiment. Perhaps a tragedy would strike in the following weeks. A shipwreck. A plague on board caused by infected ship rats. Even a war in Europe might bring the curtain down on all scientific ventures. He imagined a dire future. Eyes averted, he'd describe to Quartley all the things that could and most certainly would go wrong with their samples – a list of misfortunes drawn from his own beliefs.

Just as before, the gloom drew out his impatience, his urge to win, to show Bates 'all that was already plain'. When not at the children's camp, he spent most of his time alone, plotting his 'final argument', muttering to himself as he eyed the scavenging gulls, or mumbling in his sleep in the tree house. Every chance he could find, he escaped from the scientists' camp, as if he needed to erase Bates's face from his mind in order to dwell firmly on his arguments. Whenever they met, Belavoix would eye Quartley with suspicion, asking him repeatedly if Bates had been up to his old tricks again – unveiling a secret instrument to win unfairly at the very last moment. 'I have my surprises too, Mr Assistant . . .' he'd say darkly, wagging his finger at the absent Englishman, who had retired early to his room.

As he read Captain Perry's letter once over, Quartley could feel the familiar ship-bound nausea return, making the past week seem idyllic – the few hours' work each day, broken by naps in the hammock and wandering off into the forest or along the coast. It didn't seem to matter that the visit would end soon, yet again, without the 'final argument', the one that would allow them to go home together, with the children and Norah.

He could imagine how it would be on the way back: lying half-dead in the ship's cabin, thinking the usual things about Bates and Belavoix, the two determined never to see eye to eye. His mind would go over the arguments and counter-arguments. He could see himself lurching to the washstand and lurching back, fretting over the future of the experiment, asking himself the same unanswerable questions as he had asked before. Of what use were the log, the instruments? What use the Frenchman's notebooks? Were a dozen years enough to settle their dispute?

Whichever way he looked now, a sea of sleepless nights stared back at Nicholas Quartley.

There'd be something else to puzzle over on this trip back – a new side to the rivalry. He'd have to use his assistant's mind to piece together the evidence and motives, just as Bates had taught him. As he climbed up the hill alone, without Belavoix, Quartley recalled the scene he had dutifully recorded in his mind's log, to search through later for a clue . . .

All three men had been in the kitchen one morning, enjoying a welcome break in their work. Bates was sipping his tea, Belavoix his coconut water, while Quartley waited for Norah to bring him his favourite cocoa. As he put the goniometer back into its case, Quartley noticed Bates glancing up and down the log, his pince-nez slipping down his nose from the trickling sweat. His master wouldn't speak a word now, he knew. He was too busy dissecting the numbers. Foot up on the table, Belavoix was reading from his bulging notebook, breaking into a story every now and then, reading his scribbles aloud.

The stories relieved the tension of the morning. Quartley sensed the ease around the table. They could all hear the sea through the open window, adding a lilt to the Frenchman's singsong reading. Even Norah was relaxed, he could tell, her shoulders dropping a notch below her slender neck, as she moved about the kitchen with almost a hint of gaiety.

The scene, Quartley recalled, had started with Belavoix teasing Norah over her dwindling supplies, followed by his telling the story of a grand feast he had attended once in Africa, the 'remotest place on earth'. He had gone over the list of inedible delicacies, and then described the evening's fun. With a chuckle, he had talked about the tom-tom dancers gathered around a fire, 'each of them a queen, no less!', their glistening bodies and the shameless dancing. The custom had called for the chief of the queens to choose one of the guests as her 'paramour'. It had been a fierce contest. 'And who was the winner, sir?' Quartley had tried to hurry the story along. Among the guests had been the heads of a dozen tribes, the noblest and proudest among the savages, but the chief of the queens had made no mistake in choosing the very best.

Even before Belavoix could point at himself and smack his lips, Bates had looked up from the log. 'Rubbish.'

'Rubbish?'

'Yes. No contest at all. The negress will always choose the white man over her own sort.'

Belavoix had struggled for words. 'No, no . . . it wasn't that. It wasn't a matter of race, I can assure you . . . more a matter of . . .'

'*Simply* a matter of race. You don't really think that she'd be looking for the one who could jump the highest or yelp the loudest.'

'She took a great deal of time to decide, came over to examine us . . . it was serious, Mr Bates.'

Bates gave a snort. 'Yes, I'm sure it was serious. Your queen would take her time to assure herself that it was indeed white skin she was looking at, not white chalk that they sprinkle at times over their limbs.'

Even Quartley had been startled by his master's reaction. It was unusual for him to pay any attention to Belavoix's stories, treating them with the same indifference as he would the rustling trees and the roaring surf. Usually only something to do with the children would make him take notice and argue with his rival. He had been firm – firmer than usual. To Quartley, it had seemed that his master wasn't keen on convincing his rival, but intent on squashing him and his African queen.

'If it had been a contest among the civilised –' Bates had looked up at Belavoix and then past him to Norah – 'it would've been quite different. She'd have looked for something else, something more . . .'

Slamming his journal shut, Belavoix had left the kitchen in a huff . . .

Sitting on the hilltop, Quartley thought about Bates: his master, a solitary Ulysses. It was hard to trace anything but science in him, as if he had passed right through the womb to land in his laboratory untouched, unloved. In his years with Bates, he hadn't detected a hint of sympathy for those that surrounded him, for the kind and elderly Holmes or Jenny, even for his sick wife in her mansion in the country. On the island the silly children couldn't sway his mind, failed even to prise out a laugh. He went through the days displaying little more than the urge to complete his work. That, and arguing with Belavoix.

To Quartley, the shift in Bates's attention was the new puzzle. It seemed somehow to have spread beyond the children to cover the nurse as well – raising his voice or casting a quick look to fold her within his own presence. As he passed her on the goat path or in the kitchen, there'd be a small gesture, almost unnoticeable. A gesture to record her existence, where in the past there had been indifference. Even when he was immersed in his log, Bates would look up from time to time, glancing around the cottage as if to assure himself of Norah's whereabouts.

There were no signs that he was about to relax his vigil, or show leniency if she flouted the rules. As usual, he was quick to scold, bearing down on her with his glaring eyes at the slightest mishap. Rather, it seemed an attention without sympathy – as if, by drawing her into his fold, he was guarding her against herself, or from his rival.

Norah made up Belavoix's bed, as the Frenchman stood in the door watching her.

'Do you miss us, Norah?' He waited, hoping she'd respond with a nod or a shake of her head.

'Would you like to go back with us?'

Returning from the sanitary lodge, Bates heard him, then frowned.

'Come on. You can tell me, Norah. Which do you love more, the boy or the girl?'

'Enough!' Bates came up behind the Frenchman, gesturing beyond him to Norah, ordering her to leave the camp.

'You've scared her away, Mr Bates!' Belavoix fretted when she had gone. 'Is that what you do back in England – scare them away?' He wrung his hands in despair and began to leave the camp himself, heading for his tree house, stopping at the steps and raising his voice at Bates.

'She might be English, as you claim, But here she belongs to our experiment . . . she belongs to *both* of us, no?'

'No!' Bates shouted back.

It was a new scar. An inch long and halfway down the boy's neck, it resembled a live worm. From the looks of it, it hadn't resulted from a fall or the stab of a razor-sharp branch sticking out of the bushes like a sword. More the mark of a claw, of a deliberate wounding.

The unexpected discovery stopped Bates in his tracks. He had spent the morning playing doctor to the children, examining them from head to toe and making notes for the list he would leave Norah. Lice and scabs. An infected nail. The girl's wheezing. A coated tongue that could be the mark of a torpid liver. 'If you cannot aid nature, don't throw obstacles in her path,' – he often reminded Quartley to remind the nurse. After much arguing, he had won Belavoix over, convincing him that as long as the samples remained disease-free, the scientists would have a better chance of observing their behaviour. A sick child shows neither superiority nor equality. The Frenchman had agreed at last, secretly troubled by the prospect of being infected himself by the rabid savages.

Calling Quartley over from the instrument cupboard, Bates inspected the scar. It seemed to be very recent, acquired after their arrival in Arlinda.

'What do you make of *this*?' Bates asked him with a grim face.

Passing his hand over the mark, Quartley frowned. 'Looks like a dog bite, sir.'

'Impossible.'

As he entered the kitchen, Belavoix saw the two of them crowding over the boy. He took a look as well, coming up instantly with his own explanation.

'A fight!'

'What do you mean?' Bates raised an eyebrow.

'*Une lutte!*' Belavoix spoke cheerfully. 'A little tumble between the children. Just like two lion cubs!'

'Norah!' Bates shouted, calling the nurse over from her larder. She appeared before him with a wooden face.

'When did this happen?' Bates's face showed his growing impatience. 'Go on!'

'Wait.' Belavoix spoke quietly. He sat down in a chair and assumed his favourite posture, one leg up on the table. 'She won't be able to tell you that. Why don't you ask her to write it down?' Belavoix smiled, knowing full well that Bates didn't approve of Norah passing them notes while they were on the island. 'She *can* write, you know!' Then he turned serious. 'Ask her if she *knew* of the scar.'

'Did you?' Bates realised his mistake, his rasping voice demanding a simple nod or a shake of the head. Face stiffened and red, Norah stood motionless.

'You *must* answer. You can't pretend you've forgotten, can you?' He paused for a moment then began again, pointing at the boy's wound. 'Did you dress the wound? Or did you leave it to heal by itself?'

Quartley wished Norah could answer back, provide a simple explanation to subdue Bates. His master detested silence even more than foolish replies; he needed an answer to every one of his questions.

After a suitable silence, Bates issued the ultimate threat. 'Well then, let's remind you how it might've happened. Let me show you what his sister must have done to him.' Raising his hands over the boy, he made as if to wring his neck, causing Norah to run back to her larder, flooding the kitchen with the throttled sound of her sobbing. Until now, the boy had stood obediently among the men, his uncomprehending eyes darting between them and Norah. With the nurse in distress, he ran out behind her, deftly evading Quartley's outstretched arms.

An hour passed without further mention of the scar. Bates kept on scribbling his list of commands, while Quartley resumed sealing up the instruments in their boxes in preparation for their departure. After a while, they were interrupted by the Frenchman, who was making a funny noise with his lips, smacking and clucking them at the same time, as if he had found a satisfactory answer to a vexing problem.

'Perhaps we were wrong. Too hasty in our conclusion.'

Bates continued to scribble.

'Maybe the children didn't fight. At least not this time.'

'How do you explain the scar, then?'

'In explaining it, we might, like most scientists, have made the obvious error – followed the wrong path.'

'The explanation is obvious.' Bates was prepared to ignore the Frenchman's doubt. 'The injury was either accidental, or the result of aggression.'

'Yes, but who was the aggressor?'

'What do you mean?' Bates asked coldly.

'Let's think . . . who could it have been?'

'Must've been the girl, unless you think it was self-inflicted. We don't have too many possibilities.'

Belavoix brought his foot down from the table and leaned towards Bates. 'Ah, but you are forgetting the one other possibility.'

'Which other?'

'Norah!'

Bates stared at Belavoix's triumphant face. 'You mean . . . ?'

'It could've been her. She could've turned violent and struck the boy, slashed him with her nail.'

'But why would she do such a thing?' Bates shook his head. 'She'd have known that she was breaking the rules. What could have caused her to injure the sample?'

'Cause?' The Frenchman let out a short laugh. 'You mean you don't know? Let me give you *three* causes, Mr Bates.' Belavoix held up the fingers of his right hand. 'Anger, neurosis, insanity!'

Bates chose not to respond, returning to his notes while Belavoix continued with his explanation.

'A woman marooned on an island! Cut off for years from everyone . . . without comfort or friendship. Without love. It is enough to make anyone mad!'

Bates looked grim. 'But she was under strict instructions not to punish the samples. She was told never to—'

'Instructions!' Belavoix thumped on his notebook and laughed. 'Do you think a woman with a ravaged heart cares about instructions?'

'She agreed,' Bates went on, 'of her own free will, I should say, to come here and care for the children. She knew the conditions. Our agreement clearly stated that—'

Belavoix interrupted him again. 'Forget about agreements. An agreement might well work in an English court, not on an African island.'

Bates appeared to brood over the allegation, 'But we have no proof that she did what you say. As far as I am concerned, the nurse has kept to her agreement barring a few lapses in hygiene.'

'The scar –' Belavoix smacked his lips again – '*is* our proof.' He paused, a thought seeming to cross his mind. 'At this rate, she will end up killing the children.'

Dropping his eyes to his notes, Bates voiced his opinion on the Frenchman's speculation. 'Without proof, we cannot be certain of the cause of injury. As it stands, there are no grounds to replace the nurse with another.'

'I wasn't talking of replacing the nurse,' Belavoix appeared surprised. 'Why would we do that? *Anyone* banished to the island would go mad sooner or later. There is no reason to think that we'd find anyone better than Norah.' He glanced towards the larder. 'It could be worse. Another nurse might end up committing suicide.'

The cottage fell silent. As Bates was about to leave, Belavoix started again. This time he seemed to retract his earlier explanation, shifting the blame back to the children.

'Forget the nurse. Sooner or later, the children *will* fight. They'll cause more harm to each other than a simple scar. Our experiment is the cause of everything that happens here.'

'Are you suggesting that we stop then?'

'No, no . . . I am asking for the very opposite . . . not for *us* to stop, but for the experiment to stop itself.'

Startled, Bates shot a quick look at Belavoix across the table. 'Would you care to explain yourself?'

'I am suggesting' – the Frenchman spoke slowly, with a smile on his face – 'that we leave an instrument here for the children.'

'An instrument?'

Reaching inside his portmanteau, Belavoix took out a leather valise and from it a handsome Languiole knife, its short blade flashing and displaying Napoleon's imperial bee engraved on its handle. 'A French favourite! An English one would do just the same.'

'And the purpose would be . . . ?' Bates appeared confused.

'If the children should fight, they'd have the means to cause fatal injury rather than timid bites and scratches.'

'And what would we achieve by . . .'

'A *natural* conclusion. It would end our experiment in the best possible way. If one race is in fact superior to the other, it would be established without doubt.'

Quartley saw his master's face turn red then hard in rapid succession.

'No!'

'No? Are you sure, Mr Bates?'

'Definitely. The children are not gladiators.'

Belavoix feigned surprise. 'But isn't that the whole point? Isn't that why we are here – to identify the winner and the loser? Isn't that what your Chain of Races predicts? The one on top of the chain will certainly kill the one below, no?'

'No.' Bates raised his rasping voice to full volume. 'The test of racial superiority isn't murder. The superior isn't called upon to annihilate the inferior, although I can't say that a few misguided members of our race haven't committed such crimes. There's more to racial superiority than destroying others.'

Belavoix shook his head. 'How English, how typically English to pollute science with morals.' He shrugged his shoulders in resignation. 'What you choose to do with the inferior is your business, Mr Bates. Train them like monkeys or shoot them like dogs. But *ability* is the key. Yes, ability. The skill, the power, the cunning to kill, if necessary. That's the meaning of racial superiority.'

'That might be your view, but it certainly isn't mine.' There was a tone of finality in Bates's voice.

'The ability of the civilised, the most civilised of all, to show the highest savagery – that's the real proof of racial superiority. Nothing else will do.'

The cottage, indeed the whole camp, seemed still. Quartley sat alert. Out of the corner of his eye he saw the Frenchman shifting uncomfortably in his seat, opening and shutting his notebook and looking around him as if to find a suitable authority with whom to lodge his complaint against Bates.

'All you care about is your little measurements, playing with your toys. How sad, how silly! For twelve years you want to keep on doing the same thing. You have the English distaste for accidents, the English love of keeping records, filling up your log so that in a dozen years you can tour the academies and stun the world, proving the obvious with absolute precision. You call that science? I call it English pettifogging!'

Quartley waited for Bates's explosion. As he did with his students at the Madhouse, would he ask Belavoix to leave? He wished the children would reappear to distract them all, the boy drowning their arguments with his babble.

From the door of the cottage Bates threw his words back at a fretting Belavoix. 'Science isn't a passion play. It is more than a farce.'

BIRD OF PARADISE

He watches her for signs of madness. *It is a mystery far greater than the mystery of our experiment!* There must be a clue, he thinks, to that mystery. The kitchen holds just the two of them now: Norah and Nicholas Quartley. Half an eye on the craniograph's needle, he looks up at her sitting on the bench by her stove weaving a basket. She has foraged the jungle for leaves; he has seen them drying in a barrel at the cottage. She has laid out the dried leaves in a pattern, going over each of them to check for blemishes. He pays close attention to the eyes, cast down and fluttering each time she ties a difficult knot, pressing on the leaves with her thumbs. He waits to hear her sigh. From this, he has learned to tell if her efforts have met with success or failure.

In the hour or so together, each will spend their attention one half on their task and one half on the other.

She appears anything but mute. A rich language covers every move and gesture, her face breaking out into a volley of words with a flick of her brow. *A frown isn't just a frown,* he thinks. *The tongue darting between her lips is worthy of a dozen entries in the log.* He has caught her a few times whispering to herself, failing to catch the words. She has disappointed him in the past, offering a pair of firmly pressed lips, each time he has spoken to her.

The she-wolf.

She has fulfilled her agreement, Quartley is sure, suckling her two cubs but staying true to the rules. Perhaps just a handful of lapses, nothing more. She has been the children's nurse, not their mother; avoided cuddling and fawning. Her neglect of the samples is plain in their lice and worms. It is clear, though, that she enjoys their trust, understands the language of hisses, the babbling, and the girl's frightened silence.

Dumb, yet far from slow-witted. She has shown a passion for scrubbing and cleaning, washing up at the hot spring, ferrying pails to and fro all day. He sees her every morning, even before they have come down the hill, arriving at the scientists' camp with water for the sanitary lodge. She brings herbs for Belavoix, prepared under strict instructions to treat his 'condition', and Bates's polished boots. She stays just long enough to make up the beds, placing a fresh sprig of wildflower on the pillows, then runs back to her cottage before the men come down for their breakfast. With Norah, their camp feels like a home.

Her presence of mind surprises everyone, including Bates. During an early visit, he spotted a fire at the children's courtyard, a fire of dried leaves and nettles. Coughing heavily, he ordered Quartley to douse it with their precious water brought over by ship. Norah stopped them, running out of her kitchen and pointing up at a small dark cloud droning over their heads. The fire was her idea, they realised, to chase away the killer flies.

What does she make of their experiment, Quartley wonders, watching her in the kitchen. She must've discovered the reason behind it by now. She must understand the point of rivalry between Bates and Belavoix. Does the outcome worry her as much as it does Quartley?

He knows he will worry over Norah more than the children, when the time comes to leave them in Arlinda. He feels her burden, many times more than his: the experiment resting on her shoulders, she alone responsible for keeping it going for the next seven years. She has been true so far, weathering everything – nursing Belavoix's strange diseases, and enduring Bates's temper. She has turned into an instrument! Ready and unfeeling. What if the instrument should fail? In his mind, he turns over Norah's monthly reports, full of facts about the children and their camp, never a word about herself. Will they receive due warning should the burden become too heavy . . . ? Sitting before him now, she is more a human than an instrument. It is Norah he sees, not the nurse.

Quartley tries imagining her in their absence: the few weeks a distant memory as she goes about her chores, without the additional burden of looking after them. The strain will have died, away from the Frenchman's leer and Bates's protective armour. Does it sadden her that they're gone, or is she happy – happy to have escaped here, to a desolate Arlinda?

What will she do with her basket? he wonders.

What would she say, if she could speak but a solitary word?

Half a moon over her head, the other half drowned in the sea. She leaves the cottage to search for it under the waves. Her path will take her away from a darkness she knows, the darkness of her camp, to the sea's fireworks. She has become an explorer, crossing the last stretch of the forest, the path refusing to grant her wish, each night a different course full of obstacles. Winding her way through the trees, she discovers a new one grown overnight: a rock slid down the hill, guarding banks of soft sand. Blindness stalls her, till she hears the sound of fluttering wings – night owls hovering between their nests – to help her cross the unknown stretch.

She arrives smelling of the forest, the rotting bush and sapping bark. It's the smell of a lover who has parted unwillingly, leaving as much behind as he has extracted. She's ready now to lose the flavours to the sea, roaring louder than her screaming mind. It wins her over each time, nothing to rival its crashing whisper. Norah! Norah!

She hears more than she's heard all day. The surf repeating the same words without fail, at its peak not a question, at its drop no command. A pure sound for her pure silence.

The wet sand presents no obstacle. She runs, crushing live snails and baby crabs, to the beach's furthest point, where she hopes to find her treasure. It'll be at a different place each night, the remains buried in the seabed or lying tangled in the reef. She'll drown herself. The surf against her skin reminding her that she once lived among others. The sea becoming her other. It won't be long before she finds it – the throbbing glow that has drawn her out in the first place. The drowned half-moon.

She lives the night for the other half.

She prefers rest to sleep. Whenever she thinks of the children, her mind goes back to her first visit to the Madhouse. She'll have a job, she was told, a special job to keep her mind off her troubles. As she arrived on Arlinda with her two wrapped bundles, she started to worry over her new trouble. In the five years since, she has come to live with the fear of losing the children whenever they are out of her sight. After they learned to walk and started to leave the cottage by themselves, she tried to guess where they had been from signs they brought back – a headful of dust from climbing rocks, or clothes drenched from a swim in the sea. She found them hidden in their secret caves and nooks, fast asleep, curled up against each other. Against the scientists' wishes, she followed them, in step with their hare-like pace. They seemed somehow able to smell her presence, stopping abruptly to exchange glances then darting off in a different direction. There were times when they stopped to let her catch up, babbling excitedly as if they had been expecting her.

The island was safe, she was told even before they arrived, and reminded many times over. It seemed far from safe. How could it be safe with the two of them hanging from branches by the tips of their fingers, biting into poisonous roots, hiding in the forest amidst lightning and thunder? And the captain's messengers? She worried about them disobeying their orders. What if they were to spot the children when they arrived at the beach hut, if they followed them around, harmed them in some way? She lived constantly with her fear, worrying over the children, the *savages*, as she had heard the Frenchman call them – *her* savages.

In the kitchen she was no less than a mother, the two waiting patiently with their bowls, watching her at the stove with great interest. She watched them too, overjoyed at how quickly they ate, finishing their bowls and banging them on the table for more. How they slurped and tore at the food with their hands, stealing from each other behind her back. There were days when they were too tired to eat, bellies full of forest food, or when they smelt the stove and rushed out in disgust.

What would she do if they were to fall sick? She had examined every phial in the medicine box, listening carefully to Quartley as he taught her to spot the warning signs. The medicine box would be her saviour, she knew, hiding it under her bed away from prying fingers. 'Write to us if something happens,' Quartley had said. She had imagined a fluttering flag over the messenger's hut. How long would it be before someone arrived? Watching the boy chase a cloud of hornets, she wondered what would happen if they chased after him, bit his face and limbs. Could the flag save him in time? Fishing out a speck of dust from the girl's eye with the tip of her finger, she lost herself in worries, till the girl screamed. 'Keep them alive,' Quartley reminded her each time the visitors left. The words kept her awake at night. She had seen mothers lose their children before their very eyes. On a night of thunderstorm, she had paced the kitchen then run into the children's rooms and dragged them over into her bed – the three sleeping together just as they had on their first night in Arlinda.

She had avoided eating with the children, avoided joining in their babbles and squeals, or becoming too intimate a part of their world. She mustn't know too much, otherwise she'd end up knowing them too well, and her familiarity would be obvious to the scientists. They might think that she was raising their samples by her own rules. Even after five years the children didn't cease to puzzle her. At times both appeared to be deaf, unable to fix their attention on an object, even when she struck the floor hard with her stick. Yet she was certain their hearing was acute – acute enough for a walnut cracked across the kitchen to prick their hungry attention. At times they seemed to have no mind or memory at all. Just their human faces distinguished them from apes. Like apes, they shared a love of darkness, a craving for earth-eating. The girl liked to be stroked, but withdrew snarling into a corner whenever her mood shifted. The boy smashed and threw things, leapt about at night on his bed, cupping his head with his hands. Yet daybreak could find him inexplicably sad, waddling along with sloping shoulders and a sunken chest.

With the children, there was never an ordinary day.

Tempted as she was to teach them a thing or two, she managed to stop herself.

'Norah!' Bates's voice stopped her.

Awake after a sleepless night, she thinks of her visitors leaving. She'll miss the pleasure of words, the drone of voices in the kitchen, the men speaking in distinct notes. The comfort of common sounds – like 'I' or 'whenever' – the folding over of the tongue for a 'w'. She'll miss the way the Frenchman opens his mouth wide to speak, relying on a variety of parts to draw out his English. Words chasing words, tripping over some, scaring each other away till there is silence in the kitchen. She prepares for the silence, which will take some time coming once the echoes have found their nooks beside the stove smoke.

The row of packed instruments warns of the hectic days still ahead. Besides the last set of measurements, she must endure a few tricks from the eager Frenchman, and Bates's hawk eye watching her. Everyone turned now into observer and observed. She thinks of the assistant watching her in the kitchen, eye on his job, his thoughts elsewhere. What instrument does he turn over in his mind? From his face she has learned to tell if he is happy or sad leaving them behind.

At the tree house he turns his telescope away from the children's camp and points it towards the scientists'. It is Bates who dominates his mind now, not the savages. Each moment he is consumed by thoughts of a grand contest. An experiment is no different from a war, he knows, still smarting from his recent loss in the argument over the knife. To win, he must know his rival better than he does; he must go back over his notes to search for the weapon that will deal the perfect blow.

A tall arlinda tree stands guard as he searches for the Englishman on the veranda, pointing the telescope as if it were a gun's barrel. Even from afar, he can imagine the scene with Bates and Quartley, the two going over a list of tasks to be left for the nurse. It is easy to imagine Bates's rasping voice: 'Tell me what you mean, Quartley . . . Go on . . . !' He takes aim to destroy that pretty nest, slaying both master and assistant along with their tidy log and neat instruments. If he had been a craniologist, he would have enjoyed slicing open Bates's skull, to discover what he already knows – a neat row of honeycombs, each holding a simple fact, their owner bent on adding newer chambers with each new reading of his samples.

'But we mustn't stop with the brain, we must read the mind too, Mr Bates.' The Frenchman rehearses his argument. 'How else can we spot the traits that make up the human? There's more to a man than a body, no?' He shakes his head, knowing that his rival will be unmoved. 'Let me tell you about measurements, Mr Bates. There are scientists who roam the world with their instruments, measuring everything they see – even the hefty bottoms of Negro females! It would be foolish to trust your goniometer. What if it were to prove you wrong precisely?'

Bates will ignore all that, he knows, as he flips through his notebook to discover a stronger argument. A note he wrote some time ago during his travels makes him chuckle: his observations about a special tribe. He starts to read aloud, imagining Bates before him. 'Let me tell you about the Charibs. They have their own Chain of Races, just like yours. They taste the flesh of their prisoners, then rank them according to their merits. The French they find, of course, to be the most delicious and so place them at the top. While the Spaniards, difficult as they are to digest, must stay at the bottom!'

The test of intelligence that they are about to conduct with the children offers him a glimmer of hope. It will be the first of several tests designed to compare their samples, to decide if one is superior to the other. He and Bates agreed, before the experiment started, to wait for five years till the children were old enough for these. He hums a tune as he mulls over the mirror test, a simple procedure presenting the children with a novel object – a mirror – to see what they make of it. It might tempt and puzzle them, giving the scientists a glimpse of what happens inside their savage minds.

I'll win now, thinks Belavoix. It's a chance to engage Bates over a simple test, his only chance to win on this visit. Aware as he is of Bates's calibre, matching argument with argument, he cautions himself against hoping too much. They might end up disagreeing over the results, unable still to resolve the matter of superiority. He remembers his days travelling with the Legion. He grew used to winning his arguments easily with the soldiers, doing as he wished with their impressionable minds. But with Bates, he has had to change his line of attack. It won't be easy to unsettle his rival, upset the lines drawn with such precision on paper each morning. He needs a surprise now, otherwise the experiment might fail, the two turn dumb arguing. An accident! To win, he will need an accident in the next few days.

Turning the telescope around to the children's camp, he spots the nurse. His face lights up when he sees Norah leave the cottage with a pile of washing, running up towards the spring. He follows her through the overhanging trees, spying on her every now and then as she clears the thick line of foliage. The children seem nowhere near. Her face fills the telescope's glass. He examines it in minute detail, reaching instinctively for the notebook. A face worth a thousand visits! She could attract men as easily as she breathed! Who would let her slip through his fingers? She was too tempting to pass by, to banish to a desolate island. Did Bates love her? Was he meeting her secretly?

As he waits for her to finish, his face glows, seized by an idea. Drawing the notebook closer, he starts to scribble vigorously, not once removing his eyes from Norah. *She's the solution!* he thinks. He'll surprise Bates with Norah! *She* will be his final argument.

On his haunches at the tree house, he leans forward for a better view. He gazes fondly at Norah, finished with her washing, now stripped down to her toes and floating like a lotus in the spring.

A large mirror stood in the middle of the courtyard facing the cottage. Brought over by Bates, it gleamed in the sun. Norah had gone to look for the children in the forest. Bates sat on an iron trunk that held picks and shovels for the garden, Belavoix on a wooden stool by him, each holding open a notebook, like artists ready at their easels.

Even before Quartley had unwrapped the sheet of mirror delicately from its covers and, following Bates's instructions, carried it over to the centre of the courtyard, the scientists had started to air their predictions about how the children would behave. Complaining still of his minor scarlatina, Belavoix seemed nevertheless to be the more optimistic, flooding his rival with stories of savages and their love of civilised objects.

'These children are no different from other savages I've met. You'll see, Mr Bates . . .' His face broke out into a smile as he recalled a funny incident. 'They have no way to deal with the new. I can tell you of a tribal boy who tried to swallow a compass! Or . . .'

'You aren't suggesting that our samples will bite the mirror, are you?'

'Bite, kick, scratch, lick! They might do anything.'

'But . . .' Before Bates could finish, they caught sight of Norah herding the children back, waving her arms and ushering towards the courtyard. They ran at her flanks like a pair of obedient dogs, without a view yet of what awaited them, of the novel object. As they drew closer, the men heard them chattering in excitement, both appearing in a far friendlier mood than during their bouts with the instruments. They were close to seeing the mirror now for the very first time, glimmering under the sun, resting at a mild slope against a stump, a patch of the blue sky trapped inside its clear glass.

It took some prodding and pushing by the nurse for the children to spot it at first. Then, silence. Like the scientists themselves, the children observed the mirror from afar, as if waiting for something to happen. The girl ran a few steps towards it, struck by the puff of white cloud that had floated in from nowhere and stuck to the glass, hanging from it like fruit. A moment of distraction had her glance back to the boy, who was bounding towards the cottage, racing up the steps to disappear into the kitchen. She called after him, a sharp bleating call. Bates stopped Norah with a sign, happy to have just one of the samples in the courtyard. Sitting upright on his stool, the Frenchman wasted no time penning his notes.

The girl seemed to be measuring up the mirror, taking stock of its distance from her. A wind blew, rattling the glass against the stump. She smiled, seeing it move. The mirror turned alive by the gentle motion, as familiar to her now as a swaying branch. Small steps turned into a trot as she came up to it.

She'll bite it now! Quartley looked quickly from Bates to Belavoix. The girl seemed untroubled by her own image, facing the mirror without shock or surprise, unflinching. She didn't seem to mind that her reflection aped her – returning her fluttering eyes, frowning as she frowned, or turned blank as she went behind it to examine the stump.

Bite, kick, scratch, lick!

She left the mirror as easily as she had approached it, running back to the cottage and emerging moments later with the boy. He looked not quite himself – deeply worried eyes and slack limbs, as if just woken from sleep. She seemed to have told him something in their secret language, had him follow her reluctantly, dragging his feet and not even glancing up at their nurse as they passed.

The two stood before the mirror silently. Then she left him to go behind it once again, touching the back of the glass with her finger. The boy looked on, the scientists watching him stand still for quite some time before starting to move. They saw him bare his teeth at the mirror, let out a stream of babble and contort his little body into one impossible shape after another. Then terror struck. The mirror showed a bird flying towards him, making him race back to the kitchen once again.

Quartley gives Bates a quick look. He knows what his master thinks. A rare satisfaction for the craniologist. He has just collected a new and precious fact, seen the clearest result so far in all their tests. He has reason to be pleased with their samples for making this the most successful day of the experiment.

As Quartley puts away the mirror, Bates eyes the empty stool. Belavoix has disappeared after the test ended. He is tempted to review his own notes, then decides against it – there is the whole evening ahead for that; he'll have time to revisit the scene as he gazes at the fireflies' dance. For now, it's the girl he thinks about, praises her silently for winning the test of intellect. Her curiosity for the unknown, her inquisitive mind bent on solving the puzzle of the mirror, places her a cut above the other sample. He praises her for being true to her own kind. A great responsibility lies on her young shoulders, he knows. She has to prove the worth of her race, its superiority. She must uphold her place at the very top of the chain. No – he shakes his head. She must uphold the position of the entire species. He considers the boy as well. His conduct at the mirror showed nothing but sloth, fearfulness and vanity: the weaker sample has failed to put up a fight against his bigger-brained rival. The girl will win again, he is sure. His mind goes over the other tests that he and Belavoix have planned for the future – tests of benevolence and courage, esteem and aggression. Of sexual appetite. She'll acquit herself well in all these, using the faculties and propensities that make her superior, the *most* superior of the human races.

Arriving at the veranda, Bates glances at the Frenchman's door, which has been locked from inside. How crafty of him to suggest leaving the knife – the weapon of accident! The experiment is in constant danger, Bates thinks, at the mercy of the Frenchman's vivid imagination that is capable of upsetting the fine balance of measurements and observations. To win in the end, he must keep on winning through all these years, wear down his opponent's love of surprises. As the superior of the two, he must be prepared to wait for as long as it takes, for the final argument must invariably last long.

'Is it possible to win Mr Belavoix over, sir? He doesn't believe anything we say! At this rate . . .'

That was before the mirror test.

To himself, he scolds Quartley for believing that it is all about filling logs and notebooks, for thinking that is all there is to their science. Sipping his whisky, he prepares to lecture him, just as he would his students.

Between the experiment and the result stands the scientist, Bates whispers. He, the scientist, knows the hidden boundary between the two, whereas the onlooker sees only a coarse boundary. The scientist wins or loses in his *mind*, not by the argument of a rival. The only tragedy, Quartley – he looks around for the absent fireflies – is if he fails to read his own mind, if he fails to see it as clearly as the prize he hopes to win in the end . . .

Fresh from the mirror test, Quartley goes up to the hill top for his final task of the day. It is his duty to scan the horizons periodically with Belavoix's telescope for signs of an approaching vessel. It gives them a day or two to tidy up their camp and bring down their cases to Norah's cottage, before the outrigger docks to carry them back to the ship's hold. Between sighting and departure, he does all that is necessary, starting with sealing up the windows at their camp to hold the army of bats at bay during their absence. Sweeping the floors clean, he sprinkles them with dust of camphor to scare away the many-legged creatures that might otherwise nest in the cracks. There is the whole roof to worry about as well – the leaking spots. He has to balance on a stool to reach up and paint it over with a coat of glue. And then there is the sanitary lodge. The barrel has to be emptied lest it should become a pond of larvae or the cold resort of a water snake. He bars the doors of each room to prevent the children turning them into treasure troves of rocks, dead snails and lizards.

He scans the sea for a sighting. A dark worm winding its way past the anthills. From here, he cannot tell which flag it is flying, whether it is an English ship or not. Harder still to tell if it is a mail carrier or a trader, teeming with black and white deckhands, returning home with gold from the Gold Coast. He can tell only if it is a flagship, used to escort honest traders through this tricky passage, armed to its teeth, flashing its blunderbusses and buccaneer guns. Or a ship of the Royal Navy, patrolling the coast for slavers after the ban.

A ghost ship?

After a few trips with Captain Perry, he has learned all about the ships – the honest and the ugly, the traders and slavers, ocean tramps and convict boats. He has learned that no ship can escape the smell of Africa caught in its sails, one that seeps even into the immaculately burnished panels: the smell of disease and death. Rotting insects lie strewn all over, speckle the gold bushels.

Despite Perry's best intentions, they have had to sail on those ugly ships on a few occasions, have had to put up with the stench and cussing of sailors. English gentlemen were rare on that class of vessel. Only the captain kept them company with his grog and stories. The thought of Captain Perry draws a smile. The gentleman sailor trying to interest Bates and Belavoix in his own theories of everything and everybody. The 'unfinished scientist', he calls himself. Like most experienced sailors, Perry has learned a thing or two from his travelling companions and nurses the dream of leading his own scientific expedition some day. From each trip he brings back a novel specimen – a skull – which he presents to Bates in a special mahogany box engraved with the legend: '*A gift from Captain Charles E. Perry to the cause of British Science.*'

Scientist or not, Perry has placed his fleet at Bates's service, eager to share the glory of solving the mystery of the races. A tireless soldier, he plays his honest role in the experiment, never failing to arrange for the scientists to be ferried to Arlinda and back, while keeping the samples and their nurse alive with his supplies.

A perfect wind unfurls the sails, as the worm grows into a butterfly and skims the waves. A swallow's tail flaps like a kite from the mast. The *Rainbow*?

Quartley thinks about Captain Perry and Louisa, Bates's wife and benefactress – the two angels, the experiment's real caretakers, both as important to the samples as the scientists themselves. The captain at sea and Louisa on shore, both waiting for the results. The log is recited for their satisfaction, the samples described in utmost detail. The captain is even ready to nurse him through bouts of nausea, only to glean the secrets of the experiment. 'Tell me how the children are! Are they fighting? Have they bitten you yet? Who is the naughtier of the two . . . it is the boy, isn't it?' Quartley knows what and how much his master wishes him to divulge. Not the big secrets, but the small ones, not the arguments with the Frenchman, just tales of his madness.

Can he tell the captain about the mirror test?

When it appears, the *Rainbow* doesn't receive more than a cursory glance from Quartley. His thoughts are on another journey he must make soon when they have returned to England, to visit Mrs Bates in her country mansion, a journey no less pressing than their visit to Arlinda.

*

Back at their camp with news of the *Rainbow*'s impending arrival, Quartley found the two scientists on the veranda. Bates on his chair with a drink, and Belavoix in the hammock. On an evening of few words, he seemed to have arrived at the end of the conversation, both resting now under the night's spell full of screeching and hooting and the occasional whirr of Bates's arm battling a gnat around the oil lamp. There was no sign of notebooks or the log, no sign that the two had been sparring over the experiment.

'The *Rainbow* is a day's sail away, sir.' Quartley addressed Bates, who sat with his eyes closed. His master nodded, pointing at a half-empty case on the veranda, its contents heaped beside it. As he tidied up, Quartley glanced at the Frenchman, suspended from the ceiling like a freshly slaughtered beast. He expected Belavoix to make his demands too, ask perhaps for a supply of herbs from Norah's kitchen to treat his condition on the way back. The veranda stayed silent for a while as he finished packing, and then the Frenchman spoke in a low voice.

'We'll have much to talk about next time, Mr Bates. I'll show you a new way to settle our dispute. We'll have much to argue over.'

'Argue?' Bates feigned surprise, his eyes remaining shut. 'I thought you cared less for argument than you did for clear evidence.'

All three were woken by a loud knock on Bates's door. The scientists emerged from their rooms, both at the same time, in their night-shirts, followed by Quartley. Norah stood on the veranda with a lamp, her frightened face white in the flickering light. She held up her hand and pointed at the dark forest surrounding the camp, urging them by her gestures to follow her out.

'Stop!' Bates called after her. 'Where are we going?'

Norah struggled to explain, a rush of emotions cramping her limbs.

'Have you heard something in the forest?'

She shook her head.

'Have you seen something? A beast? A man perhaps?'

She shook her head again, and kept pointing into the darkness.

'If you're worried about something out there, it'll have to wait till dawn. Running around in the dark won't help . . .'

She grabbed Bates's arm and tried to drag him from the veranda towards the steps. 'Stop!' he shouted. 'What are you doing?'

'Is it the children?' Belavoix asked a now frantic Norah.

She nodded, a tear appearing on her cheek.

'Let me find out what's happened before you kill her with your temper, Mr Bates.' Belavoix led Norah by the hand, made her sit on the stool by the hammock and knelt by her side. 'Is it the girl? Is she sick again, unable to sleep? Has she frightened you, Norah?'

She shook her head, tears flowing freely.

'No? The boy then? Ah! The naughty one. Has he . . .'

'What has the boy done? Go on! Tell me.' Bates spoke angrily.

'Has he hit his sister? Has he scared you with *this*?' Belavoix picked up a rock from under the chair, and held it up before Norah. 'No? Has he gone into the little cupboard and smashed up the instruments?' He looked up quickly at Bates, with a smile of reassurance. 'What then?'

Exasperated, Bates dismissed the nurse with a wave of his hand.

'Has he . . .' – Belavoix looked up into the forest – 'disappeared?'

She kept silent.

'He has left the cottage without telling you. You're afraid he's lost in the forest, aren't you?'

'What?' Bates turned around and walked up to Norah. 'Has the boy gone?' He waited a moment for her to respond. 'Has he?'

She managed to nod through her tears, turning her face away.

'How can you be sure? Maybe he's just hiding . . . under the kitchen table, in the larder, the instrument cupboard. The little monkey!' Bates's voice showed his annoyance. 'Have you looked everywhere?' He brought his face close to Norah's. 'Did you scare him? You've hit him, haven't you?'

She shook her head violently, holding the arms of the chair to keep steady.

A thought seemed to cross Belavoix's mind. 'He's done this before, hasn't he, Norah?' He took her averted look for a yes. 'It's not the first time. The boy disappearing from his room at night? You hear him usually, hear his footsteps, then find him near the cottage or in the garden . . . He seems to be still sleeping, sleepwalking? But this time you can't find him anywhere. Yes?'

Norah nodded, making a throttling sound.

'Somnambulist!' Bates muttered under his breath, as he sized up the situation. Then his anger returned. 'You should've written to us about this. Didn't Quartley tell you over and over to write us about *everything*? Didn't he instruct you to do just that?'

'Let's not be too . . .'

'It will be her fault if we lose the sample.' Bates cut off Belavoix angrily. 'Had we known, it'd have been an easy problem to solve. We could have tied him to his bed at night.'

'But the boy might've released himself from his bonds, no?'

'A somnambulist isn't capable of such a wilful action.'

'Let's not quarrel over what he is or isn't capable of. Let's find him first.'

Norah rushed to the edge of the veranda, imploring the men by her gestures to follow her. As Belavoix prepared to join her, picking up the oil lamp, Bates instructed Quartley in a cold voice. 'Bring the medicine box with you, a blanket, and –' After a quick thought, he added, 'Bring the rifle too.'

It was hard to guess where the boy might have gone. At Bates's command, Norah led them to all the children's known hideouts. Leaving the goat path, they entered a small clearing surrounded by tall tamarind trees with branches joined at the top like a roof. They flashed their lamps around the clearing, circling it like an empty room. There were signs of the little visitors everywhere – a freshly dug trench, stacked up twigs – but no trace of the boy. They entered a cave through a slit in the rocks, the lamp shining on traces of ore. Would he come charging out like a bear cub? Quartley knelt low to see if he could find paw-marks. Could he be up in a tree, fast asleep? They heard noises, turned back, hoping to find him prowling behind them. The little beast. Then, rejoining the goat path, they came down to the stream. It had changed into a treacherous ditch, part muddy, part brimming with a stiff tide, its banks ready to deceive the unwary with sharp drops and jagged rocks. A stretch that appeared easy to cross during the day threatened to drag them now into unknown depths. Norah showed them the spot where she had once found the boy, curled up on a flat rock jutting out into the stream. He wasn't there. Back in the forest, they began their search of the bushes, nuts crunching under their feet, like airguns popping. Then, Belavoix cupped his mouth and started to call loudly, startling them all.

'What are you doing?' Bates barked sharply.

'If he's sleeping, he must be woken, no?' He imitated animal calls, dropping his face down or raising it to the sky. A wild boar's grunt. The yammering of a buck, a howling monkey, a pair of brawling bears. A lion's roar. The empty forest echoed with beasts. Angrily, Bates hushed him with his finger.

'We won't hear the boy, will we, if he calls for us?'

'No sound is lost in the forest. You can hear him if you want to.' Snatching the rifle from Quartley, Belavoix made as if to fire into the air.

'Stop! You'll scare him. He's hiding from us, don't you see?' Bates growled.

'It's no use being sensible now. It's time to try some new things. The boy is bound to respond to a sound he hasn't heard before.'

Stumbling over a jutting stump, Quartley almost fell, the medicine box slipping out of his hand. Norah rushed back to help him.

'Why don't you let your assistant go back to the camp? He can wait there for us. That way . . .' Belavoix stopped in mid-sentence. 'What if the boy's there?'

'Where?' Bates looked at his rival crossly.

'At our camp! Maybe he's hiding in one of the rooms, hiding under our beds!'

The thought seemed to strike Norah. She started to climb up the goat path, followed by an excited and triumphant-looking Belavoix.

'Nonsense!' Forced to follow them, Bates made no secret of what he thought about Belavoix's idea. 'To think that none of us would've heard the little scoundrel!'

When they reached their camp, the men marched into their rooms, the Frenchman peering under his bed and waving his arms about as if he was searching for a pair of missing shoes. Then they came out onto the veranda and stood in silence. Deflated, Belavoix sat down heavily on the stool and started to argue with Bates as Quartley watched Norah gazing out once again into the darkness. *We don't want you to be their mother* . . . She seemed nothing but a mother. It wasn't the fear of Bates that had her weeping, but fear for her missing boy.

'We should've stopped the experiment long ago. Norah isn't responsible for what's happened, but the foolish stubbornness that kept us going for no good reason.'

'You wanted a tragedy, didn't you?' Bates snarled back.

'A *sensible* tragedy. One that would've proved something. This tragedy proves nothing, nothing at all.'

'You mean the kind of proof you collect doodling in your notebook and twiddling your thumbs?'

'Forget me, Mr Bates. How will *you* get your proof now, without the boy? How will you explain to your academies that you have lost one of the samples, not to natural causes, but to your *stubbornness*, your *English* stubbornness?'

'I can do my own bidding, I assure you . . .'

'But can you explain away an unnecessary death?'

Norah rose and left the veranda, to climb up the steep path to the hill top. Quartley followed her, without waiting for Bates's nod. Holding his lamp up to shine on her path, he kept a close watch on Norah's steps. The fading darkness revealed her small frame, supple and steady, under a taut and determined neck. He followed her without a thought, resigned to climbing up and down the hill and wandering the forest as long as she wished to continue her search. He felt free leaving the medicine box, the blanket, and the rifle behind, free to face whatever awaited them. After a while, the two cleared the line of trees, and came up close to the top – a spot well known to Quartley. The air felt cold and still. They didn't hear the forest's sound, not even a bird call – just the spray pounding rock on the beach below. Standing behind Norah, he saw her freeze; then over her shoulders he spotted a solitary form sitting on the ledge inches away from the drop. The boy. Quartley raised his lamp. The boy didn't blink. A pair of black eyes stared ahead at the black sea.

They heard the scientists come up behind them, Bates's heavy steps and Belavoix huffing and puffing. They too fell silent as they saw the boy. Rooted to the spot, Quartley wondered who'd make the first move. They mustn't startle the boy in any way, he thought, a slight jerk could send him hurtling down the cliff. *He's asleep, doesn't know the danger he's in . . .* He'd do more damage to himself, if he woke. Quartley heard Bates creep up behind him, both arms raised, making a sign at everyone to remain still. He saw his master narrow his eyes, and start to walk towards the boy. *One, two, three . . .* Quartley counted, just as he counted Bates's steps at the laboratory in front of his scared students. Coming up to the boy, Bates stood still for a moment, kneeling gently down on the ground. He took a deep breath, then folded his powerful arms around the boy's tiny shoulders, drawing him firmly into his chest.

They sat for a good while on the hill top – the scientist and his sample, like father and son.

A piercing cry flew from Norah's lips. Then she lapsed into her savage silence.

II

In the best of all possible worlds,
all is for the best.

HEAVEN'S BRIDE

The mansion appeared even darker than before. The blue sea still shimmered in Quartley's eyes as he crossed the terrace, to encounter drab white linen and empty walls. In the five years of the experiment the island had drifted closer to Louisa's home, which they visited after each trip to deliver a full account of their findings to their benefactress.

From the carriage, sitting next to Bates, he saw John Foxton's mansion at the top of the hill. It took a while to reach. On the way up, they passed a glass-blowers' village, its chimney-black streets showing glints of shard and leprous patches at the outskirts where the soil had been dug out for the ovens. As the carriage climbed the gentle slope, the path turned cleaner, a line of trees appeared, and the air seemed fresher from the daily round of rains.

Catching sight of The Steeple was enough to distract Quartley. Like an ugly bird, a raven, it perched high on the hill with a beak-like roof jutting down from its nest. It seemed too big to his village eyes – innumerable steps leading up to the door, huge windows, and the vast grounds, like a rimless lake. A rich man's home but not a gentleman's – that's how Quartley's mother would've described it. Louisa's father had built it on the back of his vast empire of apothecaries, spread out all over the country. He was a shrewd merchant. From miners to forgers, carpenters, bricklayers and glass-blowers – working men knew the worth of his pills and ointments. A strict Quaker, he did no business with God, chose prayer and his circle of Friends over pomp and frippery. His home had been his dream, a large but plain house, built to resemble a high steeple, where he and his fellow Quakers prayed together.

Since his death The Steeple had belonged to Louisa Foxton Bates – Bates's Louisa, his milch cow, as the gossip went. He had married her for the money, taking full advantage of her charities and gifts. Some said he was waiting for her to die. The milch cow that was also a sick whale, tied to her invalid's chair. She didn't mind her husband's skulls or that he was away at his laboratory in London – just was proud to be his wife, living far from him.

Quartley had been warned about Bates's wife. She was unlike any other country lady he might've met – as devout as her father, but a worrying saint as well, with a merchant's head when it came to reading the petitions that begged her help for a variety of causes. She shared her father's mistrust of pomp, and his zeal uprooting the devil's work: slavery and opium. Quartley had been warned, too, of her mysterious illness and of her gloom, which was likely to descend at any time without a hint of warning.

On his return from Arlinda, Bates would write a detailed account of their visit to be delivered to Louisa and her small circle of friends. At first, Quartley thought it silly to present her with details of the log. What would she make of the entries? Then he had observed her pride in it first hand, seen her reading out parts of the report to an enraptured audience. Unlike the petitions that lay strewn at her feet, Bates's reports stood on a shelf of their own. They kept her and her guests alive through the evening till supper, especially when her husband was at hand to fill in additional facts, forcing him to perform a delicate dance around the subject of proof. Sometimes, Bates would send his assistant in his place, excusing himself with a lie. 'You go . . .' he'd tell Quartley. 'They won't get much out of you. Your ignorance will discourage them.'

They travelled in silence. In the hour it took to leave the brick-lined streets of London for the open fields, Quartley observed his master's face take on an extra layer of grimness. Lines deepened on his forehead, his eyelids remained still for long moments. Was it a sign of doubt? Was it gloom, or reluctance to entertain Louisa's friends yet again with his brilliance? As a frequent visitor, Quartley anticipated the evening ahead, the tittle-tattle and the chitter-chatter, the less than elaborate meal, and the cold bed at night. Like Bates, he too frowned, thinking about Louisa's friends, their 'inquisitors'. A cool breeze blew in, reminding him of the sea spraying surf on his face as he strolled along the beach. Arlinda!

Entering Louisa's parlour, Quartley saw her sitting in her invalid's chair, looking much older than Bates with her shock of white curls and her long-suffering face. She reminded Quartley of what his mother had called a 'dying saint', the incurably sick who made a virtue of their suffering. A small table by her elbow carried a variety of specie jars, ointment pots and syrup bottles. A glass eyebath sat on a smaller stool by her feet, beside an inhaling kettle with a long spout. The room was quite bare but for a settee and a few chairs in a half-circle around Louisa's seat, a darned Turkey carpet, and a cabinet of curios with a china flowerpot on its top in which a fern was wilting.

The guests had already arrived, among them Louisa's most obedient friend, Esther Graham, her spy, the social butterfly who brought her the world's silly bits. She always asked awkward questions about the children, about the boy's bedwetting or the girl's lice. Her husband, George, didn't worry Bates or Quartley so much. A horse-breeder, strictly virtuous and untalkative, except when he dwelt on his favourite hobby: reading a man's character from the bumps on his head. Dressed like an old-fashioned squire, glasses tilted far forward on his nose, he sat examining the master craniologist's head throughout the evening. Then there was the headmaster, Mr Kepler, plump and pink, speaking at a high pitch as if reading from a page of notes. The place next to him was reserved for their own Captain Perry, the oddball in Louisa's circle, an Anglican among Quakers. The captain could be relied upon for juicy stories, and for the grog he carried secretly in a flask to offer to the men after supper.

With the help of Louisa's nurse, Quartley cleared the medicine table to make room for Bates's gift: a cross of white camellias.

Acknowledging the flowers with a quick smile, Louisa took out a letter from an envelope and started to read aloud to her guests.

'I have received a very special letter from an American friend. An American *saint*, I might say!'

Quartley noticed the stylish hand on the envelope: *To Louisa Foxton Bates, from Elizabeth Moore of Pennsylvania.*

'A letter that puts all these other petitions to shame,' Louisa said, pointing to the pile at her feet. 'Worth its weight in gold! Pity we don't have many more as uplifting as hers.'

The Grahams nodded knowingly. Taking a deep breath, Louisa began.

' "A girl came to us. A Negro girl, named Jowan. There were whip marks all over her body, and scars on her back and shoulders. This was the second time she had come to us. We had sent her back a month ago, to her master, Mr Henry Tucker, an English lumberman from Richmond. Mr Tucker had threatened to file a suit against us, for harbouring a fugitive. He had denied whipping the girl, claiming the slave's marks were acquired before his purchase. He had called her a rogue and a runaway. We decided then to send her back under promises of fair treatment. We asked Mr Tucker to put it down in writing which, of course, he refused to do." '

The headmaster started to say something, then stopped at Louisa's frown.

' "This time, there were more marks – the girl seemed to have paid for the boisterous passion of her master." '

Looking up from the letter, Louisa cleared her throat, then went on. ' "Dr Anthony examined the girl. She was with child, as we had feared. After proper treatment, it was decided to keep her here in Pennsylvania till she was fit enough to travel." '

Esther sighed. A shadow fell across the settee as Captain Perry stepped into the parlour through the adjoining library.

' "We asked her to pray with us, but she refused. The poor girl was afraid of Christ. In her eyes, he was as white as her master." ' A glint of anger shone in Louisa's eyes. ' "Two of our Friends will take her up to Canada, to the colony of freed slaves. She will be safe there. We have fitted her out properly (with provisions for the baby as well). She needed a Christian name for her new life. We have given her one – Louisa." '

The nurse entered the room with a coal scuttle which she placed beside Louisa's chair, then refilled her inhaling kettle with boiling water. She helped her mistress into a special bodice, the only luxury she allowed herself, meant for those suffering from weak backs, chills and rheumatism. The sound of Mr Kepler shifting uneasily in his chair disturbed the silence. George Graham stared intently into the cabinet of curios, as if inspecting an exceptional head. Bates sat still, his face hidden behind a book. Fearing a descending gloom, Esther started on a round of resolute hiccups. By the time the nurse had hurried in with a mixture of water and calomel and waited patiently as she sipped it down, the moment had passed. It was left to Captain Perry to recover everyone's spirits with a dose of his charm.

He started by teasing Esther over her hiccups, telling her about the

Damara of Africa. 'Only time a woman hiccoughs, the Damara believe, is when she's been hiding something from her husband. When she has a secret!' Winking at her husband, he didn't spare him either, making fun of his hobby. 'Poor George,' he said, 'he knows all about it from feeling up her bumps, but he must pretend that he doesn't!' He accused Louisa of 'imbibing opium through her kettle like a Chinese Yenshee, while keeping everyone awake with her cocoa!' Then he revived the American letter to engage her in her favourite pastime: sparring with him over slavery. As usual, Perry was ready to defend the honour of Britons abroad.

'Your friend may be right about the injustices of our countrymen, but does she write about the Negro's cruelty? He may be a slave in name, but he shows less loyalty than an ox.'

Sitting upright on her chair, Louisa shot back, 'The men you've met in your journeys might've been brutish, but not every Negro is. Do you think even an African king ranks lower than a gin-swilling sailor?'

'They've produced men of talent too, haven't they?' Esther joined in the fray.

'Oh, they have their virtues, I agree. Their bodies are strong enough to survive a rattlesnake bite or yellow fever; their women, too, suffer less in childbirth than our own. And for all their romps, syphilis is practically unknown in the Dark Continent.'

'But weren't we all savages in the beginning?' the headmaster squeaked. 'It is a pity and a mystery, why some have remained savage while others have moved on.'

Taking her cue from Mr Kepler, Louisa resumed her argument with the captain, stung by his unfortunate account of the slave. 'It is our duty to convert the ox to a man, a proper man. If the Negro is taught our ways, if he learns the motives of the household, if he's made faithful to the marriage bond, I wonder if he wouldn't be able to join us here.'

'He *can* learn, I agree.' Captain Perry showed a rare concession. 'But only when he is controlled. Just like taming a wild filly.'

'Taming? If animals can be taught with kindness, why not wild men?'

Captain Perry laughed. 'Well then, Louisa, I'll fetch a Hottentot or two for our breeder friend here. See if he can perform a few miracles!'

Following a lull in the debate, Mr Kepler issued a call for expert opinion. 'Why couldn't differences arise among men in the same way as sporting occurs in horses? A dark horse isn't necessarily inferior to a white one, is it? You must know all about this; why don't you tell us, George?'

Esther nudged her husband, whose eyes had closed in deep contemplation of a golden beetle inside the cabinet of curios, a gift from Captain Perry. Waking instantly, George Graham kept his nervous eyes averted, fearing being drawn into the debate. He, along with his wife, sought the advantage of the middle ground – between the comfort of agreeing with their hostess, and the temptation of giving in to the captain's vast experience.

With her husband unwilling to help, Esther was prepared to prolong the suffering till supper time. 'But nature does nothing in vain, does she? Why would she trouble herself by creating so many races when just one would have . . .'

'Well, that's a question for science to answer.' Mr Kepler seized his chance, raising his voice as if speaking to an assembly of students. 'We've got a problem, haven't we? The number of pure whites is very small in this world. Like it or not, we've got to live with our darker siblings. But what do we know about the darkest of them? Is there hope for those who in three thousand years haven't twitched in their sleep?'

All eyes turned to Bates . . .

Even an infrequent visitor didn't take long to settle into Louisa's evenings, just one visit enough to turn him into a veteran. The gloom of the parlour was kept going by rounds of cocoa, and the dark affairs of a senseless world. Some days it would be the faltering campaign in the Crimea, or the horrors of the Indian Mutiny. Even the endless wars fought over opium in China. There was nothing darker, though, than Africa's slavery, which offered more than gloom – the prospect of a known opposition till supper. It was an opposition Louisa relished, for giving her a chance to display her agility from the invalid's chair. Her duels with the captain were meant as an example to her wavering friends. In him, she had more than an opponent, one who mouthed the devil's arguments simply to keep her pure. Whatever the captain thought, he was on her side, she knew, unwavering in his support for her venture, her most important venture as Bates's benefactress.

And the ghosts, the dark slaves, far from her sight but ever-present in her parlour, were as essential to her husband's experiment as the medicine jars were to her health. They were the reason, as visitors came to learn, for her benefaction, her generous support for Bates's craniology. She needed scientific proof for what God had intended: the unity of all races. To prove that the savage was worthy of help to raise him to the level of his superior brother, not just fit to be sold. She planned to fight the devil, the slavers, with his proof, strangle them all with the great Chain of Races. Bates must win over the Frenchman for her to win over the likes of Mr Tucker. Her husband must defend God with his science.

The worrying saint, she worried over each visit to Arlinda, read Bates's reports eagerly to find out if he was any closer to winning. How long would it take? How long must she wait? Her worries grew with each new report, delivered by the smiling assistant.

The visitor must be prepared to have supper and more – attend her prayer circle, and shiver through the night at The Steeple.

Supper failed to introduce headier matters. For the most part, they ate in silence, served by Louisa's nurse in her apron – the Grahams looking down at their plates, Louisa glancing sideways at the curtained window, and Captain Perry inspecting the portrait of John Foxton on the wall ahead. Quartley kept his eye on Bates. Over the years, he had grown familiar with the puzzle of Bates. He seemed a different person here, the only exotic specimen among the visitors and friends, not the awesome scientist, his voice never rising to the famous gravelly pitch that his students dreaded. Not the natural aggressor, but meek and withdrawn, more an obedient servant than a husband. What did he find so arresting in the book, to have hidden behind it all evening? What made him ignore the dabblers? Whenever they were together, it was Louisa who spoke in the voice of science, Bates offering his silence in her support. The silence of craniology, of all of natural history. He never corrected her errors, treating her friends with the same indifference as he gave to the cabinet of curios. Was it simply his way of keeping his wife happy?

The supper ended with just one more exchange between Louisa and Captain Perry on the subject of race. But it was much milder than before. Once again, Louisa harped on her favourite theme of upliftment.

'Even if I were to accept that the heathen Negro is vile, doesn't that suggest that it is our duty to help him?'

Putting down his fork, the captain was ready with his stock answer. 'Are you talking about conversion?' He shook his head. 'You know it won't work, don't you? I *know*, Louisa. I've carried scores of dead missionaries back – buried some at sea too. The Negro is simply unable to grasp the subtleties of our faith, I'm afraid.'

'But if we persisted . . .'

'No, Louisa. Christian or not, a Negro will always be a Negro.'

'Do the children have enough to eat?'

Quartley's mind runs back to Norah's kitchen.

'Do they get proper meals?'

Louisa has started with Quartley, the report open on her lap. Esther has come from the dining room to join them. The arrangement is different from their previous visits, Quartley can't help but notice. In place of her usual practice – reading out the report to her friends with Bates commenting – she has made a point of meeting Quartley privately, after the men have retired to the smokers' room at the end of supper. She hasn't brought the report up even once during the evening or made enquiries about their recent visit to Arlinda.

'The meals are quite good. The nurse seems to—'

'I don't mean the food that *you* eat when you're over there. I'm sure it's made specially for you. I meant for the children when they are by themselves with the nurse.'

Her face appears flushed. Her hands weigh up the report, as if she is unsure if it belongs in the petitions pile or on the special shelf. She seems not to be in the mood for Quartley's usual descriptions of their trip, but in a mood to ask questions that have been brewing in her mind.

As Quartley starts on a lengthy account of the children's meals, it is Esther who interrupts him. 'But they are suffering. You can't deny that, can you?'

'Who?'

'The children! Every report is full of disease – high fever, coughs, swollen glands, scabies.' Shuddering on the settee, she mimics holding a sick child. 'It's a miracle they haven't been struck by something more serious . . . like variola or typhus!'

'Are they tall enough for their age?' Louisa takes over from her friend. 'Would you say they are as tall as children in England?'

'Yes,' he answers without thinking. 'The boy's a bit taller than the girl.'

'How would you know?' She points at the report. 'It says here that they're both quite wild, they crouch on their knees like animals, running and hiding in the forest whenever they see you coming. They aren't being raised to be normal, are they?'

'No.'

'And the bedwetting. Has it stopped?' Esther eyes Quartley sternly as if he, not the boy, is the offender.

'The nurse could answer that if . . .'

'*Answer?* But she couldn't, even if she tried. You know that.' Turning to her friend, Esther confides her fear in a whisper loud enough for Quartley to hear. 'The bedwetting . . . children running around naked . . . it won't be long now before they start getting curious . . .' She makes a knowing face. 'Before they start to amuse themselves.'

Quartley's mind returns to the early days of the experiment. He remembers Louisa fawning over the reports, her pride bursting through the mansion's gloom. He can picture her at Bates's side when he announced the experiment and thanked his wife for her generous support. The test that would solve the puzzle of human variation. Man's gift to God! Louisa had said, as radiant as any proud wife.

The sea-change has him wondering. 'Our supporters may fail us long before the samples do' – Bates had known that even before setting out for Arlinda the very first time. 'The worriers won't stop worrying; they'll want a quick result.' As the years went by, there would be fears over the children, Quartley knew, the early thrill replaced by worries over life and death.

Is she afraid of the children dying, or of her own death?

'The boy is taller than the girl,' he blurts out again, deciding it is safer to answer Louisa's question than Esther's. 'We can see them clearly during the measurements, every day of our visit.'

Bates has been right to send him over to face Louisa and her friend while he stays with the captain. Nothing can unsettle Quartley, his instinct is more than equal to the taunts and jibes.

After a moment's silence, the ladies exchange glances, Louisa starting to turn the pages of the report. 'But your measurements don't say much about the children. Not much about their *real* character. I wonder if we'll ever know.' She speaks in a distant voice. 'Do we know anything more today than we did five years ago?'

'Do not offer facts, until asked' – Quartley hears Bates again. Should he mention the mirror test?

'Every report that you bring talks about the future, not about what's happening now, but what *might* happen later. This is what your master has to say' – she reads a passage underlined by her in red. 'The European has shown herself to be cranially superior to the African. Now we must wait for moral and intellectual superiority, which shouldn't be long in coming.' She makes a face. 'Wait! Wait!'

'The experiment is still continuing.' Quartley feels obliged to defend his master. 'When it's finished, we'll have—'

'Are you confident that the children will live that long?' Esther's voice shakes with emotion. 'The curse of the Dark Continent hurts anyone who intrudes into her bosom. She's best left alone for God to decide what He wants to do with her wretched inhabitants.'

Calming her friend with a quiet word, Louisa turns to face Quartley. 'Do *you* think the experiment should go on any longer?'

'If Mr Bates thinks so, then it must.'

'But what do *you* think?'

Louisa lets a full minute pass before asking him another question. 'And the Frenchman? Do you think he wants it to go on for much longer?'

Should he lie? Or should he remain silent?

It'd be dangerous to describe Belavoix's idea, his plan to bring the experiment to a *natural conclusion*. It might even cause Esther to faint, if he mentioned the knife. He decides to answer somewhat vaguely. 'Mr Belavoix isn't sure about his evidence yet. He's still studying the children. He's not ready to give up.' He strains his ears to catch Louisa's friend's complaint against the 'double-crossing French', her voice blending with the gurgling steam in the inhaling kettle.

'Even if the result does confirm our belief, will it be enough?' He hears Louisa, speaking almost to herself. 'Will it discourage the slavers? Will it finally stop slavery?' She sighs. 'As Mr Kepler was saying at supper: can we stop evil with science . . . ?'

The sound of footsteps saves Quartley from further questions, letting him escape to his cold and bare quarters for another night at The Steeple.

Back in London, a pair of worried eyes followed Quartley around the laboratory, even as he heard Captain Perry's cackling laugh describing the 'African Beauties' to the smokers after supper. 'Our black sisters! The Hottentot Venus! Each a piece of red-hot coal from a raging fire . . . ! And cheap as a bottle of rum!' He remembered another scene as well. Coming down to the parlour in the morning, he had seen the two of them together, Louisa and Bates. His master had pulled up a chair close to his wife, and sat speaking to her in a low voice. She was playing a game of patience, laying out the cards on a board over her lap, totting up the score on the back of an envelope. He saw her infect Bates with her worry, both sitting with frowns, till his master had risen and walked past Quartley out to the waiting carriage.

Slowly, the Madhouse returned Bates to his usual self. Exacting and strong, marching out of his study to retrieve a skull from the collection, then calling out to his assistant to record measurements in the Cranial Index. It was the same Bates Quartley knew, eager to jump into quarrels and strangle his rivals with heartless precision. Once more his curses distracted a sleepy Jenny, rushing in from her cubbyhole to remove his half-eaten breakfast, or to squiggle about on the floor cleaning up crumpled paper.

Between entries in the Index, Quartley sat at his desk and started to re-read the stack of letters that had arrived over the years from Arlinda – Norah's letters, sent through Captain Perry's messengers. The more he read, the more he was able to recover his thoughts from The Steeple's gloom, forget Louisa's hard questions.

A tall pile stood on his desk. His master examined each letter carefully on arrival, looking for clues to their samples' behaviour, for exceptional news about the children. Then he'd toss the letter to his assistant, have him settle the nurse's requests, asking him to take over her list of requirements to Captain Perry to arrange his supplies. A letter from Arlinda! Quartley grasped each one eagerly, memory of the visits returning in a flash. For the most part, they were little more than lists of things needed – an antidote for the girl's toothache, tools for the garden, a report on the leaking roof. A neat list, with even spaces between the items. Written in a schoolgirl's hand, with a slight tilt like rush-reeds bent in a breeze.

The Madhouse erupts. Suddenly he is in the world of wild dandelions and honey flies. White gulls and white surf. What would he see if he found himself at this very moment inside Norah's kitchen?

It has to be the kitchen, if he wishes to escape the torrents of rain pounding Arlinda, the moist stream of air drawn down *La Petite Route* – the south-easterly monsoon, bearer of both havoc and life to the parched islands so close to the Equator. He would hear the surging waves drive the spray high up onto the rocks close to the children's camp, swallowing the gulls' nests and along with them the stretch of beach sand. The gulls diving down to rescue their fledglings, then floating up as the surf chases them. The rain has erased the view of the hill and the garden patch, everything blended into the grey sky. With every roll of thunder, he would see a flicker in Norah's eyes, as she sits at the table gazing out without a thought on her face – watching the rain and waiting for it to stop. She knows it will leave them on the verge of drowning. She doesn't worry about the children, letting them play in their rooms. The time to worry will be later – after the rains have stopped. Then she'll follow the children to the beach, keep an eye on them as they swim in the strong currents of the receding waves.

If he had been in the kitchen, Quartley would have seen her surprise. The roof starts to shake as if hit by a shower of rocks, a drumming noise spreads rapidly around the cottage. It brings the children out, first to the kitchen and then to the courtyard, dashing to catch the hailstones, sucking on them like rare fruit. She observes them from the window – rolling over mud, dipping their heads in the small puddles, scooping up the icy pebbles and holding them high, yelling madly to announce their catch.

As he arranged the letters in proper order, he went through them again, lingering over a few. He could imagine Norah making up her list, alone in the kitchen, the children fast asleep in their rooms. Her lips breaking out every now and then into silent whispers, the frown holding firm. Occasionally he'd detect an unruly slant, wonder if she had been distracted mid-sentence. Was it the girl crying in her sleep? Had she just remembered to tie up the boy to his bed? An unusual noise outside the cottage? He could see her rise and pick up the oil lamp, then flash it over the window peering out into the dark night. What did she see? His heart throbbed. A page looked crushed, as if it had blown away from the kitchen table. The south-easterly winds had brought rain to the island, he knew. The roof leaked badly then, a wet patch inched dangerously close to her larder, Norah had written. He remembered discussing the roof with Bates, and his master's alarm – not for the larder, but for the instrument cupboard near by. He brought his face close to the page to smell the south-easterly breeze rustling in from the shore through the arlinda trees. The smell of salt and gummy bark mixed with the trace of a familiar scent. Quartley sniffed the laboratory's air. The letter smelt differently from the desiccators and the stale smoke from Bates's study. He drew in the scent again, bringing his face close to the page. It *was* different. The letter writer's breath! A faint mark caught his eye – a drop of water hurriedly wiped off, leaving a tiny speck on the page like a fading star. Could the leaking roof have spread its havoc over the kitchen table as well? He read the letter again to gauge the damage. A tear . . . ?

Do we know anything more today than we did five years ago?

'And you said what, Quartley?'

On their way to meet Sir Reginald Holmes at the Royal Society, Quartley reported his meeting with Louisa and Esther to Bates. His master heard him in silence.

'Did you point out to them the encouraging bits of our report?'

'It does nothing for their worries, sir. They've got themselves into a tizzy about the children. They fear something awful will happen, Mrs Graham is sure that . . .'

Bates nodded, waiting to hear more. Quartley kept silent, debating whether he should mention Esther's outburst. Her plea to her friend to leave the Dark Continent alone. Could she sway Mrs Bates with her fears?

'What if the next report is the same as this one, sir? Will Mrs Bates . . . ?'

'Will she what?'

He felt suddenly shy. He didn't want Bates to know that he had overheard him pleading with his wife to keep her benevolence going. He aired another possibility instead.

'What if we find something unexpected, sir? Like the girl swatting the boy or stealing from him?'

'One finds more than one expects,' Bates replied coldly. 'More than what one's prepared to reveal. The *real* evidence must be reserved for the scientists; the rest should be kept happy with the plain evidence that they expect.'

'But they aren't ready to wait another seven years for plain evidence. It's far too long . . .'

'No.' Bates cut him off. 'Not seven years. That's how long *we* are prepared to wait. They, on the other hand, must be made to think otherwise. They must feel that the answer is close, as close as the breath in our nostrils.'

As they entered the office of the President of the Royal Society, they found Holmes waiting for them. A precise geometry of beams lit the room, reflected off the glass-framed portraits of past presidents lining the walls. Bates lost no time reminding his mentor why he had asked for the meeting, but Holmes was quick to stop him with a volley of good-natured questions.

'Tell me how the children are. Do they recognise you now, or are they savages still? A pair of monkeys up to their naughty tricks!'

Bates looked at his assistant, expecting him to give a short report. Going over the cranial details quickly, Quartley started on the mirror test, only to have Bates take over.

'The girl shows promise; already her intellect is vastly superior to that of the boy.'

Holmes nodded. He seemed to be expecting a favourable result, and keen to whip up support for Bates's ultimate victory.

'It's time for an interim report. If you agree, I'll arrange for a special meeting. A private gathering with a few very senior members of the Society. They could have their say now. Suggest changes, if necessary, to help you.'

'Changes?' Bates turned his swift gaze on Holmes.

'If we change a few of the tests, the result may come sooner than expected. We might even think of bringing the children back here for –' He stopped, seeing Bates's cold stare. 'If you were prepared to be flexible with your experiment, that is.'

'But we agreed – you, me and the Frenchman – to wait till the end. We agreed to be patient.'

'Yes, but we don't want to be faulted for desperate perseverance, do we?'

'Nor for fickleness. I wouldn't want to change anything now. An interim report could be dangerous. Might make your *senior members* feel they understand what they're in fact unable to digest properly. An experiment is like a story: its middle doesn't always predict the end.'

The room fell silent. Holmes looked a touch miffed at Bates's reaction. Fidgeting with his pen, he managed to recover his genial voice and turned the meeting over to Bates.

'Perhaps we should talk about *your* reason for this meeting, rather than mine.'

'My reason . . .' Bates started, then rose to pace the room. 'My reason is to have you and the Society realise what this experiment is really about.'

'What do you mean . . . ?'

'I mean what you are witnessing now. Five years of hard work. Going over to the island twice every year, to measure the samples. It's been hard for everybody, including Quartley here.'

Holmes smiled kindly at Quartley.

'It has been hard, too, for those who support us – those who have made all this possible, borne the burden, paying for our berths, paying for the children's food and all that the nurse needs on the island to keep them alive.' Bates paused, drawing his gaze back from the portraits to Holmes. 'Loyal as they are, one can't expect them to carry on much longer. After all, they aren't men of science as we are, but those driven by good intentions.'

'Our gratitude to your—' Holmes started to say, before Bates interrupted him.

'And what will the Royal Society receive in return for the hardship of so many?' Bates stopped, waiting disdainfully to answer his own question. 'The solution to the greatest puzzle in science.' He pointed to the desk. 'There, on your desk, you'll have the reason for black and white, savage and civilised, the clue to human variation. You'll have *l'épreuve.*'

The room glowed in the criss-crossing beams.

'We know,' Bates continued, 'that it's no use asking Belavoix and his Société to help. They've been crying themselves hoarse over the *poverty of the Republic*! He might just be able to pay for his visits every now and then, but no more. I'd say it's time now for the Royal Society to stand up and do what it should've done long ago.' Bates stopped, then spoke slowly. 'I thought you could ask your senior members to . . .'

Holmes heard in silence, his pen whirring around his fingers. 'No.' He shook his head.

'No?'

'It's not beyond our means to support you. And the Society does, as you say, stand to benefit from all this. But we're best left out of it. It would raise too many eyebrows. Unusual as it is, your experiment might arouse controversy.'

'How can it be any more controversial than supporting the collection of skulls?'

'No . . .' Holmes eyed his pupil sadly. 'Our members might object. Raising the children in the wild? They might question the wisdom of such a risk. What if one, or both, were harmed in some way?'

'But children *are* being harmed even now, are they not? Slaves, or coolies – whatever you call them, they're still being carted off to America – scores of young ones.'

'Yes. But the Royal Society isn't involved in transatlantic trade. Never was. You have an English girl too, don't you? There'll be more than a few eyebrows raised if she were to . . .' Then, he changed his tack. 'You wouldn't want the experiment to be discussed too widely anyway, would you? Wouldn't want the members to tell you what to do. If they were to support it with funds, they might demand more than an interim report. Might even want to visit Arlinda to see things with their own eyes.' With Bates silent, he offered yet another reason. 'Think of the Americans.'

Quartley pricked up his ears.

'What if the Americans stole your idea and rushed into an experiment of their own? We wouldn't be satisfied with an American proof, would we? It would be full of stupid mistakes!' Clearing his throat, Holmes spoke in a kinder tone. 'It is to your advantage really, to *our* advantage, to keep this as close to our chests as possible.'

Bates started to pace again, glancing angrily at the portraits as if they were each responsible for Holmes's decision. 'So you are refusing to support me?'

'No, no. You know you have my support.'

Bates eyed him with a mock question. 'And what sort of support is that?'

'You know that I and the Royal Society stand firmly behind you,' Holmes said in a faltering voice.

'A Royal Society that refuses to fund the experiment, because it might raise *too many eyebrows*? Its president unwilling to convince its senior members that it faces the greatest opportunity of its lifetime?' He waved his hand at his mentor across the table. 'Maybe I *should* try the Americans. They'd only ask for a few rotten skulls in exchange. Even they wouldn't offer such silly excuses.'

'I'm sorry, Samuel,' Holmes said quietly, 'for all the hardship of the *others*.'

The answer is close.

Returning with Bates, Quartley feels thrilled by his words. *As close as the breath in our nostrils.*

Is it that close, really?

SUMMER THUNDERSTORM

The days have started to lengthen. The fruits on the trees are soft and green, the shrubs beneath moist with sapping buds. The children don't go near them. They have been warned of the poison since they were very young. They know the white drops could turn their skin hot with fever. I, foolishly, once ventured close to the trees while wandering in the forest and caught a drop from the branches on my neck . . .

It seemed more than a report – a letter. A letter to him, Nicholas Quartley, not to the scientists. This time, she didn't start as she had in the past with a list of essentials, followed by a report on the camp and the children's condition. It didn't contain the usual descriptions of fever or rash, of leaking roofs, or complaints over Captain Perry's supplies. Instead, she had written about the arrival of a pair of new birds in Arlinda: 'Their plumes are white like a gull's but they're smaller, like rice birds, blue-necked and fan-tailed. They don't sing, but twitter all day . . .'

He was enthralled.

Earlier, she had seemed little more than a prop, a living prop, busy minding the children – a blur of agile limbs, a silent instrument built to perfection, her frown a natural mark, just as natural as the metal ring on the wooden goniometer. She had seemed as trust-worthy as the goniometer too, requiring even less attention and displaying an evenness that the visitors had come to expect without exception till the boy's sleepwalking incident. *Her heart is empty*, Quartley had thought. *Maybe she has a secret to hide.* He thought she was at last writing him her secret after five long years. The secret of her 'wandering in the forest'. The image didn't match Norah. He knew her as fleet-footed – chasing up and down the goat path, or running after the children on the beach. *Is that what she does when the visitors have gone?* Reading the letter, he imagined Norah strolling on the island, weaving her way around the trees.

She seemed to have written more than he had read the first time around. The neat and evenly spaced words were full of puzzles, like an unknown experiment's log. Reading each sentence again carefully, he tried to solve the puzzles. At times, it seemed no more than a simple report. At others, he glimpsed a hidden sore, or a brave effort thinly disguising her sorrow. He found telltale marks of rage, and wondered who her enemy was. Was it her own condition? Or was it them – the scientists?

There are days when the children disappear for hours. When they return to the cottage, I can see that they are sad . . . glum-faced. Perhaps the two have quarrelled, they seem unfriendly to each other, refusing even to eat together at the table. I've learned not to force them. Otherwise, it might end in a fight, the children throwing their plates at each other, barking like dogs.

I've learned to follow the rules. To let them sulk, and to sulk with them.

Sometimes, he made a mental note to consult Bates about the letters, knowing full well that his master would be dismissive. 'Nonsense!' he had scoffed once when Quartley suggested that they rush to Arlinda to deal with a pressing problem.

'The nurse has written about the girl, sir . . . trouble with her . . .'

Bates had glanced up from the paper he was reading. 'It's too early for her bleeding to start. What trouble?'

'She points at her eyes and shrieks with pain.'

Bates said nothing.

'Her eyes are larger than usual, the nurse has written, the pupils large too. But she has trouble crying, shedding tears.' Quartley had read aloud from Norah's report. 'Her eyes stay open for hours even when she seems to have fallen asleep.'

Bates continued turning pages. 'And . . . ?'

'She doesn't write anything more, sir.'

'I mean what else has she written about besides the girl's trouble?'

Quartley had run his eyes back over the letter, unable to remember the rest of Norah's report. The 'larger than usual eyes' had shocked him, filling him with an urge to return to Arlinda as soon as possible. 'That's the most serious thing she has written about.' Then he had added, 'We must go and bring them back.'

'Nonsense! It's nothing but rheumatic ophthalmia, rarely found among the well-to-do but common among the poor. In time, the pupils will freeze, with painful movement and oozing of pus.'

Quartley felt certain the girl was in serious trouble. He could trust Bates's diagnosis, even when the patient was hundreds of miles away. 'Then we must go at once.'

'That won't be necessary,' Bates had said. 'The eyes will take at least a decade to close, by which time we'll have finished our experiment.'

'You mean, we'll let her go blind? We can't do that!'

'Don't argue, Quartley!'

Whenever he read Norah's letters, he felt she was sitting right beside him, speaking through her mute lips. He longed to hear more about her past, how she had come to live in the asylum, how she had been rescued. He wondered if she wasn't mute after all, but among the unfortunate few to be raised in a silent home with other mutes, learning to speak with shrugs and nods, losing her natural speech when she was very young. He wondered what she thought of his replies.

As he read the letters over again, he heard a voice he hadn't heard before: Norah's. There were the usual strains, the warnings over the children and the ever-present dangers. For the first time it made him uneasy. The more he read, the more clearly he heard the footsteps of a solitary wanderer, the sounds of the island filling in her silence: the blowing breeze, the surf and the gulls. A sound that was hers, as immaculate as her face and as disturbing as her frown.

Ever since their last visit, he had thought continually of her: weaving her basket in immense concentration. Norah pulling on Bates's arm on that eventful night. Her cry. It had taken many sleepless nights for Quartley to confess to himself that he was in love with Norah. The thought had at first filled him with shame. She belonged to Bates, like everything else about their experiment. The instruments and specimens and the nurse were all his. He felt he had gone behind his master's back, stolen a precious skull from his collection – the *most* precious one.

Did Bates suspect?

He thought of the time he had spent alone with Norah at the cottage, while the scientists were following the children around, or had simply retired to their camp for the day. He'd stay in the kitchen to wrap up the instruments, working as slowly as he could to watch Norah, taking far longer to complete his task than necessary. Bates must've known. He missed nothing. He must've made up his mind to throw the lovesick assistant out.

His love for Norah was stronger than his fear of Bates.

He held her letter, and thought hard about his reply. It always fell on him to write back. Bates intervened scarcely, leaving Quartley to pass on fresh instructions and reminders. What could he say? Should he reveal his secrets too? Tell her how he lived away from her kitchen? He thought he'd write her about the skulls, starting with number 88, the Seminole Warrior. Somehow, they seemed less than appealing, falling far short of the surprise arrival of a pair of birds. Could he write about the Madhouse, of the years spent with Bates? As he started, his unruly thoughts turned wilder, refusing to settle on paper. The laboratory blended with his visits abroad, trips to the Royal Society and home to his mother. And the dark mansion looming over a glass-blowers' village.

Day turned to night as he thought of Norah, night turning to day as he composed his reply.

The first time she dreamt of him, she woke in shock. Straight up on her bed, she gripped the pillow to hold herself steady, opening her eyes wide to catch the ending. It was afternoon in her dream, which made it easier to watch the scene inside the dark room. She saw herself in the kitchen, sitting on a chair drawn up to the window. She was watching the rain, hearing its drumming over her head, guessing how long it'd last from the sound. There was one other in her dream: the assistant, sitting beside her at the table, watching the rain over her shoulders. Watching her.

From its ending, she knew it had lasted long. The dream was as long as the rain, arriving without warning. Unstoppable. It had put her almost to sleep as she sat watching, holding her firmly in its trance. She had felt nothing for hours, not thinking about the children for even a moment – just sat in the kitchen with the rain and him.

Her skin warmed where his gaze rested. Stayed warm throughout her dream. She hadn't minded the constant attention. After a while, it felt like a pair of palms gently clasping the back of her neck, a bubble nestling in its hollow. From time to time she felt the warmth leaving, but only for a moment to travel up to the knot of hair on her head, or down past her shoulders to her waist. She felt it spreading all over her back, as she heard the drumming on the roof. The warmth as much a part of her dream as the rain.

Sitting up on her bed, she poked the dream with her finger, now ended but still floating around her like a vanishing cloud. She tried to stretch it, to look as far into it as possible to discover what had been there in the beginning.

In the beginning, there were words. She heard a voice at the table, speaking to her about the pair of new birds: the assistant finishing his work and talking to her. He was telling her how the birds might've come to Arlinda, flying on their tiny wings from another island, or sitting on the mast of a sailing ship; slipping in past the quarrelsome gulls. They preferred land to sea, staying away from the beach, near her cottage. In the time it took him to finish one instrument and start on another, he had told her about their plans. The birds would stay on in Arlinda, build a nest here, stealing the dried leaves she had saved for her baskets. He had teased her over the baskets, offered to take one and hang it from a branch to let the birds use it as their nest. 'Then you'd know where they were. You wouldn't have to search for them, like you search for the children.' Summer would fill the basket with eggs, each a gemstone with a trapped bee inside. She'd see less of one of the pair, the other busier than usual scavenging in her garden. She'd need a scarecrow.

'You'll have a flock of little birds,' he had said.

In her dream, the rain had come once and gone, then come again. The nest filled in the summer in-between. She had seen herself hanging baskets from branches, going around the island, the assistant following her, eyes on her back. His hands were free of the instruments and the log. He didn't seem to mind that their camp up on the hill was empty, without Mr Bates and the Frenchman – that he was alone with her and the children.

Thunder and lightning had come in her dream just before she had woken. She had felt the warmth leaving her body, as his gaze travelled to the darkness outside. What'll happen now to the nest, he had asked her. 'Can you see it, Norah?'

'Yes, there . . .' She had pointed at a speck outside her window. Then woken in shock at the sound of her own voice.

Nicholas Quartley. Quartley! Gradually, she has dropped that name as well. Nicholas. She likes the way it takes a full breath to say, longs to hear someone call him by that name. For him to say it himself. Even when they were together, going up the goat path, carrying a heavy bucket of hot coals between them, a remedy for M. Belavoix's 'condition', he would talk to her about the instruments. She longs to hear about more than the craniograph and the goniometer. Wishes she could shut his mouth with her palm, and distract him with the Flame of the Forest. She wishes to take him up a different path, one unknown to the scientists, past the bat cave. Have him peek inside its musty darkness.

Anything to make him forget the craniograph!

Till she knew why. Why he wanted simply to watch her and to talk, without any reason whatsoever. The instruments were his disguise, giving him a chance to draw her into his world, the world of the experiment, without the need of a reply. He'd have said more if it hadn't been for her silence, she is certain. He'd have told her how he lived away from the island in England.

She remembers him chopping wood behind her cottage – supplies that will last a few months after the visitors left. The flashing blade passing his young and determined face. Flared nostrils and a broad mouth. His mother must have trimmed those curls when he was a boy, now fussing up his neck and forehead. A village boy, as quick with the instruments as he was with the axe, he had a knack for fixing things, putting back broken parts, or getting rid of the useless. She had seen a clear mind, as clear as the scientists', behind his clean moves.

She wonders what brought him to Arlinda. He wasn't one of *them*, she knew from his looks, from the way he spoke. He didn't have the air of someone who wished to win with his words. Not sharp and piercing like Bates, or full of poison like the Frenchman. Rather, there was a bluntness in his words that felt as comforting as warm rain pelting skin.

He was easier too around the children. He watched them like Bates and Belavoix, but seemed untroubled by their wild manners. It didn't bother Quartley if the girl spilt her soup or the boy splattered the table during supper. She didn't feel embarrassed by their conduct in front of him, as she did, invariably, with the scientists.

She keeps on thinking about the assistant, about his mystery. What has brought him to Bates?

Was it a tragedy like hers?

The children are at the beach when she finds them, on the narrow stretch left undevoured by the rains. The sand appears to be little more than a bed of clay, hard to cross without slipping and sliding, digging one's heels into empty crab nests. The crabs have escaped the floods, running back to the valley of rocks, only to drown in the small lakes of rainwater trapped among the boulders. It's a garden of rotting seaweed, attracting nothing but flies.

She sees them poking around in the sand and weed with sticks – a pair of determined explorers, turning over an empty shell, as if searching for treasure. The boy carries a piece of hollowed trunk eaten by woodworms, shaped like a bowl. It is quite full with broken eggshells, collected from the gulls' nests, those wrecked by the storm. Working their way up and down the narrow stretch of beach, they move on towards higher ground, faces down like a pair of birds.

She knows now where they've been since morning. She waited with their afternoon meal, but there were no signs of them returning. She wonders if they have found their own food, as they do sometimes, digging out a juicy bulb from the earth or discovering a hidden patch of wild mushrooms. A feast of earthworms? She makes a face, remembering the girl returning one day to the cottage with a half-alive creature dangling from her lips. She looks at the eggshells in their bowl, guessing where they have come from.

They seem grown up, not children any more but two small strangers. She misses the days when they were babies, just wrapped bundles. She could do with them as she pleased, feeding them and putting them to bed. The rules didn't matter then. They were hers, to love and play with, keeping guard over herself only when the scientists were around.

She sees two strangers, growing up with each other, growing stronger by the day, a time soon to come when they will no longer return to the cottage at night. Living, perhaps, in their own cave on the island, treating her with as much curiosity as they do their visitors. *It'll be tricky,* she thinks, *to get their heads into the instruments in just a few years from now* – unless they choose to do so themselves. They are already quite strong, and it is hard for her to pull them apart when they are fighting, or to pick them up from the floor and put them to bed.

Their bodies smell different too. She follows less of their babble and grunts now.

Through the reeds, she sees them inch their way up to a nest full of eggs. A small colony of gulls stands guard. They look angrily at the raiders, stir up their wings and feathers to scare them off. The girl holds her stick out, tries to touch the nest with its tip; the boy follows behind. Both are bare on the top, wriggling up the rocks like sea crabs. They've emptied their bowl of eggshells, filled it up with pebbles. A quick signal from the boy sets the girl off at a run. She comes within a few feet of the nest then scampers back as the gulls stage their counter-attack. Beaks out, they poke at her wiry legs, flapping their wings to scare her. Then it's the boy's turn. He's not as brave as the girl, unwilling to chance his luck against the warrior birds. Perhaps he's the wiser of the two, choosing to stay hidden behind a boulder and hurl a handful of pebbles at the birds. His aim catches them off guard, striking with absolute precision. Norah hears the gulls screaming. She fears less for the children than for the eggs they are after. She wishes she could stop them, if only the rules would allow her to come between them and the nest, to pull them away and play a different game.

With each drive, the girl becomes bolder. She doesn't mind the fluttering wings and darting beaks, not even when her small frame is covered by a swooping bird. The boy yelps, spurring her on, his shouts distracting the nest's guardians. It'll all end soon, it seems, either side with a fair chance of winning over the other, their battlefield left to be overrun later by smelly weed and flies. Waving her stick over her head, the girl makes a final dash, scattering the birds, then stands still at the edge of the nest. Her eyes gleam. She smashes the eggs with a clean sweep, and dashes back to the boy. The two take off down the beach, running shoulder to shoulder like a pair of hunting beasts.

She feels like the mother gull. As she watches the scene, she imagines herself defending her eggs, swooping down on the children, scooping out their egg-like eyes with her beaks.

He isn't a scientist like them, Norah thinks of her Nicholas. In her mind, she imitates Bates. 'Bring me the goniometer, Quartley. No, not that!' She hears him shouting commands to his assistant, ordering him to recite them to her in turn. And the Frenchman – leering and teasing, unsparing of everyone. 'Shame on you, Mr Assistant! Couldn't you help our poor Norah save her garden? Where's your *English* chivalry now?'

No, he was not a scientist. Just an honest working hand. Like her.

'What is it, Quartley?'

He entered his master's study and stood facing him. He had come prepared. Bates glanced up impatiently from his notes. 'Go on.'

'It's about Arlinda, sir.'

'What about it?'

'Can we go on without anyone to support us?' He corrected himself quickly. '*If* Mrs Bates decides to stop?'

Bates looked surprised. 'I can't answer that question.'

'We'd have no choice then. We couldn't leave the children and the nurse down there.' He decided to come right out with his plan. 'It would be better to bring them back now, sir. We can do our tests here.'

'That would be wrong, Quartley. You know that. The samples would be corrupted if brought here.'

Carried away by his plan, Quartley ignored Bates, letting slip his best argument. 'It would please Mrs Bates to have the children back in England. They could even go to live with her in Surrey.'

Bates stared long and hard at his assistant. He put his notes down. 'What is this about?'

Quartley was silent.

'You think, without the means, we wouldn't be able to go regularly. And without us, the nurse won't be able to manage.'

Quartley nodded.

'Well, then.' Bates rustled up his notes and left his study with a grin. 'Why don't *you* become the children's caretaker? Send the nurse back here? You can do our work with the samples. Just remember never to open your mouth!'

He decided to add his own 'supplies' to the ones Norah had requested. Captain Perry could be relied upon, he knew, to bring over whatever she needed for her kitchen and the camp – from brooms and pegs, to clothing for the children. An item or two for the nurse as well. She needed very little for herself, he had noticed, reading the letters. Yet, on the island, she always appeared decently dressed, not in rags but presenting herself as satisfactorily as she had on her first visit to the Madhouse. She kept her eye on the children too, complaining if the captain had struck a size too short for the boy, or forgotten the girl's tunic. She'd be busy in the evenings with her needle, darning holes and patching up. She tried to keep the children decent too, even though, left to themselves, they preferred to fling away their clothes and romp around half-bare, or naked.

Quartley set off for the Brill. Unlike the rag-fairs, the Sunday market was known for its old-like-new stalls, a place where everything was cheap, but fancy – stacks of clothing going up to the ceiling in each stall, floors littered with more, and bulging cupboards. He found the din unbearable: costers announcing merchandise through trumpets, patterers preaching and a beggar's organ. The list drowned in his mind beneath the market noise. The sight of the street Arabs, dirty orphans running about over the pavements, reminded him of the children. Swimming in an ocean of rags, he managed to recover a pair of old satin slippers for the girl, and a red handkerchief. He rummaged from stall to stall, stopping only for a drink of salep, before pressing on. The boy was growing faster than the girl, he knew, measuring him up in his mind before buying a pair of knee pants and a bright blue shirt. The street urchins inspired him to go for a belt with shining buckles. He couldn't resist the temptation of Petticoat Lane, the hosiers' shops drawing him in like a magnet. On an impulse, he bought a gift for Norah: a hat embroidered with flowers.

What would she need for her idle hours? he wondered. Norah in her kitchen, waiting for the children to return. Sitting cross-legged on the beach. What would banish her frown? He eyed a kaleidoscope. A magic lantern – slides revolving under a candle's glow, showing a twinkling star or a horde of sprinting animals. Or a pack of cards? He imagined her like Louisa, playing her solitary game in her parlour. There was a moment's rush as he spotted a rusty organ among the costers' bric-a-brac, then he sobered up as he remembered the rules. The children must be raised without song.

In the end he bought a small mirror with a gilt frame and, after a quick check in his pocket, a mantel-clock with a picture of St Paul on its face.

He paid a penny and entered the Penny Gaff at the end of shopping, having spotted the brightly coloured canvas painted over with a picture of the 'Female Samson', a black dwarf and a band of 'living skeletons'. The orchestra started to play as soon as he found a seat, and the 'man without a neck' appeared on stage to enthral the crowd. Soon, he was laughing at the Fat Woman, arms sagging like bags of flour, and gasping with the crowd at the daring Flash Dancing. The best was yet to come, he was told – dolphin women swimming in a tank with nothing on – but even before that, trouble started at the back. 'Handy with their fists!' someone whispered, meaning the rowdies. Shoes started to fly amidst loud curses and bellowing. 'Fire!' – there were shrieks all around. Within moments, he had grabbed his bags and darted out of the tent, trampling over a bed of nuts scattered on the ground.

Quartley left the Penny Gaff to an approaching storm that had thinned the market crowd. Gas lamps lit the stalls, burning with a red smoky flame. A few of the smarter shops showed sparkling globes. A crimson light shone through the sieves of chestnut stoves set up by the sellers on the pavements. Under the dark sky and the blowing wind, the streets of the Brill seemed on fire. He started to run as the rain came pelting in, holding up his bags, bounding through the narrow lanes, fearful of knocking over barrows. The sky streaked with lightning, and the warm rain drenched him. The rolling thunder reminded Quartley of the crowds, and he glanced back quickly to see the empty market. The open road made it easier to run. It took less effort too, despite the weight of his soggy bundles. He felt a curious sensation, as if he was floating, his toes barely touching the ground. He leapt easily over puddles and swung his sack over his head. Passing one silent road after another, he didn't hear the pattering rain, heard nothing, till he arrived at the Madhouse and heard his echo in the empty laboratory.

'Quartley!'

He stood sodden and shivering before his master. Bates handed him a letter to pass on to Captain Perry.

'Tell him it contains an urgent message.'

He dreamt of Norah. Head down on his desk, his mind started to swirl with letters, till he heard snatches of words from the standing pile. The laboratory filled with the sounds of Norah. He could hear her snapping dead twigs for a fire in her courtyard, the breaking of each branch striking the walls like whiplash. The clash of surf over rocks drowned her steps. She was barefoot on the beach, looking for the boy. The clamouring gulls had taken up her call, flying neck-down over the spray looking for a truant head. Gradually, the sounds of the forest became her sound, following her as she went after the children – a concert of rustling trees, birdcall and the stream.

He heard the tom-tom and saw the dancers. They had circled a fire, not far from the children's camp. Chanting and clapping, arms around waists. Harps and gourds slung from their shoulders, small silvery bells ringing from a mast held aloft. The fire glistened on dark skin, against flashing white girdles and a riot of beads – on ankles and necks, and around the arms. Every now and then they broke ranks and ran under an arch of spears, swooping down to kiss the cloth of a nuptial bed laid under the trees.

Quartley saw Norah among the tom-tom dancers. A melancholy pair of eyes, small and even teeth gleaming, lips rosy and parted. Every grain of her skin shining in the glow. A slaver's kiss of hot silver on her naked back.

OTHERS

Captain Perry came to visit the Madhouse. Quartley took him straight to the collection room. 'Show him the gifts he gave us,' Bates had told his assistant a few days before. 'But beware, he'll tell you a story for each of them!' Quartley stood facing the cupboards, breathing in the desiccator's vapours, till the captain tapped him on the shoulder.

'So what do you have in them? A swarm of hornets?'

Full of apologies, Quartley ran to fetch the ladder and climbed up, unlocking number 73 to bring out the Pope – the Nubian specimen, with an exceptionally pointed head like a pontiff's hat. He passed the cranial details written on a scrap of paper to the captain.

'Oh, yes, I remember him! The skull was buried in a chamber of the sand castle. Totally unexpected – took my men by surprise. Have I told you how we . . . ?'

Leaving number 73 with the captain, Quartley climbed up the ladder again and brought out the African Bushman, making his visitor's eyes light up as if he was meeting a long-lost friend.

'Ah! The rascal!' The head, Captain Perry explained, had belonged to a Cape Town slave living in a plantation owner's home. The mistress had been fond of him, and when his master sold him off to a slaver, he had jumped ship to return and hack his mistress to death, tying up her husband and forcing him to watch. Captain Perry beamed, clearly proud of his gifts.

'We've done well, haven't we, Quartley?' He patted the young assistant on the back. 'But you've got more than skulls now. In a few years, you won't need your collection any more, will you? Your living samples will be enough.' He took Quartley's silence as doubt. 'But you *are* close, aren't you, to solving the mystery? Your master certainly seems confident. The girl was winning, he said – "She has shown her superiority already.'" He frowned at Quartley's downcast face. 'You don't seem so confident, do you?'

'It was six months ago. We don't know what they're up to now. We won't know till we go again.'

'But you *will* go, won't you? It'll be my pleasure to help.'

'When?' Quartley parried the question. 'There has never been more than six months between trips before. But now . . .' He looked down the corridor towards Bates's room. 'It's been longer than that now. He doesn't seem to be in any rush . . . hasn't asked me to get ready for our trip.'

Appearing to understand Quartley's concern, Captain Perry returned the skulls, then started to walk back with him to the laboratory. This was Quartley's chance to confide in him. He told him about his master's long absences from the Madhouse, his disinterest in the log and Arlinda's letters.

'He has forgotten about the experiment.'

'No, no . . .' the captain consoled him.

'Maybe he's busy with other things – things for which there are people to pay.' He made a face. 'Not even Mrs Bates is happy with how things are going in Arlinda.'

Captain Perry was quick to follow. 'You mean Louisa has doubts about your experiment?'

He felt awkward having raised the matter, but was compelled to go on. 'She doesn't think it'll be of much help. She and her friend.'

'Esther! She's just fanning the frenzy!'

'Both are worried about the children. Nothing we say or do can stop them from worrying.'

The captain nodded. 'It's only natural for them to worry – for the slaves, the opium sot. And now the children. Their worries are as large as their estates!'

'I don't know how long she'll go on supporting us.'

'You mean she could ask Bates to show his proof earlier than he had promised?'

Quartley pursed his lips. 'It could be worse.'

'Worse?'

'What if she were to stop right now?'

'Ah!' Captain Perry thought for a moment. 'You mean if the milch cow were to suddenly run dry?'

Quartley said nothing.

'It *would* be difficult for him then, wouldn't it?' Then he let slip a little secret to cheer Quartley up. 'Your master is well aware of what needs to be done. He's just asked me to wait a bit longer for your next trip down, while he sorts out a few things here.'

Quartley glanced up, surprised.

'From what you've told me, he must be busy finding a few reliable supporters.'

Captain Perry rose to leave. 'Is it Bates you worry about or is it something else?' Then he made up his own answer. 'You've grown close to the samples, haven't you? The savages have won you over! You're dying to see them again.' He laughed. 'I don't blame you. After all, you're not a scientist. You can't be faulted for feeling sorry for them.' Like a kind uncle, he assured Quartley, 'You shouldn't worry too much about Louisa, about what she might or might not do. There will always be financiers, *always*. For the right reward.'

He's just asked me to wait . . . while he sorts out a few things here.

With Bates out, he spent most days alone at the Madhouse, managing to work up a frenzy over the delay. As he paced the dark laboratory, he heard whispers from the crypt. The inmates of each box offered their counsel. Go back, Quartley! Go, now! He heard them warn of untold dangers. The children would suffer if they didn't return soon. He imagined them suffering the same fate as the owners of the skulls – hunted down by adventurers, their remains sold off as rare species. A letter from a year back returned to haunt him. Norah had reported an incident, a sighting off Arlinda's coast. She had gone up the hill with the children during late afternoon, to pick wild berries they had discovered in a hidden grove. They could see the coast very well from their height, and the anthills rising from the sea. It was a clear day, Norah had written. They had spotted a small flotilla of half a dozen ships approaching their island. The boy had been the first to see it, pointing with his hand. They had all gazed in silence. The ships flew unfamiliar flags and looked different too, with dark hulls and boarded forecastles, as if ready for war. She had followed the rules, running with the children further up the hill and hiding in a cave. No one could find them there easily. It was their refuge should pirates or slavers set their sights on Arlinda.

There was no sign of the ships when they came out of hiding next morning. Not a trace. Not even a message or a sack of supplies at the messenger's hut down on the beach. She had entered the camp cautiously, fearing a sudden attack.

When Quartley had raised the incident later with Captain Perry, he had brushed it aside. The nurse must have been mistaken – these islands were too well charted for a ship to approach Arlinda. Its lack of harbour was well known. His friends in the trade had been tipped off too, to avoid their *natural laboratory*. He had kept an eye on the children and their nurse from as far away as London.

Quartley remembered the incident with Norah. He saw her skull alongside the children's in the crypt's cupboards, screaming, almost killing Jenny in her cubbyhole.

Which was the more difficult task, he wondered – winning against Jean-Louis Belavoix, or winning support for their experiment back here in England? During the day, Quartley quarrelled in his mind with his master. Why must he keep on punishing the children and Norah? Punishing them all? His sharp instinct made short work of Bates's arguments, as he took Holmes's side, joined him against his master's 'desperate perseverance'.

Furore sexualis! He remembered Belavoix's words: 'It is only now that the children are becoming themselves. Growing up means more than simply a brain growing inside a skull, Mr Bates. Our savages are getting hungrier by the day. Soon, they'll feel nothing, hear nothing, but the throbbing in their loins. They'll want to devour each other alive!' He remembered Esther too: 'It won't be long now before they start to amuse themselves.' This was the moment when the races would finally come into their own. He must somehow convince Bates to return before the *furore* struck.

At night, he sensed a different *furore*. Not one to come soon, but one already arrived. His own.

Should he write to M. Belavoix? Quartley considered the unthinkable: writing to his master's rival behind his back. Perhaps the Frenchman could force Bates to finish the experiment sooner. His was a different science from the craniologist's – impatient, grasping events as they unfurled, full of a storyteller's knack for twists and turns and unexpected endings. Belavoix could be their saviour. He remembered Captain Perry warning him about the double-crossing French: 'He'll trick you if you aren't careful. Your Belavoix. Not known for following rules, are they?'

Perhaps Quartley could tempt the double-crosser. If Belavoix threatened Bates with his own visit down to Arlinda, maybe his master would hurry up.

The children have quarrelled, they are fighting with each other . . . he began to write to Belavoix. *The nurse has reported that they're unfriendly, they refuse even to sit together at mealtimes. They throw their plates at each other and bark like dogs . . .*

The other guests had already arrived when Bates and Quartley reached The Steeple. Louisa and her friends were gathered under the portrait of John Foxton in the library to celebrate the dead owner's birthday – a row of dark coats and grim faces. There were men and women Quartley hadn't met before. An evening of speeches lay ahead, the audience waiting to be treated to accounts of Louisa's charities, dutifully reported by her petitioners, followed by a plain meal at the end.

Bates waited among the petitioners. His turn would come soon. As his wife's most important venture, he expected to be the one to open the evening, or perhaps the last, providing the grand finale. The black of his tailcoat was blacker than the rest. His keen gaze rested on Mr Kepler, as he made his announcements. This evening would be his test, he knew – a test he must win to keep the experiment alive.

A page of notes twitched inside his jacket as he crossed his arms. He had a few words ready, a small set of numbers carefully picked from the log and his observations of the children, just enough ammunition to win his audience over – just enough suspense to secure their support for a few more years. He needed more than cold facts, though, he thought as he eyed the crowd. He must give them a whiff of the mystery, tempt them with the prize that waited at the end.

A thousand genera of plants in a garden, yet we, the civilised, see one – the botanical family. He rehearsed under his breath, as the head-master droned on. *There are over a score of races, yet we see one species: the human. We see order and hierarchy, while the savage sees mere profusion. If we were to believe as he does, we'd behave like ants, crawling up each leaf laboriously, treating every twig and root as a unique act of creation. We'd become ants instead of men!*

He waited as the petitioners rose to make their speeches. The Manumission Society. Prison reformers, the Anti-Opium League,

Committee for the Effective Suppression of Slavery. Mr Kepler appeared in no hurry to invite Bates. A quick glance at Louisa showed her head bent over her lap, as she penned her notes like an examiner. Captain Perry stood among the dark coats at the back, but his smile was missing. Bates began to feel the edge as the evening wore on.

Time was short, he knew only too well. A limited opportunity lay before every cause – like a bud that had just a few days to bloom, before the shifting sun shone on another hopeful bud. The academies had limited patience, and the benefactors. Even truth.

To win, he needed a small gasp of breath, just a few years more. This was his final chance. Otherwise, it would be too late. He would lose his cause to a hungrier lot.

Quartley sat with Louisa and Esther at the end of supper. Most of the guests had gone by then, a few lingering on with Captain Perry in the grounds, sharing his hidden flask. Among them was his master. He wasn't worried about another grilling from the ladies – simply baffled by Bates's exclusion from the long list of petitioners invited to speak during the evening. Didn't Louisa want to show off her most precious venture? Like Bates, Quartley too had hoped the evening would bring them rewards – Bates stumping his audience once again with his grand speech, and Louisa announcing yet another generous benefaction. Maybe they had come to a different arrangement. Sitting beside Louisa's chair, he felt he didn't need to answer back. Half his mind sided with her, wishing she'd stop her support and force Bates to bring everyone back from Arlinda. The other half urged her to go on.

'What news do you hope to offer after your next trip?' Esther started, looking like a widow in her dark veil.

'It depends on when we're able to go. The result will be different if we wait longer.'

'But you *should* know exactly, shouldn't you? If you call your-selves scientists? Unless you don't want to tell us.' She gave Louisa one of her worried looks. 'Are the children still alive?'

Quartley saw Bates enter the parlour, surprised to see him so soon after supper. He walked right up to the cabinet of curios, then answered Esther's question that he had overheard.

'We could have explained *exactly*, given a chance.'

'Do you really need to explain?' Esther sniggered.

'We could have explained to you the meaning of patience. It is a tough and a critical requirement – something you ought to have understood right at the beginning. It would take twelve years not five to get our proof. You knew that. There is no point crying over the children now.'

'Tough!' Esther snorted. 'It isn't tough on *you*. Not at all! You live and dine with pleasure, just like everyone else. It's tough on your samples. It's the poor children who suffer.'

Bates didn't appear startled by her outburst, but kept his eye on Louisa, as if these were her questions not Esther's.

'Suffer rain and howling wind. Survive on a meagre ration . . . with diseases that . . .' Her face red and shaking, Esther raised a finger. 'Do you *know* how much they suffer?'

Quartley expected Louisa to calm her friend, but she remained silent, staring back at Bates.

'The children are suffering. If they die, there will be blood on your hands.'

'Who do you think they are suffering for?' Bates retorted at last.

Unsettled by his voice, Esther took a moment before replying. 'They're suffering because we must fight the French to prove that we're better.'

'That's the silliest thing I've heard yet,' Bates growled. A wailing sound came from Esther, as she tried in vain to reach for Louisa's inhaling kettle to take a puff herself.

'The silliest drivel. One wouldn't expect it from a drunk.' He paused, then gritted his teeth. 'Do you want to know why the children are suffering? They are suffering because of *you*.'

'Me!' Esther Graham managed to utter a cry of outrage through her whimpering.

'Yes, you. They suffer so you know that you're superior to the Bushman, that you have the God-given right to civilise the savage. It's your self-indulgence, not ours. You wanted proof of God's will, didn't you?'

Calling his assistant over, Bates marched out of The Steeple.

SAVAGES

A season of complaints settled over them, starting with Quartley's seasickness, and then Belavoix's new 'condition'. The crew gave a start when the Frenchman boarded the *Rainbow*. Every inch of his body was wrapped in bandages, like a desert Arab, with just the eyes showing. He came up the gangway like a walking mummy. Hushing Quartley with his finger, he went into his cabin and shut the door. When he did emerge, without his bandages, he seemed a different person altogether. He had changed colour. His skin was dark and brassy, sallow eyes, even his shirt was stained yellow with sweat. He seemed somehow to have changed his race over just a few months.

With a quick glance, Bates announced his diagnosis. 'Ah! A case of icterus.'

'A case both acute and chronic, Mr Bates,' Belavoix whispered.

'And how did you acquire such an acute and chronic condition?'

Sitting down on the deck beside him, Belavoix wetted his lips and continued to whisper. 'The precise cause is unknown to medical science. It could've resulted from an attack of violent emotion, a drastic catharsis . . .'

'Nonsense! Its causes are well known. Errors in diet, cold in the abdomen, an infection.' Bates motioned with his hands. 'You don't need the bandages. It's not the sun that turns the skin yellow, but limited secretion in the liver.'

'But it's dangerous to have such a skin.' Belavoix seemed truly distressed. 'One could be taken for a Chinaman and put away in chains to be sold as a slave!'

Bates grinned. 'And what treatment have you started for your condition?'

'A natural cure will do, nothing else,' Belavoix sighed. 'In France, hydropathy is the only known method. In the Congo, a stew of maggots is commonly prescribed. The cure must be partly mental, if you ask me . . .'

'*Fully* mental, if you believe such nonsense!' Bates laughed. 'In England, we'd throw a wet towel over the stomach, with frequent bathing of the patient. A warm and even temperature, and foods easy to digest – no meats but gruels, lemonade and baked apples. That's all.'

Unconvinced as he was by Bates's simple cure, Belavoix did manage to find some relief over the next few days, nursed by the ship's meagre diet and hiding all day to avoid the skin-changing sun.

The weather unsettled them for a week – sultry, drizzling rain pouring noiselessly. Without the slightest hint of breeze, it irritated Perry, who wished to be away and doing. On the eighth day, the sweeps were manned, heavy oars jutting out of the gun-ports, and the *Rainbow* nudged along into the island passages. But here, the ebb left them high and dry. Where there had been water a few moments ago, now there wasn't enough to sink a sailor's chest. With the tide falling, there was no sleep for the crew. Daybreak found them in a worse state: stuck in a sea of mud. Mud ahead, mud astern. And a muddy sky frowning above them. They lay becalmed.

Bates called Quartley to his cabin. He was sitting on his bunk holding his drink, while his assistant stood at the door.

'You didn't think it'd be possible, did you?'

Quartley froze. Was this about Norah? He thought Bates had summoned him to exact a confession.

'You lost faith, didn't you?'

Or was this about his letter to Belavoix? Had Bates found out? Was he mad at his betrayal?

'You thought we would never succeed.' Bates smiled. 'And you were right to be anxious, Quartley. It was by no means certain that we would. But armed with persistence . . .' He eyed the open log on the bunk . . . 'we have won over our enemies.' He paused. 'Do you know who the enemies are? The *real* enemies?'

Quartley kept silent.

'Our supporters! Yes. Their doubts, suspicions, worries. Their frailty is the threat we must overcome. Science can only lose to human weakness. It's more dangerous than polygenism, or any such theory.'

A wave of relief swept through Quartley. So this wasn't about Norah, but about Louisa – their benefactress. He knew his master had visited The Steeple by himself quite a few times since John Foxton's birthday. He must've finally convinced his wife to keep her funds going for the experiment. He must've given her enough hope to treat her frailty.

'If we lose, it'll be because of them.'

Later, in his own cabin, Quartley went over Bates's words. They surprised him. He wasn't used to anything coming from his master except his orders. He thought he had glimpsed a Samuel Bates he hadn't before.

When they arrived finally in Arlinda, they saw a red flag fluttering over the messenger's hut. It was Norah's signal – a letter for London, or a distress call. Closer still, they spotted the children, sitting on the shore as if they were expecting visitors. They scrambled up to meet them as soon as they landed, jabbering and pointing at the cottage. Busy with his boxes, Quartley paid little attention to the two, till Belavoix nudged him.

'They have a message. Could be about the nurse. Something might've happened to her. She has raised the flag to call for help. Maybe she's dying.'

Dropping the boxes, Quartley darted from the outrigger onto the beach, leaping over the boulders, the children following him. Bates marched to the hut, to collect the message.

At the camp there were signs of neglect: an overgrown shrub, the garden turned a muddy pool by the rain, and the stench of rotting leaves everywhere. Running up the steps to the kitchen, Quartley found it just as before, but without the usual stove smell.

He found Norah in bed, propped up on a pillow. Not dying, but sick – face hot to his touch and the breath of fever. She had drawn a pitcher of water close to her bed. A plate of preserves lay on the floor – hardly nibbled. The air smelt stale from about a week's confinement, and cold without the kitchen's heat. A piece of cloth hung from a hook above the window – a clumsy effort to keep the sun out. Her face was turned towards the door, and when she saw Quartley, she sighed. A long sigh. Then she turned over on her side at his touch.

Joining his assistant, Bates took quick stock of her condition. A few checks confirmed what he had already concluded by reading her note at the messenger's hut. Inflammatory fever could be expected at any time in a variable climate. She could've got it from the incessant rains followed by the sultry air, or from her wet tunic clinging to her chest while she was on the cottage roof trying to fix a leak. Could just as easily have arisen from her windpipe, kissed by the cold sea draught, leading to a quick pulse, hurried breathing, a coated tongue, fever and restlessness. In her message, she asked for something to cure her cough that was keeping her awake, making her even weaker – and for an antidote to her weakness, which kept her from caring for the children.

Bates administered his tinctures to Norah from his own medicine box, while Quartley started the stove and scavenged around the kitchen for the supplies. All by himself at the table Belavoix scribbled, making a detailed note of the nurse's condition and offering his opinion to Quartley, warning him against callous treatment of the most alarming symptoms.

'You stay here,' Bates ordered Quartley, as the scientists left for their own camp. Alone in the kitchen, Quartley blamed himself. With Norah fast asleep, he felt troubled by the obvious mistake. He had taken pains to teach her how to check the children thoroughly, taught her which medicine was right for which sickness. He had told her to keep a log, a list of troubles, which would tell her what the children were prone to. He had prided himself on being Norah's teacher, keeping abreast of his pupil's progress from her monthly reports.

It hadn't occurred to him that she herself might fall sick, that he needed to teach her to check her own symptoms. The pulse, the skin, discharges – for her to tell if she was unwell, or simply exhausted. If indeed her symptoms were *alarming* – palpitations warning of a nervous decay, a fever foreshadowing the dreaded typhus.

Neither he nor his master had thought it wise to leave a medicine box for Norah.

He thought of the children. Without Norah, they'd suffer. He had seen hunger in their eyes as they waited on the beach. Perhaps they'd die, or turn into real savages in her absence. She's more than a goniometer – he couldn't but agree with the Frenchman. Eating with the children that evening, Quartley waited for Norah to wake, to begin his lessons and make her better prepared for the future.

The children ate in silence, holding up their plates and licking them clean at the end of the meal. They watched Quartley every now and then, but all their thought was reserved for their nurse. Unusually quiet, they moved about the kitchen lightly as if aware that she was sleeping. They avoided entering her room, staying within sight of the cottage, flitting from step to step like a pair of birds. The girl had a piece of Norah with her – an apron that she had wrapped around her arm: she could smell the stove on it, to remind her. The lush forest called them. The sea roared its invitation for a dip, to begin their game with the gulls. The surf tempted like a nest of unbroken eggs. Their island awaited them, and yet they ventured no further than their camp, no further than Norah.

They might be wary of him, Quartley thought. He might remind them of the business with the instruments, the cold metal around their heads. But they paid no attention to him as he went about his tidying up. A lid open on a jar of sugar, a line of red ants climbing up its side. Ash on the stove. Buckets of putrid berries. Ugly scales, a treacle of water in the drum, an unfinished basket. It must've pained her to leave the cottage in such a condition, dragging herself to the beach hut to leave her message. Had she gone herself, or had she sent the children? They must know how to follow her commands by now. He thought back to the children waiting on the beach.

'She will sleep,' Bates had said as he left the cottage. The tinctures would help, and the knowledge that she was no longer alone. She'd have relied on him, he thought, to take her place and care for the children. She'd trust him more than Bates and the Frenchman.

He longed to sit on the edge of her bed and see her sleeping – record each inflexion of her breath. To see with his eyes the face he had imagined, if it looked the same. To be near her. His face fell as he thought of the months – close to a full year – since their last visit. He had feared the worst – that they'd never come back, abandon Norah and the children on the island. Then, on the verge of returning, they had been stalled by yet another hurdle. This time, the Frenchman was guilty. Word came from the Société of a grand expedition. They had had to wait till he returned, in bandages, to join the *Rainbow* at Saint-Michel, the French slave port not far from Arlinda.

The experiment lived through the letters. Yet, as Quartley recalled, there had been far less of it in Norah's recent reports. Did she write less about the children than she had before? Or was it him – reading more about Norah than about the children?

The silence in the cottage distracted him, as he rose from the table to look for the children. From the creaking floor, he suspected they were in their rooms. Peeking through the girl's door, he saw her pacing, a volume of thoughts written on her young face – a scientist considering her next move. The superior savage. He saw a mind turning inside her cranium, eyes looking out into the dark moonless sky.

The boy shivered as Quartley entered his room. He slept on his side with an arm between his legs. Pulling the blanket over him, Quartley noticed the apron held tight in his fist – Norah's apron – wrested from his rival.

He resolved to speak to Norah about something other than the Ten Commandments and the instruments. He would tell her about the end of the experiment, of his plan, once they had managed to live through another half a dozen years. Earlier on, he hadn't given much thought to the matter; the experiment had covered every bit of the foreseeable future.

'What will happen to the children, sir?' he had once asked Captain Perry.

'You mean after they return to England?' The captain had chuckled. 'They'll be mine,' he had said confidently. 'I'll make proper use of them.'

Quartley had given him a surprised look.

'Oh, yes! Bates will let me have them, don't you think? I've done him more than a few favours.' He winked at Quartley, then proceeded to describe his plans for the little savages. 'They'll be a big hit, drawing a full house wherever they go. Might even take them to London. They'll be written up in all the papers. I'll build a special cage for them.' He squinted. 'Might have to paint the girl black!'

Quartley shivered, imagining the children in a Penny Gaff. It would be better for them to become Louisa's servants, or to be sent to an asylum even.

And Norah? What did Bates have in store for her? Was he thinking of turning her into a Jenny? Of holding her prisoner at the Madhouse?

He bristled at the thought.

'Stay till she wakes then come back up,' Bates had ordered. He wanted his assistant to tide Norah over her bout of sickness, fill her shoes till she recovered, then resume being the assistant. He wouldn't want Quartley to live so close to the samples, or to their nurse.

Waiting for her to wake, Quartley starts to think. He'll have little time to say all he wishes to tell. With Norah before him, the words will flow with greater ease than on paper. But after she's recovered, he'll have to wait for an opportunity for the two of them to be alone. He plans to tell her everything about himself, starting with his days at the taxidermist's. About Bates and Louisa, Captain Perry and the plans for the children. And his dream. He resolves to start even earlier. He'll tell her about his native Wallsby, the village she'll go to after the experiment. To live with him.

Settled before the stove, he feels a warmth creeping up his back – a gentler warmth than that of the burning log. It rises till it arrives at the back of his neck, holding steady, then spreads all over his shoulders like a sudden embrace. He turns.

It's Norah. Watching him from her bed.

In a flash, he's by her side, starting to say everything all at once.

She thinks he'll tell her about the instruments.

He doesn't.

The season of complaints lingers on, as the scientists wait for Norah to recover. Her absence from the kitchen has done more damage to their cause than any other obstacle. They miss the meals and her constant attention. Her sharp eye has been quick to spot a need before it turns to trouble; now they must learn to live like real explorers. Explorers without an assistant. He is busy caring for both samples and visitors during the day, returning only at night to his camp bed. Without Quartley around, they miss the diversions: Bates scolding his assistant over trifles, Belavoix confiding in him his deepest fears. It forces them to be more determined.

Already this visit is different. There's a greater resolve in each, to win and win as quickly as possible. It has quietened the Frenchman. Now he is unwilling to engage Bates in anything but the final argument, keen to restore balance on this visit. Whether at his tree house or in the hammock, he dreams of the surprise that'll demolish Bates. The mighty British Museum reduced to rubble by an earthquake! Thinking about it, he covers his ears with both hands in glee.

They have quarrelled already over the tests. The test for benevolence, that was to follow the mirror test. They knew it would be hard to judge which sample was more benevolent than the other, given their nature. A pair of fighting pups. They will need to follow the children around for days and observe them minutely, to know which of the two is the natural aggressor – which of their fights is a real tussle and which a game. Earlier, there has even been talk of a hunt. The scientists will shoot a gull, leaving a half-dead bird in the children's path to judge their reactions. The one deficient in benevolence will want to torment the unfortunate victim, will show a mean heart. The benevolent child, on the other hand, will be distressed, show its compassion.

Belavoix has scotched the hunt. After half a dozen years of note-taking, he has made up his mind on benevolence. The result is already known, he claims, the evidence clear. Lying in his hammock and waiting for Quartley to bring them their midday meal, he surprises Bates with the story of the lizard.

'We already know of their benevolence – or lack of it rather – from what they did to the lizard.'

'To the lizard?' Bates says, surprised.

'Yes. Didn't you know about that?' Smiling smugly, Belavoix opens his notebook and reads a brief description of the incident: the creature, the chase, the confinement, and the drowning.

'The girl. That's obvious,' Bates says, taking quick stock of the incident.

'What's obvious?'

'It was her courage that led to the death. The lizard must've attacked them before. It was a known offender. She, not the boy, took the lead in eliminating the danger.'

Belavoix shook his head in disbelief, his view markedly different from Bates's. 'Courage or revenge – that's a separate matter. What you can't ignore is the murder. The manner of the killing. Don't the English frown upon killing a prisoner?'

'She might not have meant to kill. Rather to set free the lizard, as you describe, picking it up from the bucket and releasing it into the forest. She might even have thought—'

'Murderers! Murderers!' Belavoix laughs wildly, shaking his head.

134

Without the test and daily measurements there isn't much that they can do but track their samples, roaming the island after them. It was easier setting off the day with their morning routine at the cottage. Then they had an early sighting of the children, gauged their mood from the bout with the instruments. The routine has fallen through. It is harder for them to find their samples now. Most days they return empty-handed to their camp. The island appears too vast a place to spot the pair of them. There are too many hidden sanctuaries. And they are certain that the children are hiding from them. At Belavoix's insistence, Bates climbs up to the tree house. But even the telescope fails to raise their hopes. The last storm has denuded the island, and they see simply more sea. Some days an unexpected discovery raises their hopes. A flat meadow, barely a turn away from the goat path – like a lush garden – appears a perfect hiding place. Or a cave in the forest. Hushing each other, they set off, expecting the children to charge out at them like a pair of lions.

Bates leads the way, swinging his walking stick. The Frenchman follows, lagging often more than a furlong behind. The sound of Belavoix's steps at times misleads Bates into thinking that the children are near. He stops and waits, then makes a grim face seeing his rival trudging up behind.

He is the more impatient of the two, the leader, the first to give up the chase and head back to the camp. He is used to a different routine, the specimen arriving at his laboratory bench, the instruments ready. The search tires his mind faster than his body. His rival overtakes him at times, keeps going even when Bates has returned.

When they do encounter their samples, it is more by chance than the result of any deliberate plan – like a shrill call in the still forest stopping them in their tracks. A call repeated over and over, sparking its own response. The voices of the children, chanting in chorus. Calling each other. Even shouting, to prove who is the louder of the two. The scientists circle the sound, getting closer, then spotting the children sitting next to each other on a tall boulder. They seem to be singing a song. Bates frowns. A song without beginning or end, but a clever blending of pure noise. They don't stop when they spot the scientists, simply raise their voices a touch to ignore the probing eyes.

Once the children were found near the scientists' camp in the morning, just as Bates and Belavoix were about to begin the trek down. They waited at the top of the goat path, like ushers ready to lead the men to their cottage. Even with grown-ups close by, they seemed in no hurry to escape, standing their ground like a pair of stubborn goats. Belavoix whistled, but they didn't shift their gaze from each other. Both were naked. The girl was urinating and the boy watching.

'Forget benevolence, Mr Bates. It's time now to test them for *hysteria libidinosa!*'

Bates disagreed. It was too early. It would be wiser to wait till the children had reached puberty. The crucial test would come then, of the sense that made one dwell on the opposite sex, and its gratification. To see which of them would be deluged by it, turned into a sensual fiend, which would take a more civilised course.

'I wouldn't recommend such an early—'

'No, no.' Belavoix protested from the hammock. 'It isn't too early at all. That organ develops more quickly in a warm climate. From what I've seen, they're warmed up already!'

Before, Quartley had always found the evenings most difficult to bear: the thought of night approaching steadily. The tide returning, driving the spray up the rocks. The setting sun taking a final shy at the forest. The gulls changing hue. Soon, darkness would set them adrift in a sinking raft, bringing out the creeping crawling creatures, and with it the island's most dangerous species: the frightening silence. Even from afar, he had suffered, thinking of Norah's long and silent nights alone with the children. But with her near by he found the evenings easier, giving him a chance to talk to her at the end of his daily chores while the children and the visitors were away.

The mornings began slowly, the two of them in the kitchen, getting ready to receive Bates and Belavoix for their breakfast. He kept his voice down, in case the children were still around the cottage, or the scientists arrived earlier than usual. Just a few words here and there, as Norah gathered strength to help him.

Mostly he was kept busy by the routine of the stove, feeding everyone at regular intervals, by the garden work and the never-ending repairs. Finished with the leaking roof, he'd slump on the cottage steps, till Norah pointed him towards the garden, to the half-dug pit where she buried the kitchen scraps. The day passed quickly, with his master adding a few chores of his own.

He didn't miss being Bates's assistant, relished the break from the experiment and its inevitable tension. He found Norah's tasks heavier than his own, yet somehow light – completion of each one requiring no further thought. *Is that how she feels too?* he wondered, eyeing her at the stove. *Or is it the experiment she craves? The thrill of a win, and the risk of loss?*

The few words turned fewer by the time they finished in the kitchen and came to sit on the steps. If he did speak at all, it was to remind them of tomorrow's tasks, Norah's shrugs and nods filling in the silent intervals. Sitting still after sunset. Not the nurse and the assistant any more, but Norah and Nicholas.

The list of unasked questions grew with each passing day – and the list of things he resolved to tell her. He knew there'd be fewer evenings together as she seemed well set on the road to recovery, that he'd have to return soon to the scientists. But it didn't worry him as much as before, especially as he saw her regain her strength and lose her only defect: the frown. It'd be absent all evening, except when she untangled their arms and frowned, spotting the returning scientists.

He brought his gifts to Norah. She took the mantel-clock out of its box, and wound the key. He offered her the mirror and the things he had bought for the children. She stood before him, arms laden with gifts. Then he pointed at the hatbox. His mind bubbled over, anticipating Norah's reaction. He helped her unfasten the clasp, then waited.

'I thought you might like to wear it . . .' he fumbled. After a few moments, she took out the hat and turned it over.

'It's new, almost.' He thought she'd notice the slight wear and tear. He should've bought a new one. He was suddenly embarrassed. What would she think . . .

'You don't have to wear it, if you don't like it . . .'

She laughed. Or so he thought, from the dancing eyes.

With Norah and Quartley on the steps, the girl enters the cottage unnoticed through the window at the back of the kitchen. Eyes darting, she crouches on the floor, then crosses over with light steps to the instrument cupboard. Her eyes glow inside the dark kitchen, like the glare of cats and dogs. Supple limbs make short work of obstacles in her way. She pushes open the door of the cupboard left unlocked by mistake, and crawls inside, pulling it shut behind her. More than a few moments pass before it opens again. The girl peeks out, spying on the nurse and her companion. She leaves the cupboard holding a box, creeping step by step back to the open window. Chest heaving, she lifts the box over her head, passing it to the boy waiting outside.

They disappear into the forest. The boy runs with a flying gallop, the box steady in both arms as he climbs the goat path, the girl following. It is a tricky business, trickier than they had expected, the narrow and slippery path posing more than a few problems. The box sways in the boy's arms. He stumbles, coming close to losing his grip. Starting with the theft, the two seem to have a definite plan. After a few near slips, the boy falls, the box rolling out of his hand and hurtling down the slope till it strikes a gnarled stump and comes to a dead stop.

Catching their breath, they set about recovering their prize. From this height, they can see the cottage below. The distance reassures them. With no one chasing after them, there's no need to run any more. The box is secure. They lift it, joining arms, and carry it carefully round the bends, entering their private garden.

It's the meadow, the lush grassland guarded by trees, their hunting ground for hidden bulbs and tubers. They land the box under a tree, then kneel before it, like diggers before a fresh grave.

Out of its box, the new instrument looks just like others – a curious tangle of metal rods and wooden arms. It gleams even in the waning light. After suitable admiration, the girl draws it closer to her, passing her hand over it, as if she is the assistant readying it for a test. Its trap is different from the ones they are used to. The boy watches, holding onto the wooden box. She imitates Quartley and his master, frowning and speaking to herself in a low gurgle. She turns the instrument over, corrects her mistake, then searches for the hidden door. It's the opening she must find in which to insert the head of her sample, a discovery that's crucial to their game.

The effort tires her, but she doesn't give up, crouching beside the instrument, observing it from all angles. Then she gets down on her belly and brings her face close to it, trying to force her head in, playing the sample herself. The frame blocks her path. She tries a dozen contortions without success. The child gets the better of the scientist. She shows her anger now, kicking the ground and raising a cloud of dust.

The two of them sit in silence, observing the instrument. Their minds run over all the routines they've learned. They hear Bates's command, and see Quartley's face calling them over for a measurement. Even Norah, encouraging them with her eyes to have a go.

The scientist returns.

Once again, the girl fiddles with a knob or two, springing open a nest large enough to hold a small cranium. The discovery startles her, but she presses on, pushing her head in. The trap fits her neatly, snapping shut with a light touch – a cage coming down to her neck, a grid of bars in a fine mesh.

The boy yelps his delight, running round the girl in circles. She screams too, face flushed with excitement, gurgling, as if to alert him to record the vital measurements. She crouches on the ground, head inside the trap, triumphant with success.

After a while she fiddles the knobs to release her head from the trap. It's time for her to play the scientist. And the boy's turn to be the sample. Much as she tries, the trap remains shut. It refuses to open despite her frantic efforts. She tries to wriggle her way out, but the snap has tightened around her neck, bitten into her skin. Each time she jerks her head to bring it out of the instrument, like the devil it pulls her back. Face red, pupils enlarged in fear, she screams, tears streaming down. Her chest starts to heave as she tries in vain to rise from her squat, bearing the weight of the instrument on her shoulders. It is an impossible task. She gives up after a few tries. The heavy frame threatens to snap her neck. Muscles twitch, froth dribbles from her mouth. She cries for help.

The boy watches silently. He has made no move to help her. A pair of unblinking eyes watching the horror from a few paces away, he sees the girl writhing on the ground. His face shows no dismay at their game gone astray. As if *this* is the game. *His* game.

The trapped scientist, watched by the savage.

Will he leave her to wring her neck and die? Is it the germ, turning inside his head? Will he use his intellect and run down to the cottage, fetch Quartley with groans and babbles?

Will he or won't he?

It seems to take an age for the girl to lose the last ounce of her energy. She lies flat on the ground like a trapped animal, all thoughts of escape given up. It's all over for her, the garden now dark as evening passes to night. Her eyes have closed, just a whimpering noise remaining.

The boy rises. He bends to examine the girl's condition, then releases the trap with a deft move, turning the knobs like an expert, as if he has known how to all along. He pulls her out of the frame without the mesh biting any deeper into her skin. Lifting up the instrument, the boy hurls it down the hill with one powerful fling of his arm.

Half a moon over Arlinda.

The cottage is quiet. An empty kitchen table. A cold stove. The lock on the instrument cupboard secure once again. The children are fast asleep in their rooms, the wall between them, their faces turned towards each other. The nurse sits alone on the steps, her heart flooded with nightdew.

'*Bonjour*, Norah!'

She snapped her head back, the basket slipping out of her hand. It was unusual for Belavoix to arrive at the cottage so early in the morning, ahead of Bates and Quartley. Their normal routine had resumed soon after the mysterious disappearance of the new instrument. After a thorough grilling, Bates had warned everyone. The offender was unknown, but his motive was plain: to disrupt the experiment. He had made much of the missing item, claimed it would've tipped the result in his favour. 'It's absurd to blame the children,' he had told Quartley. 'They couldn't possibly have made off with such a heavy box.' Naturally, his suspicion fell on Belavoix. 'He's acting like a true Frenchman, doing what the French do best: foul play.' Their rivalry had hardened after the instrument went missing. Bates was on the prowl now, following Belavoix around the island, filling his log with his rival's movements.

The Frenchman came up to the table. Despite the exertion of the trek down, he looked cheerful.

'Ah! A new basket. It must be for Mr Bates's missing instrument! The one he has hidden under his bed!'

She rose to return to her stove. 'Sit down, Norah. I've something to tell you. Something that'll make your heart go mad!'

He waited for her to pick up her unfinished basket and sit, drawing up a chair beside her. With a quick glance at the cottage door, he started to whisper.

'You want to leave Arlinda, don't you? Want this experiment to end, no?' He nodded, expecting Norah to nod too. 'I *know* you do. It has been a long time since you lived like a . . . like a *real* woman. You must miss what you've left behind . . . miss *everything*.' He paused, bringing his face nearer to her. 'And who has made you suffer like this? Who has kept you as a prisoner?'

She turned her gaze away to the window.

'Yes, Bates. The mad Englishman. He wants to keep you a prisoner for six more years. Six years!' Belavoix put his hand behind her neck and turned her face towards him. 'But I, the mad Frenchman, want to stop it. Stop it now. End the experiment and take you back with us on the ship. Do you want to come home with us, Norah?'

Her frown returned, muscles of her neck tightening in Belavoix's palm. He released his hold and rose from his chair, circling the table with measured steps.

'We can stop it if you want to. If you're willing to help. I can tell you my plan.' He lowered his voice. 'Nobody will know. *Nobody*.' Then, seeing her frown deepen, he tried to tease back her spirit. 'No, no, I'm not asking you to elope with me! Something even better . . .'

The plan made her heart go mad. With fear. As long as the children were alive and well, the experiment would go on, Belavoix said. It could go on even after the dozen years had ended. *Neither will win if neither is ready to lose.* The battle of nerves between him and Bates could continue as long as either had an ounce of breath left. Belavoix had taken out his Languiole knife from his satchel, and flashed its blade. 'It'll only end,' he said, 'if either he or I are to die.'

Then he revealed his plan.

If they lost a sample, they would have to stop. 'If one of the children was found . . .' He stopped, seeing her shudder. 'You'd win your freedom, if you gave up one of the two. That way you could leave with your favourite child. Before they go wild and kill each other. You could have the one you love most. For ever!' He had repeated it over and over – his famous prediction: the murder of one sample by the other. It was bound to happen, but they might have to wait for many years more. 'Unless it happens now . . .'

He ignored her ashen face. 'You decide. The black or the white?' Kneeling beside Norah, he held her crossed arms over the table in an act of consolation. 'A serious injury would do, if you can't bear for one of them to die. Anything that'll stop it from being a healthy sample.' The plan called for her, the nurse, to play the witness, to vouch that the damage had been inflicted by one child on the other.

'You must think about our plan, Norah . . .'

Entering the kitchen, Bates saw the two of them at the table. His face clouded. Before he could apply a suitable phrase to his thought, Belavoix leapt up and offered an excuse.

'Ah! You've caught us, Mr Bates. I was just proposing to Norah! Proposing to take her back with me to France after the experiment.'

Bates looked stunned, as did his assistant who stood behind him.

'You don't believe me? Ask her. She's sick of everything here, the suspicions, the lies.' Belavoix waved his arms about. 'She knows it's all a hoax. Just made up for you to prove you're better than me!'

'What are you saying?' Bates growled.

'I'm saying, she's ready. Ready to leave. But she knows she has to wait for six more years before she can be with me. That's why she's upset. Isn't that so, Norah?' Belavoix waited as the whimpering grew, then slumped down at the table.

'You can't blame her for crying. She's *English*, after all. If she was French, she'd be dancing right now!'

Bates troubled Quartley more than the Frenchman. He found Belavoix's comical fears – even his comical outbursts – amusing. His crush on Norah seemed absurd, just like one of his farcical diseases. Surprised as he was to stumble upon the two of them, the prospect of Norah going to live with Jean-Louis Belavoix didn't trouble Quartley. If anything, he felt more concern about the Frenchman when he was around the children. A murderous look entered his eyes sometimes when he spotted them. He found it odd that the Frenchman should call their samples killers, even when they appeared as harmless as pups, curled up on the kitchen floor. He'd pretend taking aim at them from the tree house, lowering his gun to mutter curses.

But it was Bates who troubled him – his rising interest in Norah following Belavoix's proposal. He was bent on guarding her like his instruments. Guarding her day and night, making it impossible for

Quartley to be alone with her. Waking up one night, he heard noises in Bates's room: stomping boots, the trunk slamming, a stifled curse. He wondered if his master was alone, his blood turning cold at the thought of nocturnal visitors. Belavoix had warned him not long ago of the anthropophagi who roamed the islands, devouring white men wherever they could find them. Thoughts of the eyeless creatures left Quartley paralysed on his bed for a while. He found Bates's room empty, the door ajar, when he managed to free himself from his fear. His mind started to spin. Perhaps a danger had arisen at the children's camp, with Bates rushing off to help. Running down the goat path, he saw the cottage lit by the moon, its contours etched sharply against the night sky. A shadowy figure stood at the steps, peering into the cottage through the kitchen window: Bates.

Another night he was awoken again. But before he could rise, a similar noise came from Belavoix's room. It surprised him even more, as he knew the Frenchman to be the soundest sleeper of them all. He heard both doors opening, and Belavoix calling after Bates in the dark.

'How *un-English*, Mr Bates! Turning into a Frenchman at night!' He had made a funny sound with his mouth, then raised his voice to wake Quartley. 'Are you sure you won't need your assistant to help with your special measurements?'

Through a crack in the door, Quartley saw them both, standing on the veranda in their nightshirts.

'I don't mind your adventuring. In France, it would be considered most gallant! But let's settle our little experiment first before turning Arlinda into a paradise . . . you, me and Norah, no?'

Bates glared back. Clearing his throat, he started to say something, but Belavoix interrupted him. 'No, no . . . there can't be any measuring of the children so late. Your assistant is sound asleep. Your instruments too are sleeping. Even foolish Belavoix can't be fooled like that.'

'I was about to say—'

'Say what you wish, but you'll have to do a lot more to win the nurse over. It won't be easy!'

A loud bang announced Bates's return to his room.

Neither was prepared to lose, Quartley fretted. What would they do? Fight a duel on Arlinda's beach? The winner killing his rival and claiming Norah as his prize?

In a rare moment alone with Norah, he brings up the experiment. Maybe he should ask her, he thinks. She knows more about the children than they do. She can tell him which is the cleverer of the two, the kinder – if there is one who shows a deviant mind. It's a mistake not to have consulted Norah before. Perhaps *she* can help to end the experiment.

Eye on the setting sun, he asks her which sample she'd keep if she was a scientist and needed an assistant – someone quick and firm, loyal and steady. She'd have to choose one of the two.

'Is it the *girl* . . . ?' He waits, giving her time to make up her mind.

A shadow crosses her face. The question seems unexpected and unwelcome. Getting up from the steps, she returns to the kitchen table and picks up her unfinished basket.

'Come!' Belavoix grasped Bates's arm, urging him and everyone to follow him out of the kitchen. 'They're fighting! The savages . . . !' Gasping for breath, he raised his voice at Quartley, who was readying an instrument on the table. 'You won't need that any more. The mischief has spread to their bones!'

'Is it just child's play or . . . ?' Bates was guarded, but curious.

'No, no. Blood has been spilt already!'

Following the Frenchman out, they spotted the children easily. A dozen paces apart, they stood facing each other at the valley of rocks – the narrow strip at the foot of the hill. Not the children, but two creatures. Hideous. The boy hunched, his head barely raised from the ground, fangs bared, ready to fight with his jaws and teeth. A cry came from the back of his throat. The girl stood taller than usual, on her toes, arms flung out, a rock in each hand. Her scorched skin showed marks of a tussle, a deep gash on the knee dripping blood.

'See!' Belavoix pointed.

Throwing back her head and bursting into a wail, she charged towards the boy, and aimed a rock at him. He dodged her deftly, threw up a handful of rubble that covered her in a cloud. She chased him around the rocks, taking a few tumbles but picking herself up and resuming the chase instantly. They saw her other wound, a nasty cut above the eyes, inflicted no doubt by the master rock-thrower.

'Didn't I tell you!' Belavoix kept up his nervous commentary, eyes darting between Bates and the fighting children. 'The final act! You are about to see what we came here for! Racial murder!' He waved his telescope about like a wand.

The boy seemed to have conserved his strength better than the girl. He waited for his enemy to wear herself out. She wasn't without her advantages, though, using her speed to make him scramble about, getting within a hair's breadth of her target.

Quartley waited for Bates to intervene. He felt confident that his master would choose the right moment, before the samples damaged each other mortally. With every passing moment he hoped to hear the deep gravelly voice barking out enough fury to subdue the fighters.

What were they fighting over?

Climbing on top of a boulder, Quartley tried to get a better view of the children. The fight had taken a bitter turn, with the boy changing tacks. Standing his ground as the girl charged in, he bore her full thrust, knocking her over and landing on top. Then he held her face down and unleashed a flurry of blows.

'Bravo!' Belavoix screamed, jumping up and down and ignoring Bates's stern look.

A pair of jaws snapped. They fought hard, pounding madly, scrambling around for a piece of rock to smash open a skull. A flurry of black and white limbs. A cockfight.

Where's Norah? Quartley saw a pair of cold eyes watching the fight. *Why doesn't she stop them?* Was she following the rules? Didn't she worry about the bleeding girl? Perhaps her heart has frozen, he thought. *Perhaps she has seen it all before . . .*

As the girl broke free, the boy chased her. They went bounding over the rocks, then up towards the hill, towards a different battleground, flat and clear of obstacles. Belavoix ran after them, yelling at the others. 'Come on!'

'Stop!' Bates shouted after him. 'There's no need to follow them . . .'

Belavoix screamed back. 'We need to know how it ends. We need to *see* the end.'

The rock caught him then, on the head. It downed the Frenchman before he could catch up with the children.

He lay bleeding.

Reviving Belavoix and bringing him back to the cottage took

longer than the fight itself. Head bleeding profusely, he lay motionless, forcing Bates to prop him up like a child and tie his vest around his head like a turban. When he was fit to walk, he looked like a wounded soldier, using Bates and Quartley as crutches to inch back to safety. He stopped after every few steps to turn around, fearful of another hail of rocks. Bates got busy at the cottage, ordering Norah to boil water, cleaning the gash with a stinging tincture. When he was finished, his patient looked like a monk with a white cape.

It took Belavoix a few glasses of laudanum to get over the sting. He made no mention of the lost telescope that had fallen from his hand. Just one plea to his rival.

'You must go and find the children now. Bring back the corpse before it's eaten. Among the cannibals of Guinea, it's common to . . .'

Bates hushed him.

They started a wretched week – wretched on every count. Lying in the hammock all day, Belavoix no longer showed any interest in the children or in his notebooks. The day began and ended with a few attempted measurements – the children often missing from the cottage. After the Frenchman had recovered from the attack, Quartley had run back to the forest to find the children. He had searched for them everywhere. In his heart, he knew that the fight was likely to have ended with just cuts and bruises – a sad, but not the dramatic end they had feared. He had failed to find the two at once, but knew them to be around from the echoing calls, and later from the empty bowls he found near the cottage. He had seen Norah take food out to the forest, hiding the bowls in a basket, knew that she fed them, even when they chose to stay away from her sight.

When he had found them at last, back at their camp, the girl had a scar on her forehead. Not a festering wound, but dressed and healing. There was a bandage on her knee too. A few scratches showed on the boy's chest – beads of dried blood on his skin. They were edgy around each other, but edgier still around their visitors – ignored the nurse even, though not the food she offered them.

The Frenchman dined all by himself at the scientists' camp. Even when the pain had gone, he didn't venture down. For him, the visit had lost its purpose. He kept his gaze averted from Bates, who was his usual self, busy tracking the children. When he was awake,

Belavoix lay in his hammock, mind in a trance. His stories appeared to have congealed into one single story, Quartley noticed: cannibals, grave-robbers, pirates, feral children – all sharing the same tragic ending.

He saw a different Belavoix. For the first time Quartley saw a helpless man, suffering in mind as well as in body – the scientist defeated by his science. Despite his shocking predictions, he seemed truly downcast over the 'savages'.

'I knew what the result would be even before . . . before we started all this,' he mumbled. Wiping his face on his sleeve, he called Quartley over. 'Do you know what he was like in the beginning?'

'Who, sir?'

'Primitive man.' Belavoix smiled weakly. 'When he was a stranger, living on an island like this . . . ?'

Quartley kept silent, glad of his master's absence.

'I know. He was half-brute, half-angel. Born with a rock in his hand . . .' After a long silence, Belavoix picked up his thread. 'I know what you're going to ask me, Mr Clever Assistant. What happened to the angel? Aren't you going to ask? I know the answer to that too. The brute killed the angel.' He shivered in the evening breeze, drawing his robe around himself. 'That's how it turned out. For him. And for us.'

Quartley felt his heart grow heavy, listening to the Frenchman.

But Bates refused to show sympathy. Suspicious as ever, he held Belavoix responsible, thought he had somehow provoked the children into a fight. He must have set the whole thing up, he told Quartley.

'Set what up, sir?'

'This unnecessary event. Just to prove his point.'

'But . . .'

'But, what?'

'Could he really have done that?'

Bates replied with a questioning look.

'Could the fight have ended as he says, sir, with one child dead?'

'It could've ended in any number of ways. Accidents aren't uncommon even back in England. Children do sometimes get into tumbles.'

Without the Frenchman to egg him on, even Bates seemed to lose something of his zeal – the odd measurement wasn't enough to keep it alive; his observations of the samples dwindled to nothing. Without Belavoix by his side he knew that his reports would be meaningless: the Frenchman could deny anything he hadn't seen himself. He drove Quartley to unending chores, a frantic routine of checking and re-checking, like a general readying his arsenal before battle. He berated Norah for letting the children out of her sight. Breaking his own Ten Commandments, he ordered her to lock the doors when they were at the cottage, and to stop leaving them food.

A sick Belavoix and a raging Bates. The week passed slowly.

'When will you get up?'

'Why do you want me to get up?' The Frenchman offers Bates a teasing smile. 'Ah! I know, Mr Bates. You want me to go down to the messenger's hut and raise the flag. Quartley could do that for us, no?'

'The flag?'

'Yes. To let the captain know that we're ready to leave.'

Bates grimaces.

'To tell our kind Perry that he must suffer for us one last time. He won't have to come to Arlinda any more. Just this time, to take us all back.'

He tries to tempt Belavoix out of his torpor with arguments, pretends he is ready to match his log to the Frenchman's notebooks. Returning early to their camp, he sees Belavoix packing his case, sitting on the veranda floor. Bates offers an olive branch.

'The samples are yet to reconcile. They are still acting as strangers to each other. I'd say there's a chance of another fight.'

The Frenchman maintains his indifference. 'You can go if you wish, but I see no reason to . . .'

'The next fight might be even more ferocious than the last. After all, they've had time now to think about each other's weaknesses. This next one could be fatal.'

'I've learned all there is to learn.'

Bates sits down facing Belavoix. 'And what have you learned?'

From Belavoix's smile it's difficult to tell if he has given in to Bates's persistence, if he is ready to start his 'final argument', or is simply thinking of his notes in the stacked-up volumes. When he speaks, it is as if he is reading aloud.

'I've learned that they are both wild. And mad. Untamed. Free.'

He seems almost delirious. 'I've observed them now for six years, preyed on them, waited to catch them at their best and their worst. They've shown nothing more than a *plain* character. Yes, plain and vicious, stubborn, quarrelsome, awkward, comical, slow. They are tiring to observe, they show no reaction even when they know they're being observed. They are no better than a pair of hedgehogs, spending every waking hour digging, burrowing, scraping. Even their games are dull.'

'Our experiment, if you recall, isn't about how attractive the samples are, but—'

Bates cuts in, but the Frenchman pays him no attention. 'They have nothing to offer but the dull routine of a pointless life. It's futile to try to judge which one of them is smarter, wiser or superior. They are both incapable of any significant act that will allow us to judge their moral character.'

'And so you suggest waiting longer for that act?'

'No! Just the opposite. I suggest stopping now. More years can't change my conclusion.'

'But the samples did perform a *significant* act, a rather unfortunate one I should say.' Glancing quickly at Quartley, Bates goes on. 'Didn't they strike you down?' He pauses to gauge Belavoix's reaction. 'They were acting on their instincts, I suggest. Stopping an outsider from intruding into their affairs.'

Belavoix laughs. 'Is that your understanding of the act?'

'Whatever it was, it wasn't *dull*, was it?' Bates's eyes twinkle.

Quartley expects an outburst, but Belavoix appears unusually calm, his whimpering voice turned sonorous again. 'Plain and dull. In his primitive state, man is no more than a small animal. The brute in him waits to strike at the precise moment, transforms him into a ferocious animal. The fight wasn't an isolated act, but a rare glimpse of the truth. We've witnessed the germ. Anything might happen, now that they're awake to their instincts. *Anything!* Rape, murder, mutilation . . .' He stops to catch his breath. 'It won't end here.'

Bates raises an eyebrow.

'They've tasted blood. They know how good it feels! Did you see how they both stopped to relish the blood on my face? Now they'll look for more victims. The nurse will be next, I predict. Yes. They could ambush her in the forest, plunge down on her from a branch above, tie her to a tree trunk and begin their torture . . .' Belavoix's eyes gleam. 'When you return to Arlinda, you will find her gone. Disappeared! In a few years' time, the children will be ready for men.' He gives Bates a murderous look, imitating the children. 'Oh, yes! They'll come up to this camp in the dead of night and enter the rooms. Smash your skull with a rock!'

'Nonsense!' Bates slams down his glass, shattering it to pieces. 'That's the most grotesque thing I've heard. Not the least bit scientific. Don't children fight in France? Do they grow up without ever seeing blood? No! Do they all turn out to be murderers then?' He drops his voice. 'What are you writing in your notebooks? Stories? Your stories, I must say, are excellent, might charm a few ladies back home who have nothing better to do than while away their time reading romances. I wouldn't recommend that you present them to an academy. You might raise more than a few eyebrows there. The audience might take the author, not the children, to be mad!'

'It wasn't a normal fight, but . . .'

Before he can finish, Bates rises, ready to leave. Belavoix calls after him. 'And your log? What does your precious log tell you? I don't trust your observations. Skulls are more important to you than living samples. No? No wonder the children have confused you. You and your poor assistant have nothing better to do than feed them opium and slip their sleepy heads into your instruments. Your log can't excite even you, let alone the members of an academy.'

'Our observations are as sound as our measurements. They point to an awakening in *both* samples, particularly the European.'

'How interesting! How wrong but interesting! Why don't we go back then, and present our arguments to the gentlemen of Europe?'

'Because we must observe more to finalise our conclusions.'

Belavoix raises his hands in despair. 'More! How typically *English* to be so over-cautious! What have you to fear, except—'

'The gentlemen of Europe – English, French, German, Prussian – want more than arguments. They want facts. Hard facts about how the samples behave.'

'You can't force me to go on.' Belavoix seems upset at Bates's refusal.

'If you don't come back, it will stop the experiment. I couldn't test your predictions for you, could I? You'd be breaking our agreement.' Quartley hears Bates's voice rising.

'I agreed to a principle. A principle to work together to—'

'Work together! Our views are in exact opposition. Let's not forget that! We agreed as gentlemen to conduct a fair test to resolve our disagreement.'

'The ungentlemanly Frenchman will leave you to resolve it all by yourself then.'

Quartley waits to hear Bates's reply. After a long silence, he hears the gravelly voice. 'Is that your final word?'

Then he hears Belavoix. 'You are a patient man. But I won't keep you waiting for too long. I shall send you my word *very quickly* once I return to France.'

The inferior European. Bates narrows his eyes as if examining Belavoix's head through the open door as he lies on his bed. He peers through the shock of curls to detect the parietal bones on both sides of the skull. A Celtic specimen. A mischief-maker. Puckish, quarrelsome – no match for his Saxon rival.

He tries one last time.

'I thought you loved the children. You played with the boy – didn't think they were soulless criminals in the beginning, did you?'

'*Soul!* You talk of *soul!*' Belavoix exclaims.

'And your God? Where is He in your notebooks? Have you left Him out by mistake? Or is He just a silent observer to the killing?'

Turning over on his side, the Frenchman faces Bates. 'He *is* left out. Just as He is absent in your log. Do you want Him to be included? Are you sure?'

'Aren't you coming back, sir? Ever?'

Belavoix said nothing. The two of them had resumed their evening walks on the island as they waited for Captain Perry's ship to arrive. The Frenchman stared at the sea, as if he hadn't heard Quartley.

'Won't you miss Arlinda?'

Belavoix sighed. 'What would you do, Quartley? I mean, if you were me? The mad Frenchman? If *you* were Bates's rival?'

FLAME OF THE FOREST

I t was Quartley's turn next. A painful boil on his leg, which he had kept hidden all through the wretched week as they prepared to leave. He had tried his mother's herbs, tried to disguise his limp as best he could. Till it bloomed into a raging fever.

'Making a habit of it,' Bates muttered, angry at having to play the doctor yet again.

'Could it be scarlet fever, sir?' Quartley turned pale with terror. He had heard its effects described by Belavoix.

'Don't be silly. Genuine scarlatina seldom strikes beyond the age of twelve. If you had it, you'd look like a boiled lobster by now.'

Still, it was too dangerous to travel with fever, Bates announced to an aching Quartley – not for *his* safety, but for that of the captain and sailors. The crew would be suspicious. A fear of contagion might lead them to refuse berths to all of them. It was better that Bates and Belavoix leave together, with Quartley to follow when he was recovered fully.

But first, the boil would have to be removed.

'Dangerous and unnecessary,' Belavoix whispered into Quartley's ear as he held both arms in a lock, and Bates prepared to lance the boil with a surgical knife. He had prescribed a glass of laudanum for his patient. A bucket for pus stood at the foot of the bed alongside a pot of boiling water. Norah waited with a tray of bandages.

'Hold steady or we'll have to tie you to the bed,' Bates said as he dipped the knife into the boiling water.

'Yes, sir.'

'Nothing but an *English* fetish. An obsession with the knife. Doing things in a hurry that should be left to nature,' Belavoix whispered, holding Quartley's arms tightly. 'The knife will cut more than necessary, it will damage the fine tissues, the veins, even the bone . . .'

Bates looked up with a frown, then continued disinfecting the knife.

'And the risk of infection is great.' This time he addressed Bates directly. 'Why don't you simply puncture the boil, if you must use the knife, and let it drain by itself?'

'Because I don't want poor Quartley to die of tetanus.'

'But if you sprinkled salt over it?'

'Then he might suffer concussion from the pain.'

'No, no. It's a mistake to assume such an unfriendly nervous system. If he drinks enough of your laudanum, he will not feel anything at all.'

'More than the prescribed dose and he'd start vomiting. Dehydration will halt recovery.'

'But if you tried hydropathy . . .'

'Why don't you leave Quartley to me and go quacking over your own disease?' Bates growled. 'Leave the room, if you can't be silent. The nurse and I are perfectly capable of handling this ourselves.' With the tip of the knife, he traced a circle around the boil then cut open the skin with one quick motion, draining the pus swiftly into the bucket. Norah plied Bates with gauzes, helped him to wrap a neat bandage while Belavoix stared, balefully silent.

After Bates and Belavoix had gone, the camp felt empty, their island home like an abandoned outpost. Sipping barley water, Quartley stared past his door to the veranda and the darkening forest. A swarm of bats flew into the last cone of light, swirling in the rays of the sun, then changed trajectory. He heard a cawing bird and the twitter of busy nests on the tall tamarinds that surrounded their camp. With effort, he could decipher the surf from the assorted noise, before it grew into a solitary presence over the silent island.

The night fog slipped in through the draughty window.

He heard a low sound. Fear froze Quartley to his bed. He looked around the room in the faint light of the oil lamp. He heard the sound again, then flailed around his bed, searching for the rifle he hoped Bates had left behind. It was too early for Norah to bring up his meal. And the children weren't ever expected here, at least while the visitors were present. A ghost? Moments stretched to minutes as he tried to calm his rapidly beating heart. Bathed in sweat, he tried as best he could to distract himself. He thought of the sleepwalking boy. The mirror test. Norah. Gradually, the veranda started to fill with the sound of creaking boots. He heard Belavoix's sad voice. What would you do? If *you* were Bates's rival?

He puzzled over the question. His mind, once firmly on Bates's side, now wished desperately for the experiment to end. For Norah's sake. The thought made him forget the intruder, filling him with a rush of emotions. Had he joined the shameless Pharisees, as Bates called them – those looking for a quick result? Had he abandoned science for love? He blamed his own defect for failing to come up with a firm view of the races: his background and his half-baked village mind. Was the girl better than the boy? Would he ever know from his own writing in the log? Not a scientist, he rued. Just a pair of working hands.

Quartley dreamt he was roaming Arlinda's forest. All by himself at night, finding his way around by the light of his oil lamp. The goat path appeared more familiar than any other he had taken in his entire life, as were the hidden alleys and openings in the forest. He was searching for something, but his mind was tranquil and it seemed like a pleasant stroll. He dreamt coming down the hill to the beach in a flash, and climbing back without even a trace of exhaustion. Finding the object of his search, he felt the comfort of meeting long-lost friends. The birds' nests hung low in the trees. He walked to each one of them, holding up his lamp to view the interiors. Yes! They were all there. Each nest held a skull, lovingly cleaned and measured many times in the past. The names rattled off his lips: the Red Devil, the Dwarf, the Eskimo from Baffin Bay, the Laplander. He recited their measurements with ease. The parietal diameters, the inter-mastoid arches, the facial angles. A few of the nest-cabinets were empty, but there were plenty still to keep him busy. He ran from one tree to another, calling out for the skulls to make their appearance, inviting them to descend to his imaginary table for a routine investigation.

In one of the nests he found not a skull but a living head: Norah's. She was delighted as ever to see him, and started to tell him everything that had happened since his operation. She told him about the visitors leaving – the Frenchman kissing her on both cheeks like an ardent lover, as Bates looked on frowning. And about the sulking children. In his dream, he felt exhausted by his walk around the island, lying down on soft grass under a tree. Norah sat with him, cradling his head in her lap and speaking quietly, her face close to his, the words flowing from her mute lips as if she had been speaking to him all her life.

Quartley woke drenched in sweat. He saw Norah come in with his meal and sit down on a stool by his bed.

She spoke to him, just as she had in his dream.

'Norah . . . !'

Quartley shot straight up in his bed. It took a moment or two to be fully awake, to match the Norah of his dream with the one sitting before him. By then he had lost his speech. A million questions surged, as he gazed at Norah helplessly. Ignoring his shock, she started to recite the special diet prescribed by Bates, full of cautions and warnings. When she stopped to smile, the shock left him in a shudder, each word ringing in echoes. An impulse, unlike any he had ever felt, made him reach forward and grasp her shoulders, bring her face close to examine if indeed the lips had moved, if the echoes had come from a living source. 'Speak . . . ?'

She showed no surprise at his surprise. Wiping the sweat off his forehead, she raised a spoon to help him start his meal.

'But you knew, didn't you?'

He shook his head.

'I thought you knew.'

'Knew what, Norah?'

She started to say something, then stopped. She pointed to her lips. 'That I've lied.' The frown returned. 'Lied to everyone. Lied for years.'

'But?' He stopped himself, eager to hear more of her voice.

'Thought it was for the best. It made it easier to keep it all hidden, till it didn't matter any more. No harm would come to us if my lips were sealed.' She looked up at him as if she had said enough for him to understand it all. As if she had given a simple reason for her lie.

His hands shook as he held her.

She brought the spoon down to the full plate. 'But with you, I knew I couldn't hide. *He must know!* I thought. I knew you did . . . observed *everything* about me. You must've spotted my lie. Didn't you?'

155

'Norah!'

She dropped her eyes. '*He knows because he loves me*, I thought. *Just as I do.*'

He heard the same sound he had heard before he had fallen asleep and dreamt his dream. A flutter, as she threw back her shawl and turned to look at Quartley defiantly.

'If you didn't love me, you'd have told your master, wouldn't you? Then they would've found out about me. Sent me back and brought another nurse over. A truly dumb nurse. It'd be hard to hide from you, I knew.'

'Why?' He listened, still in wonder at her voice.

'From being so close to me all day in the kitchen, hearing me whisper and mumble. *He knows, but he has kept my secret*, I thought. I wanted to surprise you and speak when the other two were away, just to hear how my voice sounded mixed with yours. But I didn't know if it would upset you, if you wanted to keep the lie. I thought you might be angry . . .' She gave him a searching look. 'Did you want me to speak?'

Quartley shivered.

'I'd peek into your log to see if you had recorded anything about me. If you had noticed that something was wrong. *He must know! He must know! But he hasn't told anyone. Why hasn't he?* I didn't have an answer.'

'What made you so sure I loved you?'

Norah fell silent for a moment. 'I knew it from the way you were.'

'You mean from my letters?'

Quartley wondered if she had read something in his replies, but she shook her head. 'No . . .'

'Then what, Norah?'

'I knew you'd come sooner, if you could. From your face, I knew you didn't want to leave.'

He started to say something, but she went on. 'The scientists returned for their samples. But you came for me.'

She runs down to her cottage to feed the children, leaving Quartley dazed. He feels elated, but too tired to hold her back, managing only to ask, before she left, why she waited so long to speak. She had worried about confessing to him, she said. Worried that she'd be unable to keep her lie any longer, that she'd betray herself to Bates and Belavoix. Her love, once spoken, would kill her silence. Unable to sleep, Quartley goes over every word she has said, his excitement getting the better of his fever and the knife's wound on his leg. He had often wondered how she would sound if she could speak. He had imagined her laugh, crafting the sound to match her delicate throat and mouth. When she spoke, he heard the twitter of a newly arrived bird – a sound like Norah's, just like her – as if he had known all along. With much effort, he overcomes the urge to get up and hobble down the goat path to her cottage. The night's silence suits him now, as he hears the only sound he wishes to hear. If he frowns, it is because he remembers something she has said – likewise for his sighs. He dwells on the mystery, the reason behind her lie, and the mystery of her last words. Weren't you afraid to come to Arlinda? he had asked. She had shaken her head. Not even on your first night alone? No.

'But I am afraid now,' she had said before leaving. 'More afraid than ever.'

She brought him out onto the veranda next day, helping him limp along and sit on Bates's chair. Then she started tidying up, sweeping the floors and sealing up the windows. He paid no attention to her agile limbs, the flurry of action – just waited for her lips to move.

'Did you talk to yourself when we were gone?'

She raised her face as if recalling the years of silence, after just one evening of speech. 'More in the beginning than later. Twittering all day, like a bird,' she laughed. 'Couldn't stop mumbling and cooing, singing whenever I was alone in the forest . . . screaming, cursing . . .'

He worried the memory of those days might have her lapse into silence. 'What did you say to yourself?'

'Told myself all the unspeakable things I had seen, the unspeakable things I wished upon others. Went over everything that had happened to me. Everything that had gone wrong.' Her voice broke. 'All about Norah, Norah, Norah . . .'

He waited for her to recover, holding back his curiosity.

'Then Norah vanished. Like magic! There was nothing more to say. I lost my voice in the island. Became the mute nurse. Just whispering in silence the rules that you had taught me. After each visit, I scolded myself, just like your master.' She stopped, eyes flickering as she remembered Bates's harsh words. 'I learned the names of your instruments, imagined my head being measured. ' "Hold steady, Quartley!" ' She imitated Bates's gravelly voice. ' "Her head shows definite marks of madness! Fetch the goniometer. Don't dither!" '

Quartley laughed. 'So you've observed everything about *us* too!'

She imitated the Frenchman, the two giggling like children over his melodious snoring.

'Then the lists. I read out my letters and reports many times over to hear how they'd sound. What will Mr Quartley think? I asked myself. Will he read these words and imagine me speaking to him? Will he put me down as just a dumb nurse?'

'Did you read Mr Quartley's replies aloud too?'

She nodded.

'Weren't you worried you'd slip up?' Quartley asked, reaching for her hand to help him rise. 'That you'd lose your silence by accident before your visitors? How did you learn to stay dumb?'

'I reminded myself of all the terrible things that could happen, if . . .'

'And the children?' Quartley could barely contain himself. 'Didn't you talk to the children?'

Only when they kissed did they fall silent. Both turned mute after the very first time, losing the words they had saved for each other. The spell lasted longer each time, till silence was no stranger between the two.

He goes wandering with Norah, once his fever has gone. Still hobbling, he holds her hand and follows her lead. She avoids the goat path, choosing the longer way through the forest. They don't go down to her cottage, as he had hoped, but venture deeper into the hillside, winding their way around trees.

The forest is her destination. A place full of surprises. It seems a different island from the one he knew before. They set out on a familiar path, only to reach a place that seems to have risen overnight from the sea. Untrodden woodlands. Nooks hiding extravagant foliage. Trails that start suddenly and end nowhere.

He recognises the sulphurous stream, but it appears to have sprung from elsewhere – not a fissure as he had guessed, but a waterfall, flowing down an unvisited face of the hill. She takes him wading across the shallow pool at the foot of the waterfall. Hot currents soothe his aching leg. The water is clearer here than in the spring, and they can see their reflections on the bed. The spray drenches them, but there's no risk of slipping, even in the deeper parts, as the gravel is free of mud. She holds onto him with a firm grip.

From the falls, he can see the cottage. It seems far away, barely visible among the clumps of trees, its dull roof shaded green. The cove is visible too from where they stand, and the Flame of the Forest – a swarm of red ants crawling out of the bush for a dip in the sea.

She avoids the children's camp. Their stroll in the forest ends at the veranda, as Quartley's leg starts to ache. Then she runs down to fetch his meal. She wishes no reminder of the experiment yet, its traces alive in the instrument cupboard and on the kitchen table. As if her memory might turn her mute, take her back to playing the nurse. As if the cottage might turn her lover back into an obedient assistant.

They can be themselves, as long as they remain in the forest.

He avoids reminding her of her lie. A speaking Norah he finds more mysterious than the mystery of her silence. With her beside him, he doesn't need to know anything more about the past, his mind kept busy with her presence. She isn't a puzzle waiting to be solved.

He follows her to the bat cave. It is higher up on the hill than the falls, a place without trees. They enter through a narrow opening, leaving the afternoon's glare behind. A step behind Norah, Quartley feels the damp air rising like mist from the ground. The bats are inside, covering the dark walls with an even darker layer. There's dead silence. The smell of warm and musty flesh. The occasional flutter of something fleeting across the mist, and displacing its neighbour with a screeching noise. Then silence once again. He hears them breathing – a million of them, inhaling and exhaling, filling the cave with their breath. He looks around for Norah, but she has disappeared. It feels darker without her, as if a sudden landslide has blocked the cave's opening, trapping him inside. Just him, alone with the bats. A moan rises with a shadow closing in behind him. He feels breath on his neck. The breath of a primitive creature, long extinct. The island's beast. Eyeless.

Arms grasp him. A delicate mane covers his face. His skin burns with bites. Each thrust of the assailant leads to greater entanglement. He can't escape. The beast stirs a beast in him as he returns the favours, matching force with force, lunging back to plant his own bite. The two are ready to crush each other, to swallow and be swallowed – withdrawing for a moment, only to entangle again.

They hear the roar of a million wings. The bats aroused by their smell, and taking flight in droves. With every thrust, they sense every bit of themselves – the cave's prisoners.

They added their own sounds to the forest. Leaving the cave behind, they came down the flank of the hill to the secret meadow. The tickling grass on their backs mixed laughter with sighs. The tree-walls echoed. When they swam in the spring, they seemed like two giant lizards lashing the rock steps with their naked limbs, waking a water snake from its sleep and setting it off hissing. Even at the valley of rocks, their mating would silence the gulls, which stopped their cawing to examine the larger-than-life crabs basking over a rock bed. Only the sea paid no attention to them, all the squeals and shrieks drowned untraced.

Whenever they entered the cottage, they checked to see if they were alone. Then, a quick visit to the stove and larder to recover their share of the meal that Norah had cooked, leaving the rest for the children on the kitchen table. The empty cottage didn't excite them, nor the comfort of a bed. They must return to the forest, eating under the shade of a tree, or in the tree house. Eating with their hands, and talking till sleep silenced them.

It was a routine that neither was used to, yet both found easy to follow: waking and sleeping, roaming the forest, with Norah vanishing from time to time to return to the cottage and care for the children. Like them, she had started to spend some nights away from the camp, coming up to share the hammock on the veranda with Quartley. It felt like a part of the forest, their own little tree house on the hill. There were nights when he was alone at the scientists' camp, unable to sleep, quarrelling with himself over whether he should join her down at her cottage. What if the children saw them together? Would they be jealous? He remembered the bleeding Belavoix. Would they be surprised to see her talk like their visitors?

It didn't take him long to win his quarrel. Then he'd dash down the goat path on his rapidly healing leg. A knock on the window would let him in, the bed becoming their hammock. They'd sleep soundly, waking in the middle of the night only if the girl cried out in a nightmare.

He saw a different dawn whenever he spent the night at the cottage. Waking to find Norah gone from his side, he'd hear her humming in the kitchen. It reminded him of when he lived with his mother, of the time before the experiment. Before the journeys. Before science. A dawn to set off simply another day. For them, a day of roaming, and aimless pleasures.

He surprised Norah in the kitchen, coming up behind her to smell the pot on her stove.

'Will you miss me when I go?'

He saw pain in her eyes.

What have the children seen?

Great observers of the forest, they've spotted their nurse and the assistant, hushing each other as they trail them. The boy aimed a rock once at the tangled flesh – the intruders in their secret garden. The girl stopped him, the two creeping up for a closer look, then creeping back. They have heard the splashing in the spring, the cave's echoes.

Their routine has changed. The nurse has turned into a stranger, rarely present at the cottage, day or night.

When they are all together, it seems different from when the scientists were around. The cottage is a happier place, the kitchen just another playground. The children pile heaps of shells they've collected from the beach on the floor, like a string of hills – each hill made up of shells that are of the same shape and colour; piling higher and higher, till a heap explodes and forms its own string of hillocks.

It's their own game. Sometimes Norah and Quartley sit and watch them turn the kitchen floor into an ocean bed. It's hard to walk around without crunching their precious possessions. The children surround their feet with shells, make it impossible to move, turn them into prisoners. Raising her feet, Norah laughs, Quartley follows her – their feet tangled up over the table.

The children don't mind them laughing or watching the games. If anything, they want them to join in. It doesn't take long for Quartley and Norah to discover that they are spied upon, whether at the cottage or in the forest. At times, the children's desire to be with the adults gets the better of them, and they barge into the tree house or splash suddenly into the spring.

Whenever they are with Norah and Quartley, the children appear far from wild. Only their lack of speech makes them different from normal children. They are unable to express a sudden inspiration or warn of a change of mood, unable to warn them of a sudden departure. Then it is the grown-ups' turn to follow the children, to spy on them.

The boy was sitting cross-legged on his bed with the girl on the floor when Quartley entered his room. They watched their visitor silently kneel before them and take out a sailor's pouch, emptying it on to the floor. A handful of cowries, shining like pearls. He smiled proudly at the children, admiring his catch, bought from a deckhand on his way over. He lined them up in two rows, facing each other, like rival armies. Then, he offered them the cowries.

'Go on . . . they're yours.' He spoke, looking from one to the other.

Two pairs of unblinking eyes stared back.

'You can have them.'

They kept on staring . . .

They were woken at night by pattering feet coming into their room. The children had arrived to steal the cowries. They searched under the bed and turned over a few things till they saw that Norah and Quartley were awake, and observing them. The thieves left with a serious look on their faces.

Strolling over the beach at dawn, they saw the children running ahead of them. They dived into the surf and floated on the waves. Within moments, they were gone. A touch of panic gripped Quartley when they disappeared underwater, staying submerged for eternal moments, till Norah spotted them swimming far ahead like a pair of dolphins, frightening the gulls with their screams.

Mornings reminded her of her lie. The frown returned as she busied herself with the supplies, with Quartley still asleep. As she lit the stove, she mumbled to herself, much like the dumb nurse she once had been. When he did wake one morning and entered the kitchen, Quartley saw Norah sitting head down at the table, idle fingers braiding and unbraiding her hair. He saw the Norah of the cottage, waiting for her visitors to arrive.

She told him all in one breath.

Listening to her, he could imagine Norah before the experiment. The orphan raised among costers, living in workhouses and filthy courts. A kind seamstress had taught her to read and write, taken her as an apprentice. But her luck had drawn more than her kindness: the attention of the seamstress's husband. It hadn't been long before she found herself back where she was before. Her litany of tragedy had taken her to grimier slums. She had been reduced to living worse than the street Arabs. Prey to bullies and gaolbirds, she had escaped on the verge of becoming an 'upper-floor girl', one of those who were forced to escort customers up the stairs or go behind the counter. Another lucky break found her a job as a nursery maid, dreaming of becoming something more – a midwife, even. A job she lost to yet another tragedy, forced back to fleeting between bullies and hawkers, to a life on the streets.

Her birth was her tragedy. She had thought of escaping once and for all, with a penny-stick of pills. She'd sleep with her eyes open, she had decided, till she thought of the asylum. She had lied to get in, feigned her defect. She could've pretended to be anything – even the owner of a wobbly head, which would have kept her locked up for life, barred her from the workhouse for ever. Losing her voice would be easier, she had thought, making her way through the years with nods and shrugs. Dumb Norah. She had slept with a blanket over her face, done her duties in silence at the asylum, lived in fear of her minders, who'd have thrown her out if they'd known. She'd have had to go back to the streets, if they'd found out.

The last tragedy was the child she'd had, but lost: a baby girl, fathered by one of the bullying minders. She had lived only a few days, died just before Bates's friends came to the asylum looking for a nurse. They'd wanted a dumb caretaker, someone to wet-nurse newborns – a nurse with a strong will, and willing to live far away. She had fitted the bill.

Had she thought she'd speak again?

In her dreams, she had seen herself in a place where no one could keep an eye on her – where she was free to talk, to sing, to scream . . .

Arlinda was her dream. She'd been grateful to be chosen.

Quartley could've guessed much of her story from knowing what happened to the unlucky ones. He had managed to avoid the streets, coming down to London from his village. His mother had kept an eye out for him from far away – he had found promising jobs that hadn't let him down. But he knew of the less fortunate, having passed them on the streets or stepped aside lest their paths crossed.

Tragedy has made her what she is, he thought, listening to Norah. She had avoided the worst only to live, her frown her guard against hope.

He thought of her climbing onto the cottage roof, determined to stop the flooding rain – determined to go on. The barren island was her dream, her escape. He saw her cowering before Bates. She had learned how to appear dumb before bullies. Lying and struggling. Being a mother had taught her how to care for children. She didn't mind them being wild, having lived in the asylum.

'If the scientists take back their samples, you'd have to come with them, wouldn't you?'

'Back?'

'Yes.' His mind skipped over the next six years. 'Back to England. Once the experiment ends.' He imagined her as a nursemaid at Louisa's mansion, its gloom relieved finally by these adopted children.

'They won't need me then. They'll look for a proper nurse who can speak, to teach them.'

He toyed with the other possibility: if the scientists agree to go back early. 'What if we went back to the laboratory now? Finished the experiment there?'

'You mean, if I went to live with you at your Madhouse?'

The rush lasted a moment, then he remembered the obstacles. The scientists would never agree.

'Will they end the experiment early?' From her face, Quartley knew that even Norah had her doubts. 'They've been arguing, haven't they?'

'They would have to end it if something happened.'

She jerked her head up. 'What could happen?'

'If . . .' His mind compiled a long list of tragedies, but he decided against reciting them to Norah.

She smiled a sad smile. 'I won't leave until I die.'

He shut her mouth with his.

*

Silence descended whenever either of them mentioned the fate of the experiment. Playground turned to prison when they started to think about what might happen. They avoided the hill top, for fear of seeing a ship heading towards Arlinda. The inevitable kept them awake at night.

Lying beside Norah, Quartley recalled the night she spoke for the first time. She was afraid now, more than ever, she had said then. Was she afraid her visitors would stop coming, abandon her, leave her marooned?

She was afraid for their samples, Norah told him – afraid they'd turn truly wild as they grew older. The fight had scared her. They weren't like the children she'd known so well. Her face clouded. She didn't know what was on their minds any longer – if their play was just play or a sinister plan; if they might, as the Frenchman boasted, end up preying on each other.

Quartley held Norah as she started to shake.

'I haven't spoken a word to them. Ever. I have raised them just as I was ordered. If they'd lived among other children, they would have grown up as just another boy and girl. They would have known what it was to be human, even if they couldn't speak a single word. But here? Even I can't save them from themselves.' She broke free of his arm.

'Arlinda will turn them into savages.'

He surprised himself. Thoughts that had made him shudder only a few years back now raced through his mind – thoughts both worrying and delicious. Since arriving at the Madhouse, he had lived only with the hope of becoming the perfect assistant. He had always sided with Bates, certain of his eventual victory over all his rivals, including the Frenchman. Now he discovered another hope, a more powerful one: of spending a whole life with Norah. A hope strong enough to crush his loyalty to Bates. Nothing in his life had quite prepared him for the near-impossible task that faced him now, that of escaping with Norah from Arlinda.

He didn't doubt for a moment that the experiment needed to end. He knew Bates wouldn't agree to stop before the dozen years were over, despite Belavoix's threats never to return to Arlinda. The master craniologist was fighting for his own sake, fighting to solve the puzzle of human variation, to prove that he was right. Bates would soldier on, weather the wavering supporters. He would keep Norah and the children at the island as long as it suited him.

He himself must stop the experiment, Quartley thought. Not the scientists, or Louisa, but the humble assistant. The faithful recorder of the log. He must finish what the scientists couldn't.

It was time for him to rise from Bates's shadow.

Quartley described his plan, as Norah joined him on the hill top. She beamed as he pointed past the anthills towards the setting sun.

'You mean we'll go to another place like this?'

He shook his head. 'A different kind of place.'

'But who will take us there?'

He started to tell her what he'd do once he returned to London, but she stopped him before he could go further.

'And the children? Who will help us to take the children with us?'

The boy's scream tells them that the ship is close to landing. He has spotted the flag and comes running in from the beach, covered in sand. His babbles draw Norah from the garden; she and Quartley exchange glances. The girl enters the kitchen holding her head, squeezing herself in between the two grown-ups.

It's hard for them to slip away from the children now. They refuse to leave their sight, as if they've sensed something. There's no list of tasks for Norah, no final check of the instrument cupboard for Quartley. Just the wait at the steps for a sighting of the outrigger.

All four wait. The children disappear to their rooms for a moment; they both seem to have thought of the same thing, a final task before Quartley leaves. The sound of pattering feet announces their return after a while.

They've come with gifts. A gift from each, in exchange for the cowries.

The girl has a basket in her hand, a row of uneven knots to show for her brave effort. The leaves stolen from Norah's bucket. A basket large enough for a pair of birds.

Then the boy. He holds something in his closed fist. It takes Quartley a while to pry open the fingers, requiring the usual run of tricks. A tooth. Lost recently, and saved among his precious shells. Gleaming. A nest-egg.

*

The horizon swallows Arlinda. Only an exact count of nautical miles remains between him and his destination.

Is it more than that?

On the voyage back with Captain Perry, he finds his thoughts as troubling as the boisterous sea. Arlinda and the Madhouse. The children and the skulls. Assistant or lover? He can't be both.

A new rivalry keeps him awake.

III

There is grandeur in this view of life . . .

CHARLES DARWIN

MADHOUSE

It's grim at the Madhouse. Since their return from Arlinda there's been nothing but trouble. After a year of misgivings, Louisa has finally given in to her fear and to her friend's urging. Seeing no sign of hope in the reports, she has cut off her gift to her husband's experiment. It hasn't brought the result she thought it would. Or at least not as soon as she wished. The cause of racial science has been dropped in favour of other causes. The cow has turned into a mule, kicking Bates where it hurts most. Quartley hears all the gossip. Mrs Bates has rescinded her gift, but passed on The Steeple's gloom to the Madhouse.

Now there's mess and muddle where once there was order. Nothing is to be found in its right place, the laboratory reduced to an ugly warehouse, floors cluttered with boxes and instruments. Bundles of reports lie stacked high on the bench, dust gathers on the Cranial Index. The collection room is no better. Faulty desiccators have left a mouldy touch on the cabinets, and a foul smell.

The master of the Madhouse is no longer a hermit cloistered in his laboratory, but a restless traveller, a travelling lecturer, willing to go wherever there's a fee waiting for him – lecturing on anything, just to keep the funds dribbling in. Never one to stoop, he walks now with a limp from carrying around heavy boxes of instruments and specimens for his lectures. When he's at the Madhouse, he's a different being altogether. Rarely leaving his study, he calls Quartley over to run his errands. Passing letters, getting the items ready for his travelling show. In the months since their return, Bates hasn't devised a single new instrument. Dozens of unfinished ones tangle up his window sill. He brushes Quartley aside when he tries to bring Norah's reports to his attention. 'You decide if her requests are reasonable. If they could be supplied within a moderate cost.'

Calculations of the children's crania meet with a similar answer. 'Let's wait till our next visit, Quartley.' A mention of the Frenchman doesn't arouse him either.

Quartley watched his master climb the ladder as he held it steady, and open cabinet 241. He brought the skull down, laying it on the floor next to the other five. Then he ordered Quartley to move the ladder and fetch the Pope.

When they had finished, seven skulls stood in a row. The Egyptian Nubian, a Papuan from the Oceanic-Negro family, a child's cranium belonging to an ancient Peruvian tribe, a fiery and revengeful Ashanti known to be hostile to colonists, a wobbly-headed Chinese Yenshee, the Villain, and the Mississippi Mermaid. But Bates didn't want them on the laboratory bench this time.

'Put each in a box and sprinkle camphor around the lids.'

'Are they going somewhere, sir?'

'We wouldn't be putting them in boxes if they weren't, would we?'

After a pause, Quartley asked, 'Where are they going?'

'Baltimore and Philadelphia.'

America! A tour of America with the skulls! British racial science embarking on a conquest of the New World? Perhaps Bates planned to thrill his supporters with a glimpse of his treasures? A grand viewing in exchange for their help in keeping the experiment going. Would Quartley be asked to come too? Another voyage!

'Shall we prepare for a trip?'

'Not us. Just the specimens.'

Another thought entered Quartley's mind. He remembered the frequent letters from America – the requests to purchase rare skulls in order to strengthen the fledgling collections there. Museum directors wrote of a rising interest in racial science, with savages arriving in a great tidal wave. *America trails behind Europe; our knowledge of the races is barely greater than that of the slaves themselves and their traders.* There had been offers of exchange – Bates's skulls for a generous benefaction to his science. Quartley's master cracked jokes about American scientists. 'They want to buy up everything. Knowledge equals possessions! Dollars! Even body-snatchers would spit at these offers!'

Now he knew. Bates was selling his skulls! This then was his way of winning supporters, of keeping his experiment going – his way of fighting Louisa and the Royal Society.

'Are we selling them?'

Bates frowned. 'I wouldn't say *selling*. No. Having exhausted these crania of the necessary facts, we're passing them on to the novices.' He doubled his argument for the benefit of a silent Quartley. 'They are all here anyway, in the Index. Nothing will be lost. We don't need the skulls to remind us of their measurements, do we?'

As Bates left the crypt, Quartley started packing up the skulls. He felt saddened by the coming departures. The Pope, found in the desert. Mississippi Mermaid – the object of much ribaldry. 'You might fancy her tail, Quartley! Just don't get trapped under her apron skin!' He remembered Captain Perry's cackle. The Villain he was happy to pack away. Holding up the Peruvian child, he was reminded of their excitement the day it had arrived. A gift from an admirer. A baby! A new baby at the Madhouse!

Would he stop with the seven? Or would the rest go too?

Quartley gazed sadly around the collection room.

The plans had started on Arlinda's hill top, and grown in leaps and bounds before he had taken them to Captain Perry. Despite his unkind scheme for using the children after the experiment, Quartley had come to trust the captain. He had stood by them all unwaveringly, always ready to give in to the scientists' whims, never shy, though, of offering his opinion and advice about the children.

Perry had sighed at the sad turn of events. 'I don't blame Louisa, really. All financiers are like that. Even if they are your wives! One shouldn't rely on their patience. If Bates was a shipping man, he'd have had to deliver his results even more quickly.' He had stopped. 'But you're worried about something else, aren't you?'

Quartley had nodded.

'You're worried that Bates will simply plough on with what he's got, even if there are no supporters.'

'Yes.'

'Now *that's* something a shipping man would never do! If I were him, I'd stop right now and bring the children back.'

'That's exactly what I think, sir.' Quartley had felt excited.

'Bring them back while the white is still ahead of the black. Declare her the winner based on your mirror test and whatever else you've got. The longer you leave them there, the bigger the chance of something going wrong.'

'I'm ready, sir.' Quartley had bitten his lips. 'Ready to bring them back. If you will help.'

The captain had stared at him for a moment. 'You mean behind Bates's back?'

'Yes. If he won't stop, then . . .'

'And you're sure you want to do that? Take on Bates, no matter what happens?' Captain Perry had kept on staring at him.

'It's a risk one must take.'

'Why must *you* take the risk, Quartley?'

Quartley had taken a deep breath. This was his moment, his chance to win a friend, a key ally. He mustn't lose his nerve. He had delivered the short speech he had rehearsed over and over at his desk, adding bits taken from Norah's reports.

'Otherwise, M. Belavoix will win. Certainly. It'll be the end of British science.'

Taken aback, the captain had narrowed his eyes.

'With every passing day the risk grows,' Quartley had gone on. 'The nurse has reported to me that the children have been fighting regularly. Vicious fights. There was one while we were there last time. They attacked M. Belavoix, left him bleeding from a nasty cut.'

'You mean . . . ?'

'There's more. If the children don't harm each other, then there's a possibility that someone else might.'

At a loss for words, Captain Perry had only been able to manage sounds of encouragement, urging Quartley to go on.

'I fear that M. Belavoix has a plan. He plans to kill one of the children and blame the other for the murder. Then claim victory over Mr Bates. He has already asked the nurse to help him.'

'Does Bates know?'

Quartley had shaken his head. 'Belavoix has suggested leaving behind a knife. Something for the children to use. Now I fear he plans to use it himself.'

It had taken a while for the captain to digest everything. 'You're saying Bates's experiment is doomed. Either way, he loses. A dead child would make Belavoix the winner.'

'Yes.' Quartley had nodded calmly.

'The double-crossing French!'

'It would be a disaster, sir. Word could leak out if a child died. Our enemies would pounce on it. It might even become impossible to ever study the races again.'

Captain Perry had looked horrified. 'That would be a pity. The future of racial science ruined on Arlinda!'

When they had met again, Quartley's plans seemed to have taken root. As they strolled along the Strand, the captain had appeared to have gone even a few steps ahead of him.

'It's a pity your master can't be persuaded that he is in danger of losing.' He had gazed at the afternoon strollers, tipping his hat at a few familiar faces. 'Do you think he can be persuaded?'

Quartley had told him about the meeting between Bates and Sir Reginald Holmes, taking pains to explain how strongly Bates felt about the experiment lasting its full course, imitating his voice even. ' "We agreed to wait till the end, to be patient . . ." '

Captain Perry had grimaced. 'No hope then.'

'He won't willingly dissolve it, until he is sure that he has won.'

'It could be dissolved for him . . . that's what you're thinking, isn't it? An escape?'

Quartley had stayed silent.

'With the children *and* the nurse?'

'If they are brought back here, Mr Bates will have no option but to end the argument openly with M. Belavoix. Whatever happens, he couldn't lose unfairly. The children too could be saved.'

'And then?'

'The experiment would end, sir. *Naturally.* Without an accident, I mean.'

'But what would happen next? To the woman and the children?' Captain Perry had given Quartley a searching look. 'You'd want to have the nurse live with you, I suppose?'

He had known the captain was bound to suspect. Sooner or later. Perhaps he'd have guessed from those letters, the ones that came so frequently from Arlinda for Nicholas Quartley.

'And the children?'

'She'd want to have the children with her.'

'Hardly surprising. She has become their mother, nothing less.' He had startled Quartley with his next question. 'Where do you suppose they'll live?'

'I don't know exactly . . . here in London, or . . .' He had felt

Captain Perry was worried about the children's wild manners, by their lack of speech. 'They can learn our ways quickly, I think, given a chance.'

'But they can't live in England, can they? I mean, *together*. You know slave-holding is illegal in this country.'

'Slave-holding!'

'The black boy would have to live as a slave, wouldn't he? You couldn't raise him as a brother to the girl, could you?'

'What do you mean?'

'I mean, where in the civilised world can you raise these two as equals, in the way they've been raised in Arlinda? You could have him as a houseboy, of course, or a stable hand. You could raise him with kindness, but at a distance.'

'What if they were taken elsewhere, sir?' Quartley had felt awkward. He hadn't considered this complication.

'You mean to another island? That would be hard. If it was a slave port, the boy would be shipped off to America in no time. It would be hard for Norah too . . . with so many hungry sailors around her. No. If you're thinking of escaping, I wouldn't recommend another island.'

Seeing a dark cloud gathering over Quartley's face, Captain Perry had tried to cheer him up. 'There's no problem a sailor can't solve! You might just have to make two escapes rather than one! The first from Arlinda to here, to finish off the experiment. The second from here to some other place, for your *domestic reasons*.'

'But to where, sir?'

'We'll get to that when we have to, Quartley. Got a good pair of sea-legs, have you?'

The perfect assistant. It had taken him almost a decade to get here. From a skull-cleaner to one who knew almost as much as the scientist. He could recite from memory the columns in the log, as well as the list of supplies delivered to Arlinda in half a dozen years. He had seen more of the samples; he had lived in the cottage with them. He had been more than a visitor.

The thought of betraying Bates didn't trouble Quartley. The puzzle sorted itself out in the only way possible. He didn't see the end simply as a win or a loss. A triumphant Bates bringing home a pair of savages and their broken nurse after twelve long years; or the

Frenchman holding up a dead child. It wasn't just the settling of an argument. Quartley dreamt of more than that: the chance to settle the mess now, to end the experiment and prevent loss.

To win over Bates he'd have to do even better – encircle him, tempt him, madden him, till he slipped on his own resolve. He must match him word for word, he must trick him with his superior grasp of the experiment. Bates couldn't tell lies from fact, couldn't verify his account of Arlinda without rifling through Norah's reports.

Away from the island, Belavoix worried him less. The Frenchman would be on his side; he too wanted a quick end. But he must be tempted to fight one last time with Bates, to settle the rivalry. Without that, Arlinda would be worthless to all of them, simply another anthill on *La Petite Route*.

There were just two ways left, Quartley thought: first, getting the scientists back to the island for a final test. After their argument had been resolved, they would return together, with Norah and the children. If Bates won, he might want to take his samples to the academies, present them in place of the skulls to boast of his victory over Belavoix. After all that was over, Quartley would escape with Norah and the children with Perry's help to somewhere they could all live together.

But if the scientists delayed any longer, he would have to think of the other plan: going down to Arlinda by himself and escaping with Norah and the children. Then they wouldn't have to return to England, but would go wherever Perry took them.

Of all the years at the Madhouse this was the busiest. His mind was kept even busier than his hands. He spent hours at his desk, waiting to ambush Bates when he returned from his lectures. He wrote to Norah, keeping her abreast of his plans – wrote to Belavoix too, hoping to tease out his interest. Then there were meetings with Captain Perry, each meeting driving him to a frenzy of hope.

He imagined Arlinda twenty years from now. The camp now overgrown, the forest reclaiming it from the visitors. The bat cave. Gaping holes in the cottage roof and puddles underneath – a sanctuary for lizards. The hammock hanging over the veranda like a giant cobweb.

It would be a quieter island without the children. Both camps in similar disarray, but one saved from total havoc by the shading trees.

It looked habitable, once the encroaching garden had been pruned back and the rocks cleared from the courtyard. Sand had blown in through the open windows, painting the stove and the table with the same brush.

Only the evening star, shining as old, on the steps.

Norah's letter in his hand, Quartley entered Bates's study. It was hard to spot him at first behind a tall stack of books, as if he was hiding in the shadows.

'What is it?'

His master looked weary and a touch wet. He was drinking quick shots from his little travelling bottle, and kept his eyes glued on his book. After Quartley had presented the alarming report – the girl suffering from frequent spells of dizziness – he kept on reading without comment.

'We must go immediately to Arlinda,' Quartley said.

'It's common vertigo. Nothing serious. Derangement of the stomach is the likeliest cause. Couldn't be apoplexy, or she'd have reported severe headache and vomiting.'

'The nurse has tried everything. Given her drops from the medicine box, kept her in bed for days, but . . .'

'It'll pass.' Bates turned his eyes back to the book.

'And if it gets worse?'

'We'll wait for her next report to decide. No need to rush. There's no evidence of a systemic disorder.'

'But meanwhile . . .' He hated Bates's patience. Patience in the face of a suffering girl and a distressed Norah. How could he care so much about human variation, without the slightest concern for the humans he knew?

'We must go *now*.'

'You go, Quartley. Go back to your desk. I order you to copy the Cranial Index from beginning to end. Start again when you've finished. It'll keep your mind off your stupidity.'

'I warn you of the consequences, sir. If we don't go, the experiment will be lost.'

'You warn me!'

'If we don't go, I think something will happen to the girl.'

'*You* think!' Bates let out a snort. 'So in six years, not only have our samples changed, but the assistant has become a thinker!'

Quartley ignored Bates's jibe. 'We can't let the girl die. It would play into M. Belavoix's hands.'

'Are you mad or drunk, or both!' Bates glared at him. 'We can't rush to Arlinda every time there is a minor hiccup.'

'We don't know if it's minor. If the children are—'

'The children are rubbish, Quartley.'

'Rubbish?'

'Yes, rubbish. I thought you'd know that by now. This isn't about the *children*. It's about two great arguments.'

'So it doesn't matter if they suffer? As long as they are alive?'

'Absolutely! As long as they meet our purposes. That's all.' Bates slammed his book shut, and leaned across the table. 'Tell me, do you care about a cadaver, after you've finished slicing it up?'

Whenever he met him at the Madhouse, he found Bates's sight hard to bear. He saw not one but two faces: an arrogant Bates crushing a suffering Norah. Yet he followed him around, waiting for a chance to pounce on him.

'I'm prepared to go to Arlinda alone, sir, if you're not.'

'You?' Bates appeared taken aback.

Quartley nodded, preparing himself for yet another speech he had rehearsed carefully. He'd need to go alone, to put into action the escape he had planned with Captain Perry.

Bates stared long and hard at him. 'And what do you think Belavoix will say? We can't go to Arlinda by ourselves, even if we want to, can we? *That* would break the rules. We must give him time to decide if he wants to come with us, I'm afraid.'

'He's had months to think now.'

Secretly, Quartley hoped his letter to the Frenchman might help. His plea to him to return quickly for the *final act*.

Bates shrugged. 'It's all about patience. One must have patience to do a proper job.'

Damn Bates!

Fretting at his desk, Quartley went over the offence. The words had cut through him like a scalpel. He wished he could equal Bates's savagery.

'You're just as afraid as the others,' Bates had told him during their last encounter. 'You should've known our work wouldn't be easy. Dangerous even.'

'It's most oppressive for the nurse.'

'*Oppressive?*' Bates looked at him quizzically. 'Is that why you bring her gifts? To lighten her oppression? Does it help her to sleep better, listening to the ticking of your clock?'

He forgot he was the assistant. 'She's not a goniometer. Even *you* would go mad, if you had to do what she's done already. She's not a . . .'

'She's a whore, Quartley. Arlinda is her paradise. In London, she'd have starved to death.' He had brought his face close to Quartley's. 'Go, if it's too much for you – this oppression. There'll be other assistants. You can go back to the taxidermist. They might still need a few bird-stuffers over there.'

Damn Bates!

He went back to his plans.

NUMBER 88

'The Frenchman has failed to keep his word. It's time to call him back to Arlinda.'

Unlike himself, Bates apologised for his lateness as he and Quartley arrived to meet Holmes at the Royal Society. But true to himself, he wasted no time starting his argument, opening with a complaint against Belavoix.

'He has threatened to withdraw before, but he has never waited this long to change his mind.'

Holmes nodded, showing only faint interest.

'We have quarrelled in the past. Indeed in the last six years we have done nothing but quarrel. It isn't unusual. We knew this was how it would be right from the beginning. The moral tests were bound to draw out our arguments. And it was no different on the last visit. We disagreed about why the children had fought, why . . .'

Holmes interrupted calmly. 'And you're asking me to do what?'

'To write to him immediately, to order him back. A proper scolding will do him the world of good. And if he doesn't listen, then . . .'

'Then what?'

'Write to his mentor – Leconte, or whatever he's called. The Société Ethnologique should reprimand such an irresponsible member.'

'But I thought you didn't like that sort of thing,' Holmes said, turning pages of a report.

'What sort of thing?'

'Others meddling in any way – coming between you and your rival. After so many years, one would've thought the two of you needed no coaxing to work together. You are not children, after all.'

Bates looked surprised. 'But I am only asking you to do what you agreed.'

'I –' Holmes started – 'agreed to nothing more than keeping my silence till the two of you had finished, then hearing your conclusions. I agreed to help the winner spread his view of the races to the academies. I agreed *not* to support you, *not* to suggest changes, *not* to influence either. That's all I agreed.'

'But you did suggest that we change a few tests, didn't you? You did warn me against *desperate perseverance*.'

'I've suffered for my blunders,' Holmes replied drily.

Quartley detected a strange note in Bates's voice. 'But we're close now to the answer. If Belavoix returns, if we agree to a final test with the children, if the results are clear, then we will have our proof. *L'épreuve!* Finally!'

Holmes appeared unimpressed by the 'ifs'. 'How many angels do you want to balance on the point of your pin?'

Quartley was puzzled by Holmes's air. The kind uncle was incapable of refusing Bates, he had thought. Beyond the usual differences, had there been a deeper parting of ways? What was one more letter to the prolific statesman of science?

Before Bates could come up with a suitable argument in his favour, Holmes rose to welcome his other guests, Dr Edward Burnett, the retired captain with a keen interest in the natural sciences, and Lord Skeene, the Head of Anatomy at the Royal College of Physicians, both respected members of the Society. Holmes seemed to be expecting them.

'Ah! The jewels of British science! What have we to reveal to each other, that the world waits to hear with an ear at our door!'

With an arch look at Bates, Dr Burnett parried the question. 'Bates is the one to reveal, I'd have thought. He has kept us waiting outside his door for a while now, has he not?'

'We must wait for good news. We mustn't hurry.' Holmes, not Bates, was the one to counsel patience.

'But are we sure it *will* be good news?' Skeene was less willing to share Holmes's optimism. 'What if we are waiting outside the wrong door?'

Bates didn't speak. It was not his way to respond to conjecture. If he was drawn into a debate, he'd have to reveal more than he wished.

'What if it was neither monogenism nor polygenism, but something else that explained the racial puzzle?'

'You mean if . . . ?'

'I mean if Mr Darwin and his friends are right,' Skeene put in quickly. Then he turned to Bates. 'Have you heard of the new theory of evolution?'

With Bates silent, Skeene seized the chance to lecture. 'It's a theory that explains what we've been trying to explain for so long. It claims that we – men – were born not of Adam and Eve, but—'

'But that all the races have evolved from a common origin,' Burnett joined in. 'And it's a peculiar origin that is claimed. One wouldn't think of it normally, but there seems to be a lot of evidence in its favour.'

'What origin does it claim?' Bates looked up, curiosity overcoming his silence.

Holmes leaned forward in his chair, brought his face close to his pipe as if to examine the contents of the bowl carefully. He, not Burnett, answered Bates's question. 'There seems to be evidence that we – *all* races of mankind, including the superior and the inferior – came from the great apes, that we all share animal ancestry.'

There was silence in the room. Bates didn't pay much attention to the new theory, prompting Lord Skeene to raise his squeaky voice. 'If Mr Darwin is indeed right, then it means that we, the European races, aren't special after all. Not the possessors of a divine soul, morally superior to the Negro, say. It'd prove that the races are different only in degree.'

Burnett was even more emphatic. 'There would be no ideal race then – each known to evolve in its own way, adapting to nature's struggles.'

'But' – Bates raised his hand, before the others could get carried away – 'does it explain why the Negro is black? Why he has a smaller cranium? Why he loses every time we fight him? Does the new theory explain why he's closer to our common ancestor – if he is the common ancestor – in behaviour and character than us?' Gazing around the room, he aired his final opinion on evolution. 'At best, it's a half-baked idea, not equal to the precision of ours.'

'Better a half-baked idea than a burnt one!' Skeene squeaked again. 'Who do you think will be interested to know that the white man is superior to the black, if both are known to have descended from the chimpanzee!'

Bates ignored him, speaking directly to Holmes. 'One must consider what evidence exists for these claims. Otherwise they'd be no better than yarns.'

The evidence,' Holmes started to say, 'has been painstakingly collected from a number of species, molluscs to aquatic—'

'Our experiment can claim no less pain in collecting facts from two human samples, comparing their races directly. When complete, it will end all theorising that offers little more than cheap surprises.'

'But your experiment will take years to complete, while the evolutionists are already knocking on our doors.' Dr Burnett was quick to rebut Bates.

'I'm sorry, Samuel.' Holmes returned to the discussion after Skeene and Burnett had gone. 'Our two societies are best left out of this. It's now a matter between you and Jean-Louis Belavoix. I'm afraid, you have to do your own letter-writing.'

'You are threatening science with anarchy.'

Quartley recalled Bates attacking Holmes at the end of their meeting. The statesman kept his temper. 'We must welcome new ideas. We can't rule unfairly in favour of one. It isn't one argument or another that we're loyal to – but to the puzzle of human variation.'

'And yet you'll happily betray our experiment, when the answer to the puzzle is within reach.'

'Yes . . .' Holmes sighed. '*An* answer is within reach, I agree with you. But . . .'

'But, what?'

'Will it be the right answer?'

Quartley!'

He rushed into Bates's study. A letter, a letter! His heart sank, when he saw Bates reading yet another letter from America. From another prospective skull-buyer.

'Fetch the Tartar.'

Quartley made a face. 'He's gone already. We can give them a Mongol. Same racial family.'

'That will be fine. They can't tell one from the other anyway.' Then he barked out another number.

Quartley felt shocked. Number 88! The Seminole Warrior? Selling off Buffalo Tail! The pride of the Madhouse? He struggled to find words. 'I don't think we should sell it, sir. It's vital to our—'

Bates pointed to the door. 'Go! It's a pity they haven't asked for a foolish assistant's skull. We could have a large benefaction, if we put you inside a box instead!'

Quartley entered the crypt and moved the ladder over to the stack. His heart grew heavy as he climbed each step and saw the empty cupboards surrounding him – the cabinets with their doors open, no specimen left inside most, just scraps of paper bearing the details of their former owners. He lifted out the skull, came down the ladder and carried it wearily back to the laboratory.

'What have you got there?' Bates's angry voice froze him.

'Number 88, sir,' he fumbled. 'As you said, Buffalo Tail. A member of the American family, a Seminole warrior killed by a single shot . . .'

'Who asked you for number 88? I said 98. Leave him right where he was. Go on . . . don't dither, Quartley!'

'In the name of the experiment, we have fought each other. For six years! We have kept faith in our rivalry and suffered for the sake of science. We've struck out like savages . . . knowing no other way, ready to die in order to win . . '

His heart pounded, he was afraid to go on. The *quick answer* from Belavoix had finally arrived. It spoke of things Quartley could barely understand.

The children ceased to interest me. Rather than observing them, I started observing you. Professor Samuel Bates. The great craniologist, the heartless taskmaster – a sick man, addicted to drink. In England, you could hide behind your skulls, but in Arlinda you were naked. Here you revealed everything. At first, it seemed funny the way you measured the children then measured them again. How upset you became at the slightest mistake made by poor Quartley! And how you refused to see what your instruments didn't show. It was more than your science, I realised later; it was your way of protecting yourself. Your mind was a greater threat to you than the silly Frenchman.

I observed you at the children's cottage and at our camp – reading, scolding the nurse, crossing the stream while I struggled behind. Your mistakes – I recorded them too. It was hard for you to argue with me, because you wished to win without argument. Every time we quarrelled, you came a step closer. But you would've been disappointed if I had let you win. You trusted neither my arguments nor your own, just those stupid instruments recording truth without thought, without feelings.

His heart sank: was this Belavoix's way of calling off their rivalry?

And so, I fought myself in the name of fighting Samuel Bates. Observed more than I've ever observed, filled up more notebooks, tried to entrap you with surprise. Even if I didn't believe in a tale, I tried hard to have you believe it, hoping to overcome you with lies. It would've pleased me if I had succeeded and saddened me at the same time. To think that you had lost not to truth but to a clever and pathetic Jean-Louis Belavoix.

He felt hollow as he started to read the final words.

Our rivalry has ended. Just the last rites remain. A final meeting in Arlinda. I am hoping for a dramatic conclusion, something to remind the world of our experiment decades later. A sudden and brilliant ending. I shall come prepared, as I hope you will too.

Quartley's cry would have startled Bates had he been at the laboratory. The dramatic conclusion! If Bates agreed, this would be the end, the final visit, the perfect solution. Belavoix had laid down his conditions in the letter: he would arrive separately from Bates in a month from now by a French boat, for just a brief visit. Meeting only in Arlinda. The Société had been informed of his intentions; the members were as eager to learn the experiment's outcome as the Royal Society's.

A month! A mere month to plan the trip, buy supplies, prepare a new instrument if necessary. It left Quartley breathless. He had followed his master's orders and opened the letter in his absence. When Bates returned, he rushed to his room and dropped it on his desk. With a quick look at Quartley, Bates read.

'Have you told Perry?'

'Yes.'

'And?'

'He'll make the necessary arrangements. He thinks we can reach Arlinda at the same time as M. Belavoix.'

Quartley thought of the 'brilliant ending', eager to ask Bates as many questions as he could before his master disappeared again.

'Shall we take something special with us this time, sir?'

Bates shook his head. 'No.'

'No new instrument?' He expected Bates to unfurl his surprise weapon, his best, at the final battle.

'Nothing more than our brains,' Bates replied gruffly, then got busy with his files.

As they waited for their departure, Quartley thought continuously of Captain Perry's reassuring words . . . *There's no problem a sailor can't solve* . . . He felt hopeful that the experiment would end soon, but less so when he considered his escape with Norah and the children. There were many hurdles still. Many journeys ahead of him.

Bates called him to his study on the eve of their voyage. Quartley found a similar jumble of stacks to before, with his master hiding among them. He looked sick – haggard, eyes sunk into craters. He didn't seem ready.

'Do you know where you'll be going?'

The question caught him by surprise.

'We board the *Maverick* at Portsmouth, sir. Captain Perry has arranged it.'

'I mean, after we return. Once the experiment is over.'

Quartley stood speechless, stunned. Was Bates planning to get rid of him?

'Our success will prove the worth of craniology. We won't need to keep a collection here any more. The principle will have been established.' He paused, staring ahead. 'I won't need an assistant. You'll be free to go.'

Quartley's mind started to spin madly. Freedom! Banishment! Rival emotions drained him.

'It won't be hard for you to find work in another laboratory. I'm sure Holmes will help.' Bates stopped for a swig from his bottle. 'You can go now if you want. Unless you relish another bout of *mal de mer*!'

'What will *you* do afterwards, sir?' He managed to draw words out of his dry mouth. 'Will you continue to . . . ?'

'But, of course, Quartley!' Bates let out a laugh. 'Go right on! There's much more left to prove. We've all heard of this new pest called *evolution*, haven't we?'

The coast of Gibraltar receding under moonlight reminds Quartley of Louisa's final words at The Steeple. Will it be enough? He wonders about her question, awake in his cabin. It forces his thoughts away from Norah. Will this solve the puzzle finally? Will the academies fall silent when the last word has been spoken?

The voyage ends without sickness.

Is it Belavoix he is thinking about, as he paces the veranda? Or Mr Darwin? The polygenist, or the rival-to-be?

His assistant is busy getting their camp ready for the days ahead. Winter on the island has dried the natural ponds, and the drums have to be filled with the ration of water brought over on ship. Quartley has to run up and down the goat path with a canister balanced on his shoulder. He has to check every crack in the cottage floor for scorpions.

Their visit has caught Norah by surprise; the captain's messenger has failed to inform her on time. Arranging the new supplies has kept her busy, though, as well as preparing for Belavoix's 'special needs' once he arrives to join the others.

There's much on his mind, judging by his frown, as Bates sits down with his drink. He must be taking stock of the past six years, weighing up his chance of winning over the Frenchman. He must be sharpening his beak and claws. Or is he is thinking of the aftermath?

Speeches he has rehearsed many a time ring in his ears. He imagines himself standing before a packed audience. In the Royal Society's jubilee hall, in Florence's Academici, in the smoky salon of the Société Ethnologique.

He hears Holmes's question, not the applause of his audience . . .
Will it be the right answer?

Rising, Bates starts to pace the veranda. Another rival occupies his mind now. An Englishman like himself, the anti-creationist. He rehearses a fresh set of arguments. If the evolutionists challenge him, it will be a different matter, he knows. Proving that one race is superior to another won't be enough. Simply throwing an instrument on a head or two won't do. He'll have to test man against beast. He'll have to challenge the evolutionists' origin.

Did we rise from barbaric roots, Mr Darwin? he whispers under his breath, *or have we fallen from a civilised Eden?*

He drains his glass, then pours another.

In Holmes, he sees a more troubling rival – the father abandoning his son before his true worth can be proven. It is men like Holmes, who keep the puzzle alive, keep the scientists busy purely by their fickleness. This is his other rivalry. He must win against Holmes and his friends before he can offer his final argument.

Or has he lost that argument already? Lost by the very fickleness, even before he has had a chance to cross swords with Mr Darwin?

He curses the dark veranda. Only the glass escapes his wrath.

They see less of the children than before. At times they seem to disappear altogether. Or to have been forbidden by someone to appear before the visitors. Whenever Norah comes up to their camp, Bates asks her routine questions about the samples' health and habits, receives the usual nods and shrugs in reply. Breakfast at the cottage feels different now that there are no measurements to do. There's really no need for the children to be around. Only an occasional check of the instrument cupboard revives the memory of previous visits.

Norah stiffens when Quartley brings out the goniometer for Bates to examine. She fears that the routine will start again, fears for herself – that she'll break her silence. The thought of the children struggling inside the traps reminds her of the dismay that she confided in Quartley. The children treated like animals. Forced into obedience if they resisted. Put to sleep with opium, then measured. 'How would Bates like to have the craniograph around *his* head?'

It would only take a small incident now to loosen her tongue.

She listens to the men talk about Belavoix. Word has come of him leaving Marseilles on a cutter full of troops bound for Dahomy. The *Soldat Patriote* has been spotted making brisk passage through the island channels. She hears Bates mention a 'final test'. Her body stiffens again, as she remembers the Frenchman's plan. What does he mean by the final test?

She avoids looking at Quartley, relying on her frown to build a wall between them. Otherwise, she can't be mute. She still goes up to the scientists' camp to do her chores, but avoids entering his room – finds it hard to touch the bed that she tumbled on in his absence, hoping to steal a moment from the time they were together. The pain, she keeps telling herself, will soon be over, the arguing scientists will keep her busy, drown her urge to be alone with her lover.

Back at her cottage, the children absent, she waits for Nicholas. She thinks he will come to tell her of his plan. He has one, she knows from the way he avoids her, knows it too from their sudden return to Arlinda.

*

Every time he enters the cottage with Bates, his heart starts to pound. He can hear Norah speak beneath her silence – fill the kitchen with her words, her laugh. He worries the sight of him will break her composure. He'd have felt more secure had Belavoix been around, the scientists kept too busy with each other to pay the nurse any attention. The two would be arguing at their camp, leaving him free to steal a visit to the forest with Norah. They could disappear like the children. Hide in the bat cave.

He wishes Norah would ignore Bates's stricture and leave him a note, with her very own words that he longs to hear.

One evening, Bates surprises him, calls him over for a chat. After all these years, he shows a mind to consult with his assistant.

'What do you make of our friend?'

'M. Belavoix, sir?'

Bates nods, gazing out of the veranda as if expecting to sight an approaching ship. Then he chuckles, providing his own answer. 'I'd say he was a man of superior sentiments – *too* superior, if you ask me.'

'An adventurer, I've heard people say,' Quartley mumbles.

'A man of superior but reckless energy. His imagination borders on fanaticism. He's fond of the ludicrous, full of tricks and in love with confusion. In short, he has all the qualities of a successful crook!'

'A crook?'

'Yes!' Bates laughs. 'Like a crook, he suffers no remorse. Just the urge to repeat his crime.'

'I wonder what disease he'll bring with him this time!'

Bates pours himself another drink. 'A scientist, a crook *and* a soldier.'

Is Bates thinking of the young Belavoix, of his days with the Legion?

'But I thought he didn't stay long with . . .' Quartley begins.

'Like a soldier, he wishes the war will never end. Without it, he will die. He has taught me a valuable lesson, Quartley.'

He is surprised to hear Bates praise his rival.

'The pure instinct. I've seen that in him. The instinct that keeps him going, makes him believe he might still win when the experiment is all but over.' He raises his flushed face from the glass. 'Only the instinct is pure, Quartley – I've learned that observing the

Frenchman. It is more powerful than reason . . . takes more than argument to overcome.'

Quartley remains silent.

'Is it instinct that keeps *us* going, sir?'

Bates stares at him. 'What else can you call it? Madness or instinct.'

The breeze calls out his name – in Norah's voice. The surf. The gulls. The aching waterfall. Quartley goes looking for the children.

The scientists have discovered all their hideaways, they know; to stay hidden they must find other places. Their private garden is no longer their own, spoilt by the visitors' footsteps; the spring changed beyond recognition when Norah and Quartley splashed about in it, unsettling the rock shelves left untouched for years. The water lizards have disappeared mysteriously.

Quartley blames himself for having ignored the children for so long. Before his last visit he viewed them simply as samples. It didn't matter to him if they howled or screamed, slept with open eyes, or threw rocks. Or if they managed to catch a fish in the spring. As long as one of them could be proved superior to the other.

Norah too has made him forget the children. His obsession with the report-writer has made him neglect the subject of her reports. The boy's fever or the girl's dizziness hasn't worried him as much as Norah's loneliness. Nothing has been more serious than her predicament. It has been just Norah, and Norah . . .

It all changed, he thinks, during the last visit. He remembers the time spent with the children. Their gifts. He expects them to treat him differently now, come over to the scientists' camp, perhaps, and invite him to join in their games. He expects them to be his friends. Or are they savages still, as Belavoix claimed, living from moment to moment? Savages without a mind, without memory?

How will their samples be remembered? Will the brilliant conclusion they expect be brilliant for the children too? Quartley strolls on the sand, looking out for a pair of heads in the surf. The rocks remind him of the day the children fought. What must they endure in this, their last test? He recalls Norah's fear as she explained Belavoix's plan. 'You'd win freedom if you gave up one of the two.' Will the final act be the final test? Will they stand the children on the beach, face to face, with rocks in their hands?

The proof of racial superiority is murder.

The germ waits to be released into a clear sky, to spread in Arlinda's poisonous breeze. He imagines Norah in her cottage, doors barred to prevent her from trying to stop the test. An excited Belavoix, notebook in hand. Will Bates allow the Frenchman to go ahead with it?

He turns back from the surf and walks towards the valley of rocks. The children are there, plainly before his eyes. They make no move to escape. Quartley expects they'll come bounding in, throw themselves all over him. He sees them building something with rocks, piling one on top of another, like a tall column or a lighthouse facing the sea. From a distance, it looks like a solitary figure – a marooned sailor. He hears them chatter.

He must prevent the test, he decides, if it comes to it. Step in between the children, even if it means catching a rock on his head.

A week passes without a sighting of the *Soldat*. Bates restlessly paces the veranda, cursing Belavoix, cursing Holmes and all his enemies back in England. A family of scorpions keeps Quartley busy. He drives them from crack to crack, till the cottage floor appears to be one giant nest of cunning killers. He feels anxious too. Without Belavoix, there will be no end to the experiment. He'll have to rethink his plans.

Water empties in the drum. Supplies dwindle. The children come and go as they please. Norah waits to speak.

Quartley woke in the night, disturbed by a stirring in Bates's room. He heard the trunk lid slam, followed by a curse. Then he heard footsteps on the veranda. Perhaps the Frenchman had finally arrived. He waited on his bed to hear sounds of greeting, the huffing and puffing, loud exclamations. Silence forced Quartley to think of another explanation. Perhaps Bates had left his stifling room to enjoy the breeze on the veranda, perhaps he was restless for another drink.

Then his heart froze. Could Bates have gone down to the children's cottage?

Norah!

He jumped out of bed and rushed onto the veranda, just caught sight of Bates's nightgown disappearing down the track to the lower camp. The Englishman turned French for his adventuring . . . ! An image fleeted through Quartley's mind: a helpless Norah crushed by Bates on the kitchen table; the silent nurse suffering under a savage scientist. Recovering his senses, he began to run down the goat path after Bates, then stopped, overcome by a sudden instinct. Darting back to their camp, he grabbed Bates's rifle, then started down again. Leaping over trenches, turning sharply at bends, his mind spun in a frenzy and came to rest on a brilliant idea. He knew the solution, wondered why it hadn't occurred to him before. He forgot his anxiety about Norah. He knew now how to stop the experiment. He would kill Bates, and blame his death on an unfortunate accident. He could see himself breaking the tragic news to Perry and to Holmes back in London. It would be just a matter of choosing an accident: a fatal fall from the tree house, or drowning in the sea. The body buried in Arlinda, or lost for ever. What could be simpler? The solution, superior by far to any he had thought of before, made his hair stand on end.

Quartley saw the lamp burning in Norah's room when he drew near the children's camp. Careful not to bump into Bates, he hid among the shrubs that surrounded the cottage. He heard a sound, the sound of laughter and a few scattered words. Suddenly horrified, he realised he was hearing Norah speak to the children, her voice rising above their blabber as if she was trying to calm them. The boy's gurgle mixed with a drumming sound – bare feet running over the wooden floor. The she-wolf playing with her cubs! Quartley edged closer to the kitchen window. He saw Bates arrived there already, unaware of his approach, gazing in through the window just as he was.

He has heard her! Heard Norah speak!

Quartley felt dizzy and leaned on the rifle to steady himself. Her secret was out now! The lie had been broken at last. She had betrayed herself at the very end. The cottage fell silent, Norah's voice and the laughter stopping, as if in anticipation of an event. Then he heard a different sound: the cottage coming alive once again. He heard Norah singing – a tired but pleasant voice, soothing the children with a familiar song. He saw Bates take a step forward, tilting his head to one side to catch the words.

So this was how the samples lived when they were alone in the island. Quartley felt like an intruder. He turned his attention to

Bates. He was standing motionless. The dim light made it impossible to read the reaction on his face.

Quartley waited till the song had ended, and the lamp had been blown out. The cottage was dark, but he could sense Norah's presence in the kitchen. Perhaps she was sitting at the table by herself, the children locked in their rooms to prevent them venturing out at night. He longed to go in and join her – longed to hear the song again. Suddenly he could no longer see Bates, and started to worry. Maybe he'd go in now, attack her like an animal inside the dark cottage. Instinct held him back still. He checked the rifle. Bates had taught him the proper use of this instrument too, in case they were ever ambushed on the voyage down. He raised it to his shoulder, and peered down the barrel. He would have one chance, one shot, he told himself. Just enough time for a single bullet to the head, entering the skull at the coronal suture and leaving through the parietal bones – just as it had done with the Seminole Warrior, number 88.

As she lit a lamp and brought it over to the kitchen table, Quartley saw Norah. She was wearing a white tunic, her hair hanging loose over her shoulders. She was busy cleaning the stove, scarcely glancing out through the window. From her ways, she could have been anywhere, simply getting ready to end a long day. Then he saw a dark shadow in the cottage doorway. Bates entered the kitchen.

Shaking himself free of the scene, Quartley followed swiftly, going up the steps but stopping short of the open door. He heard Bates's rasping voice.

'Liar!'

Norah spun around, a cry escaping her throat.

'Liar!' Bates took menacing steps, closing in on Norah. 'Rotten lying whore!'

Now! Quartley raised the rifle. Blood rushed to his head.

'Is that what you do with your filthy tongue?'

She turned her face from Bates.

'Don't act dumb now!' He reached out and grabbed Norah by the hair and shoulder. 'Let's hear it again! Sing!'

She snapped free of his hold.

'Won't sing? Won't sing!' Bates slurred. 'Why don't you tell me about your little monkeys then – what rotten lies you've taught them?' His face within inches of Norah's was black with anger. 'You bitch! You've spoilt everything. You've broken every rule. Whore! I won't let you get away with it! I'll *make* you dumb, tear out that bloody tongue of yours!'

She was shaking now. Quartley entered the kitchen and stood behind the two. The children! Where were the children? A quick look at their locked doors reassured him.

Bates swayed, unsteady. 'Our pure experiment! Our *pure* samples! Pure as hell! You've made them into little devils – stinking scum, like you . . .'

Suddenly she spun around to face him. 'Yes, I lied. What are you going to do now?'

Unsettled, Bates grabbed Norah and drew her by the neck towards him. 'Go on, tell me . . . Who's your *real* master? Who sent you here?'

She shook her head vigorously. Veins throbbed on her temple, her face red and contorted in pain.

'No one? You mean you've broken the rules just because you wanted to?' Bates almost wailed.

'The children are pure.'

'Pure as dirt. Ready to vomit words like you.'

'They can't speak!' Norah burst out.

'But they know how to play games. You've made sure of that. You told the boy to hide. You taught the girl to pretend she was sick. You even taught them to fight.'

'No!'

'Tell me –' Bates suddenly dropped his voice, still grasping Norah's neck – 'which of your monkeys is the better one? You must know that.'

She looked at him speechless.

'Black or white? You *know*.' He breathed into her face. 'Tell me, or I'll wring your neck.' He tightened his grip, brought his lips closer to her ear. 'Or would you rather speak with something up your cute arse?'

Kill him now! Finger on the trigger, Quartley took a step forward. It was hard to aim, with Bates holding Norah so close to him. Her face next to his face, her shoulders locked against his. A single bullet could kill them both.

'You know your rotten answer.' Tearing away from Bates, Norah screamed at him. 'You bastard! What do you care about them.

You'd leave us all here to die!' She stopped, a glint of fire streaked from her clear blue eyes. 'I lied! I lied for *them*. To save them from wild beasts!'

Bates let her go and made as if to turn and go into the children's rooms. 'They're rubbish! Dead or alive, they mean nothing! They're worse than useless to us! I'll show you what we do to dirt.'

In a flash, she picked up the axe which lay by the stove. 'You've got to show me first.'

Bates stopped, eye on the blade. 'Are you sure?'

'I'll kill you first, before you touch them!'

Suddenly she caught sight of Quartley and screamed as hard as she could before lunging at Bates. He swayed out of her way at the very last moment, and shot a glance at the door. He saw Quartley and the gun.

'*You* . . . ?'

Quartley didn't move. The assistant facing his master.

'What are you doing here, Quartley? Get out until I call you. Who said to take that?' He pointed at the gun, which was aimed at his head.

Quartley stepped nearer to the flickering lamp, facing Bates squarely with the table between them.

Bates's look turned from shock to seething anger. 'You knew all about this, didn't you? Knew it all along. You snake!' Ignoring Norah, he turned his fury on Quartley. 'You stupid boy! How dare you! I should've left you in London. Stuffing boxes – that's all you're good for.' He raised a finger, 'I order you to –' then saw the barrel inching closer. His voice turned hoarse. 'I warn you not to come between us. I order you to leave the cottage now!'

Quartley held his ground, his shoulder touching Norah's.

'Caught you like a fly,' Bates hissed at him. 'Turned your head. You half-witted boy! You've become her slave. A whore's slave! You've gone behind my back just for a piece of her.'

'She's not a whore.'

'No? What is she then?' Bates snorted. 'She's wrecked the experiment – *our* experiment, Quartley!'

'*You* wrecked the experiment.' Quartley kept his finger steady on the trigger.

All at once Bates started to laugh. 'You must be mad. What do you know? What do you think this is?' With a quick glance at

Norah, he went on. 'This isn't what you think. This isn't just a silly little test. This is more than a few damn skulls, more than anything you've ever seen in your pathetic life.' He stopped to catch his breath.

'Do you know what you've done? You've killed the experiment. You and the whore.'

Bates heard the click of the gun's lock. He strode past Quartley out of the cottage, to march back to their camp.

MIDDLE PASSAGE

At daybreak, the children find them on the kitchen floor, rolled up, head to toe. Norah had brought them over to her room after Bates had left, held them tightly, shaking and sobbing, while Quartley locked the cottage door. Then they had returned to the kitchen, determined to spend the whole night awake to watch over the children and be on their guard against Bates.

The discovery begins a flurry of activity. The boy and the girl observe the scene for a few moments then start on their duties. They try lifting Quartley first, pulling on his arm. But it's twice as heavy as normal, caught between the floor and Norah's waist. They try to lift her instead, and manage to push her along the floor, accidentally banging her head against a table leg.

She wakes with a start – then cries out for Quartley as the night returns in a flash. He wakes too. They observe their busy caretakers doing their very best to carry them to bed.

Both wake to a sense of relief. There is no need to hide any more. They can simply be themselves, speak together whenever they wish, and live with the children at the cottage.

Bates is their worry. What will he do now? Will he storm back to their camp? Will he have his revenge for their 'betrayals'? Rifle in hand, Quartley sits on the cottage steps, keeping a lookout for Bates.

He knows his master. He is not one to give in easily. He will have stayed awake all night, cursing and damning, pacing the veranda, smashing glasses. His eyes will have sunk even deeper into the hollows above his chin. The mighty Bates – his glory marred by a pair of servants. The greatest experiment in racial science lost to a pair of foolish lovers.

The beast is out in Arlinda's forest. It's only a matter of time before it strikes. Bates will soon settle on a plan, decide to take the final step with or without his rival. Quartley is sure of it, just as he can imagine him now at daybreak after a night of madness – doubled up on the veranda amidst a shower of broken glass, and a few curious scorpions.

They go about protecting their camp from Bates, working up a frenzy. It could be any moment now that he arrives, marching down the hill as always and leaping over the fence. His stomach will bring him down here, and more. They pile a heap of rocks within reach to use as cannonballs. Quartley runs to fetch logs from the garden, chopped for firewood. He starts to board up the windows with Norah's help, turning the cottage into a barred prison within hours. Then a more frightening thought strikes. What if Bates sets fire to the cottage, burns them alive? They fill the courtyard with nettles and thorny branches brought from the forest, to build an obstacle course.

Norah brings up the Frenchman. Will Belavoix seek revenge too, when he comes? He might make much of Norah's lie: 'I knew it, Mr Bates! I was going to tell you everything about the lying *English* nurse when we met. I thought I'd surprise you . . . !'

After six long years, will the scientists be united at last? Against them?

They might take the children away, Norah fears, leave her and Quartley behind on the island. Capture their samples, corrupted as they might be, and take them to another island to start the experiment again. They might find another nurse. Even raise the children themselves. The possibility alarms them. Both rush to the garden where the children are playing, and escort them back to the cottage, locking them up like prisoners. The boy and the girl watch them in silence, uncomprehending.

Even if they did manage to steal the children, how would they resume their measurements? It won't be easy, Norah says. 'The children will become wilder; they'll refuse to be treated like animals.'

As they sit on the cottage steps, they see scenes of vivid unrest, vicious fights.

Norah climbs up to the tree house first, followed by Quartley. After a whole day of waiting, they have come now to look for the enemy, armed with Belavoix's telescope, which Norah has saved.

She looks up at the goat path and the spring, to the scientists' camp hidden almost entirely by the trees. She stiffens, seeing a shadow. But it isn't Bates – just a swaying branch. She ignores the beach. Bates isn't likely to fancy a swim. As sunset nears, their anxiety mounts. Could he be hiding close to them, close enough to hear them breathing?

Quartley spots it first. Even without the telescope, he sees the flag on the horizon. The swallow's tail flapping on the mast. The *Rainbow*! Captain Perry! His heart starts to race. A swarm of possibilities runs through his mind, as he clambers down from the tree house and runs towards the beach.

Captain Perry waved at Quartley from the outrigger. He seemed as sprightly as ever, dragging the boat himself a few yards over the sand, then leaving it for Quartley to secure against a rock.

'Where's the great man?'

They started to climb the goat path together, Perry with his hands tucked into his pockets, chattering away. Relief flooded Quartley's mind as he kept up with the captain's pace. The familiar and the friendly almost made him forget the terrible night they had passed. It seemed like a bad dream now, its traces beginning to vanish with the captain's arrival. He toyed with the idea of telling Captain Perry what had happened, but stopped himself. It would be easier to face Bates with the captain, he thought. He might not need the rifle. The captain could help subdue Bates should he turn violent.

They found the scientists' camp empty. The veranda and the rooms were just as before, the hammock rolled up into a ball. The trees cast a pattern of shadow on the floor – it appeared oddly pleasant, a restful place tucked into the hills. A quick look around assured Quartley that everything was in order.

Captain Perry fidgeted with an envelope as they waited for Bates. He gave Quartley a serious look.

'You must be wondering why I am here.'

Quartley said nothing.

'I've brought a letter for Bates.' He looked around him, then whispered, 'It's important. *Very* important. It's improper for me to show it to you, but –' he cleared his throat – 'it's pardonable under the circumstances.' He handed Quartley the envelope. 'Read it, while we wait for your master.'

Quartley spotted a flying lark on top of the blue-lined sheet, the watermark of the Société Ethnologique de Paris. He started to read eagerly, skipping over the usual beginning.

'It came just after you left on the *Maverick*,' Captain Perry said, eye on the setting sun. 'I tried to have the message passed on earlier, but . . .'

Quartley read with growing astonishment. A senior official of the Société described the voyage of the *Soldat Patriote*, which had left Marseilles on an important mission. She carried troops to Africa to quell a mutiny. She was the best warship of the French fleet, a veteran of many campaigns. There was nothing to suspect that things could go wrong. But then, there had been a terrible accident . . .

Quartley looked up at Captain Perry, who nodded knowingly.

. . . She struck a reef and sank like a rock – captain, sailors and passengers all lost, including M. Jean-Louis Belavoix, scientist extraordinaire, who was rumoured to be on his way to conduct one of his marvellous studies.

Quartley gasped, then read on:

It is a pity that this tragedy has nipped the youngest bud from the blossoming tree of European science. It is a pity that the world won't profit any more from the brilliant mind of M. Belavoix. The Société considers it its duty to inform his colleague, Professor Samuel Bates, of this terrible loss and expresses its deepest sympathy.

Belavoix dead! Quartley's heart skipped a beat.

'Has his body been found . . . ? Are they sure?' His questions sounded hollow. At that very moment they saw Bates coming out of the sanitary lodge in his drawers. Without even a glance at Quartley, he walked up to Captain Perry and took the letter as if he was expecting it. He read swiftly.

'Most tragic . . .' Captain Perry murmured.

'Does Holmes know about this?' Bates asked in a matter-of-fact way.

'Yes. I informed him before we sailed.'

Without another word, Bates left the captain and Quartley on the veranda, went back to his room and shut the door.

From the tree house, they watch the outrigger leave. Bates sits with his back to the captain, the boat weighed down with his personal effects, packed by himself. Not a single instrument box rides with him, all of them still locked up in the cottage cupboard.

A solitary passenger.

What does he think, as he leaves Arlinda? What turns inside the skull of the skull doctor? Quartley wonders. Bates is not one to moan over what might have been, he knows. Has he already left it all behind? He must know that his cause is lost, that it is impossible to win over a dead rival. The Frenchman has outfoxed him.

Does his mind dwell on the betrayers? 'Science can only lose to human weakness,' Quartley remembers his master saying in the ship's cabin. 'The frail are our *real* enemies!' Does he conjure up the faces, as he gazes at the horizon ahead? Louisa and her friends. Sir Reginald Holmes. Quartley and Norah.

What will Bates do when he returns to the Madhouse? Quartley tries to guess. Will the dark laboratory remind him of the misspent years? Remind him of his lost collection? And the log that he tore page by page in Arlinda, the shreds crawling and floating around the forest like a new species?

What will remain of him without his science? Will the empty Madhouse finally strike fear into the legendary Samuel Bates?

'Your turn will come next!' Captain Perry had winked at Quartley before he left with Bates. The captain didn't think it was necessary for Quartley, Norah and the children to return to England. It was better that they should stay in Arlinda, till he found a way to send them off to their final destination, to a place where they could live as a family. Bates, he reported, hadn't said a word about them as he got ready to leave. He didn't care any more about the samples, their nurse – even his assistant. Cared about nobody.

'I'll find a friend to take you over –' Perry had gestured with his eyes – 'over the ocean. You've told Norah about the plan, haven't you?'

Quartley nodded. His letters to Norah from England had been full of details about the plan. He had written to her about the 'middle passage', crossing the Atlantic as the slavers did with their cargo of black gold. But unlike them, they wouldn't be bound for America or the Sugar Islands, but for Canada.

He knew he could trust the captain. It was a matter of waiting for a few more days, before they could be berthed on the right ship bound for the right destination.

'You have told her it won't be easy, haven't you?' Captain Perry had said, before leaving.

They return slowly to living by themselves on the island. Memory has them lapse into old habits. The mornings still feel tense, the children are edgy around the table, and Norah puts back her frown. The instrument cupboard reminds Quartley of his old chores. He feels strangely responsible, just as he used to feel responsible for the skulls. Whenever he goes up to the scientists' camp or walks to the top of the hill, he expects to find Belavoix – expects to hear his singsong voice. 'Hello, Mr Assistant! Tell me, is it true what they say about the English . . . ?' It's difficult for him to imagine a dead Belavoix, despite the Frenchman's much vaunted bouts with deadly diseases. It seems he's merely away on the trail of yet another fantastic adventure. It is difficult for Quartley to imagine that the experiment has finally ended, after all his desperate worries.

Eventually, Norah brings up the plan. 'Is it safer to go to Canada then?'

Quartley tells her what he learned at Mrs Bates's home, as he listened to her talk about her Quaker friends, about her *American saint* – Elizabeth Moore of Pennsylvania and the Underground Railroad: the grand conspiracy that assists runaway slaves to escape north. Louisa's charity helped to keep the labyrinth of safe houses and wagon runs going. They hid the slaves during the day and helped them to slip into Canada at night in carts with false bottoms or in barges, sometimes with little more than the North Star to guide them.

The thought of the railroad worries her. 'But we aren't going to America, are we?'

'No. There'd be problems for the boy if we did.'

'Are there no slaves in Canada?'

Quartley shakes his head. 'They are free when they set foot in that country. Slave-catchers from the south aren't allowed to get in. The boy will be safe there.'

'How will we know if we have found the right boat to take us there?'

It would have to be a whaler or a fur trader, Captain Perry had told Quartley. They'd have to be patient till the right ship came along.

He smiles at Norah. 'It'll bring a note from Perry, just as before.'

The children worry them as much as the thought of the journey ahead. Even if they manage to find the right berth, what will the other passengers make of the wild children? And how will the children view strangers? Their fights and mischief might lead to much commotion. They might run helter-skelter on the deck or climb up a mast. Might even fall into the sea.

They agree to begin to civilise the children, to do the best they can in the time remaining. They must get them to speak – just a few words, just enough for them to reach their destination safely. Both have already started to talk in the children's presence, doing the things with them that they would normally do if they lived back in England.

'Even if we fail to escape from Arlinda, if we all die here, they should spend their last days as humans,' Norah says. 'And if they survive, they must live as humans not savages.'

'But will they ever be like us?' Quartley asks aloud.

'It might be too late,' she replies. 'But, they must still know who they are. They must know that this island is not their real home.'

'And if they should ever ask who they *really* are?'

Norah looks at him. 'What do you mean?'

'Why the sister is white and the brother black?'

She leaves without answering.

They spend a morning with the children at the cottage, or spend an afternoon by the waterfall, bathing in the shallow pool, trying to rid them of the fear of being touched. Norah tries to distract them, when they quarrel, by humming a song. It is Quartley's job to hold the boy's hand and scold him gently should he dig out an earthworm to taste. They try not to laugh or show anger, reminding themselves that they are on an almost impossible mission.

They decide to name the children, then spend hours arguing over names.

Another fear rises as a week passes without the sighting of a ship. It'll be soon, Quartley reassures Norah as he goes up to the hill top to scan the island channels. Maybe the captain is still trying to coax a friend, to win them a supporter. Maybe he'd come back himself with the *Rainbow*, all else failing.

But what if nobody comes? If they are left marooned on Arlinda? Left to die slowly, supplies dwindling and the water drum running dry. They'll be forced to forage in the forest, digging up roots and boiling leaves, cracking open the arlinda fruit to die by its poison.

After a whole day with the children, they come down to the beach to dream about their future. The past seems ever-present, the experiment still unconcluded, till they escape. They sit silently for hours, watching the flag flutter over the messenger's hut – their signal to passing ships, to let them know that they are ready for the middle passage.

Quartley wakes to a silent cottage. From the kitchen window he sees Norah in the garden, plucking out dead leaves. He goes out to join her, feels the cool breeze – the haze yet to lift over the forest. He longs to feel the spray and the surf, to run through the trees with Norah to the sea. The tide is high now, the roaring sea answering the call of screaming gulls.

When they arrive at the beach, they find the birds busier than usual, noisier, rushing around as if they are chasing a juicy prey. Standing at the edge of the sea, they find the horizon blocked by a giant sail, risen like a rock overnight. Puzzled, they look around, hear the gulls screaming in human voices. Quartley hears another cry: the children darting over the beach, chased by a band of men dressed in white. They seem to be playing a game of hide and seek, the strange men shouting at each other in their strange tongue, encircling the children and swooping down on them.

Quartley freezes, but his mind comes suddenly alive. Arabs! He remembers Captain Perry's stories on their voyages. The oldest slavers of Africa, buying and stealing children for centuries. Their traders don't take the middle passage, their captives are bound for Damascus and Baghdad, the Bosporus kingdoms, as far away as Persia. The girls to become harem maids, the boys eunuchs.

'You can't blame us Europeans, you know; the Arabs were at it first!' Perry had exclaimed.

Quartley sees the white-robed gulls chase their prey, sprinting over sand, running around the rocks, and splashing in the breaking surf.

He hears Norah scream, dashing wildly after the men with a rock in each hand. Quartley runs too, closing in on the girl. He sees her frightened face. Before he can lunge at one of the men, a rock flies in, hits the Arab between his eyes and splatters his face with blood. It's the boy, the master rock-thrower, coming to the girl's aid while being chased himself. The wounded man yells, then draws a musket from his waist, fires shots into the air. The boy scrambles like a crab and hides behind a boulder.

Leaving the girl for a moment, Quartley runs after Norah, who has started to swim out to the ship's outrigger, pressed into the kidnappers' service. It is loaded with clubs and muskets. She tries to climb aboard, to grab a weapon with which to fight back. They need more than rocks to hold back the bandits. Quartley dives in to join her, dragging a man off the boat by his feet, the two of them scuffling, churning the waves. He strikes out with both hands, taking blows and fighting back. Between the two of them, he and Norah seem on the verge of capturing the raft, when the sound of screaming brings their attention back to the beach. Norah swims back towards the girl, leaving Quartley to hold off the boatmen.

At the beach the men have regrouped. They are chasing the children, and forcing them towards the sea. They form a semicircle, then go after the boy, who looks around, unable to spot either Norah or Quartley. He is shrieking and yelping at the girl. He can't lay his hands on rocks any more, can't strike back. He must keep running to evade the tightening cordon – the men closing in on all sides, making a bleating sound with their tongues, as if they are out to trap a young and frightened animal.

Norah spots the boy in danger and screams at Quartley. He lets go of the oar he has managed to wrench from one of the boatmen, and loosens his hold on the raft. At that moment, a club comes crashing down on his head.

Norah and the girl run towards the ring of men around the boy. They can barely see him, dwarfed by the wall of robes. Just a few steps away they see one of the men catch the boy with a deft move, then dive into the sea, swimming fast towards the boat. The others join him, firing their muskets at Norah and the girl, strafing the waves at their feet.

Head bleeding, Quartley stumbles out of the surf and chases after the men. The girl joins him. They swim neck and neck, till they're within reach of the raft once more. They see the boy, held by powerful hands, bobbing over the robes. They see him shaking his head, terrified.

'Ari!' the boy screams.

The girl screams back.

Suddenly the girl lunges ahead of Quartley, within inches of the boat, reaching out towards the boy. A boatman raises his oar, aims it at the girl's head.

'No!' With the last gasp of breath, Quartley splashes over the waves, pulling her under him, shielding her from the oar. The boat pulls away rapidly, now drawn by several powerful arms, leaving Quartley, Norah and the girl behind. The surf drowns their scream.

They see the anchor rise, and the sail ripple.

Quartley raises his throbbing head from the sand, now that the gulls have fallen silent. The beach is empty once again, the tide receded. The sun over Arlinda has warmed the air and driven the haze away. He sees neither Norah nor the girl. Head reeling, he starts to walk back to the camp, crossing the valley of rocks with some difficulty.

Inside, Quartley finds Norah sitting at the kitchen table, gazing out of the window with a vacant look. A broken mother. Her tears dried. Sobbing comes from the girl's room. Quartley sways past the table and makes for the instrument cupboard. He kicks the door open, breaking the lock. Picking up a box, he strides back through the kitchen to hurl it into the courtyard. Then returns for another one. Each and every one of them. The torsiometer, the craniograph, the orbiostat, the goniometer and many more. Emptying the cupboard, he throws himself on the courtyard, on the mangled heap, groaning and wailing. Norah joins him. The two lie writhing on the ground, grieving for the boy, their son.

The three sit around the rock column the children built a few days back. They've buried the boy's things in a pit at its foot. His clothes, the shells. They wait patiently till the sun dips behind Arlinda, till the only light comes from the stars. The column stands up to the sky. As dark as the boy.

Indestructible.

IV

The last bird to fly will know.

AFRICAN PROVERB

RACISTS

Where did he go, after the Madhouse was shut down? The new owners of the building didn't know. They didn't care for Bates or his collection, surprised though, as they must've been, to enter the crypt. A spooky room, they must've thought, shaking their heads over the broken desiccators perched liked aged turtles on the floor.

There were rumours for a while that he had gone to be a prison doctor in Ireland. Or had become a pamphleteer, even, writing under a pseudonym, joining the gutter press to continue his fight. Perhaps. It was just as likely that he simply vanished.

The brilliant century didn't spare a thought for a failed experiment or two. Much was soon to change after Bates's return from Arlinda. Rampaging evolutionists turned everything upside down. A new hankering replaced the old. It took decades more for racial science to stage a return, along with the scientists who claimed that it was race, and race alone, that could solve the eternal puzzle of human variation. The racists were still to have their day arguing over skin and skull, and intrinsic worth that marked the superior over the inferior. But by then, the last of Bates's toads had croaked.

And what of Jean-Louis Belavoix? Did his notebooks go down with him, robbing scientists and storytellers alike? Did the art of tantalising speculation disappear for ever? Without him, the Société had lost – none left to match *English* science or the *English* scientists.

The *real* experiment, though, was about to begin, after the failed experiment. The battle to raise the races together, to have them live among each other, was to start soon in America – the war against the slaving South. Abolition took just five years to win, but the sea captains were kept busy for a decade more, before the bunt fell on black gold. *La Petite Route* and the middle passage were left to dry up at last.

But for the likes of Louisa, the evil still lurked.

'Ari!'

Norah goes looking for the girl in the woods behind the cottage. She often comes here at the end of the day, when she has finished at school. It's her private playground, from which she must be called back before darkness sets in. Norah knows where to find her, although she can't tell if the girl will be in a tree or lying flat on the ground looking up. Some days she answers Norah's call, runs out of the woods to meet her. At other times she appears to be in her own world, barely aware of her mother.

Her father sits at the kitchen table to help her with her lessons after supper. The notebook fills slowly and laboriously. Hurrying won't help, Quartley knows; he needs to be patient. He reads out each word, waits for a nod – waits for a light to shine in her eyes.

She is a rare species in Wallsby. Runs faster than other children her age, climbs trees fearlessly, and is adept at all forms of physical endeavour. At school, she's quieter than the others, her big bright eyes unblinking for long periods behind a pair of spectacles that her father, the village pharmacist, has her wear. Why does she always have a serious look? her teacher wonders. Is it nature or sadness that makes her keep to herself? Her friends have learned never to tease her into a fight, for fear of a mauling.

In the woods, she loses her serious look. Badgers and squirrels have her in raptures. She chatters and squeals at them, swings from branches at will. This is her true nature.

Norah finds her under a tree with a nest in her hand. It must've fallen from a branch above. She sees her slither up the trunk, like a little monkey, returning the nest to a leafy hollow. Then come slithering down.

She brings her home for a bath.

The mirror shows a common face. An English girl. Unruly locks hang over a small forehead. A scar between her brows. She looks at the mark and frowns, just as her mother does; touches it with the tip of her finger, tracing it all the way through.

It reminds her of who she was.